OTHERWORLD CHRONICLES: BOOK THREE
THE DRAGON KING

OTHERWORLD CHRONICLES: BOOK THREE

The DRAGON KING

NILS JOHNSON-SHELTON

HARPER
An Imprint of HarperCollinsPublishers

DISCARD

Otherworld Chronicles: The Dragon King

Copyright © 2014 by Full Fathom Five, LLC

www.harpercollinschildrens.com

Library of Congress Cataloging-in-Publication Data
Johnson-Shelton, Nils.
    The dragon king / Nils Johnson-Shelton.
        pages cm. — (Otherworld chronicles ; #3)
    Summary: "Artie Kingfisher's quest to claim his throne as King
Arthur reborn approaches its end as he reaches the mythical isle of Avalon,
sets off in search of the Holy Grail, and prepares to face off in battle against
the wizard Merlin"— Provided by publisher.
    ISBN 978-0-06-207097-5 (hardback)
    1. Arthur, King—Juvenile fiction. [1. Arthur, King—Fiction.
2. Adventure and adventurers—Fiction.]   I. Title.
PZ7.J6398Dr   2014   2013032168
[Fic]—dc23   CIP
                                                                  AC

Typography by Torborg Davern

13 14 15 16 17   CG/RRDH   10 9 8 7 6 5 4 3 2 1

First Edition

For Daisy,
whose heart and imagination know no bounds

The DRAGON KING

TABLE OF CONTENTS

𝔐erlin reached down with dark fingers and opened a worn, decrepit book, its fragile pages yellow with age. Without searching, he turned right to the part he wanted, as if among the thousands of sheets the wizard knew the place by heart. He read aloud:

15 May 1558
Sangrealite! You tricky element. Like a woodland sprite, hidden in bark and moss and branch, you bewitch and tease. I could not find your secret for so long. . . .
  Sangrealite! You strengthen the steel of Excalibur, make its blade true and ever sharp.
  Sangrealite! You alone give the Grail its restorative abilities. . . .
  Sangrealite, sangrealite, sangrealite . . .
  How I loathe you. . . .
  You element of magic, you mysterious essence of Otherworldly power. Without you there is no wizardry, no conjuration, no vision. No Otherworld . . .
  Sangrealite. I have been unable to escape this prison—this invisible tower—because I have been

1

unable to rediscover your potency. I have been a wizard without magic for all these long years. . . .

But now! The woodland sprite is discovered. I have felled his tree, and he will whisper all his knowledge into my ears.

For not more than an hour has passed since I gleaned the method of your liquefaction, Sangrealite.

I have gone mad looking for this technique, and it has nearly destroyed me, but today I succeeded in transforming a dark and kingly key—resistant to all heat, all light, all the urgings of the storm-filled sky— into a pool of gray liquid. I will rub you into my skin, and you will mark me, and I will rediscover my magic.

Soon I will see if our power is sufficient to break the walls of this prison. If it is not, then I will require the help of another. It will be tricky to bring him hither, but if I must then I will. . . .

This wizard may yet be jailed, but the king will set me free. If all else fails, the king will set me free. . . .

Merlin let his fingers linger on the last words. "I remember them as if written yesterday," he mused. "Perfectly, pet."

He turned to a large cage wedged into the rock of a vast stone cavern. Light from electrical wall sconces glowed around the periphery, casting the room in a warm glow.

A guttural snarl came from the cage. The creature inside could not be seen.

"Yes, you are right," Merlin said slowly. "We no longer need this king—this *Artie Kingfisher*." His words were laced with disgust.

The wizard turned to a full-length mirror and stared. He was different from when he had fled the field of battle on Fenland, running from Morgaine and her cursed dragon, Scarm. The muttonchop sideburns remained, as well as the little paunch beneath his robe, but there was nothing light or whimsical about him. Every inch of his skin was the color of ash. His fingernails were long and pointed. And his eyes, as if they'd been dipped in dye, were as red as August roses.

He squinted with pleasure at his reflection. "I am remade," he said. "A new, old wizard. I have all the sangrealite I'll ever require. And I am making you, pet, a creature that is more dangerous than any dragon." The thing shifted restlessly and growled. "Yes, you are right." Merlin smiled. Even his gums were black with magic. "I no longer have need of him at all. . . ."

𝔄 **burst of energy shot through** Artie. He toppled over, hitting the ground hard, and that was all he could remember. After this shock he felt nothing. Heard nothing. Smelled nothing.

For him, there was nothing.

Then a dull pain grew in his shoulder as his consciousness slowly returned, sound filling his ears in waves—literally. The periodic swish of the ocean breaking on the shore hissed in the near distance.

He remembered—he was on a beach. He had been fighting. *All* of them had been fighting. They'd been fighting against . . .

Morgaine!

Artie's eyes snapped open as fear gripped his gut. He

attempted to sit but the pain was too great. He blinked furiously and tried to get his bearings, looking in every direction that he could for the witch. Was Morgaine still there, about to finish him off?

But there was no sign of her. If she had been around, she would be taunting and threatening Artie. Had she left, then? Or had he been thrown to the opposite side of the Fenlandian beach? Where *was* he exactly? He just couldn't be sure. Aside from the sand, all Artie could see was a gray mist surrounding everything. He couldn't even see his friends. . . .

His friends! Had Morgaine taken them and left him here to die? Artie rolled from his back onto his side, searching for Kay or Thumb or anyone else, and when he did an excruciating jolt of pain seized his hip. He looked down the length of his thin but strong body. Blood soaked the ground. His shirt was hiked around his chest and he could see that he had a deep gash along his abdomen.

How am I hurt? he thought. Is Excalibur's scabbard not working?

With great effort he reached over his shoulder and patted the top of his back. He didn't have the scabbard—that precious thing that healed all wounds!

He craned his neck as far as it would go in every direction to search for the sheath and could see no sign of it. . . . But then . . . Yes. There. Something dark rose out of the sand a few feet away. He lifted his head as high as he could. There was no doubt. He had to reach it.

Artie ignored the pain and pushed himself with his legs toward the scabbard. He couldn't get his upper body off the ground, so he plowed forward, his head, face, and shoulders gritting through the sand. It was not fun. Tears streamed from his eyes and his face reddened with the strain. It took him several minutes to just reach the scabbard, and when he did he was exhausted. As soon as he stopped exerting himself, the color drained from his face and he became lightheaded. If he didn't touch that magical sheath soon it would be the end of him.

Fighting a sudden urge to sleep, Artie flopped his arm forward, his hand slapping the scabbard's old leather. At that same moment, his eyes closed. . . .

He felt nothing. But then a strange energy began to flow through him, as if the scabbard understood just how dire the king's wounds were—which it probably did. His eyes went wide, his pupils shrunk, and he could feel his heart and veins filling with blood. The gash on his side drew itself together and went all warm and tingly, and the dull pain in his shoulder dissolved as quickly as a teaspoon of sugar thrown into a cup of bubbling hot tea.

He was pushed upright by invisible hands. Reflexively his fingers wrapped around the top of the scabbard. He pulled it out of the sand and jumped to his feet, his lungs filling with cool, salty air. He slung the scabbard over his back and ran his hands over his body.

He was a mess. His hundred-pound body had been tossed like a salad and his face was speckled with sand and dried blood. His clothes—jeans, graphene shirt, sneakers—were ripped here and there and really needed a wash.

But who cared? He was alive. He had survived.

Artie wiped the sand from his face and tried to shake it out of his light brown hair. He spat a mouthful of gritty saliva to the ground. Then he spun in a circle, searching, and spied his sword jutting from the sand at an angle. It reminded him of the first time he'd seen Cleomede, stuck in the stone way back when.

He lunged and grabbed Excalibur.

Excalibur!

Its grip felt familiar, like a game controller or a favorite baseball bat. The black pommel swirled with anticipation. The sword was still light in his hands—way lighter than a broadsword should have been—and still deadly. Holding it felt so right. Even though Morgaine had stolen it, every inch and ounce of Excalibur was still *his.*

Artie's happiness at reuniting with Excalibur didn't last long, though, as he remembered that aside from his strange and remarkable sword, he was completely alone. Yes, he had survived. But had the others?

"Hello?" he choked faintly. He cleared his throat.

"HELLO!" he said more loudly, and his voice bounced over the mist-covered beach. But no answer came. "Kay? Tom?" he pleaded.

He started to walk. The heavy fog hung everywhere—Artie could almost reach out and feel it with his hands—and he could only see a few feet in front of him. He walked thirty paces through the mist before stopping. "Where am I?" he asked out loud, his memory still patchy.

But then it came rushing back like a video clip played in reverse. How Morgaine had nearly won before Artie's twin, Dred, showed up. How they killed Morgaine's dragon, and how Morgaine had retaliated by killing the mute fairy Bors le Fey. How Morgaine had trapped Artie's friends in huge bubbles, and how Numinae kept popping his bubble only to be trapped instantly in a new one. How they had fought Morgaine's army of soldiers and bears and archers. How Merlin, who'd fled from the battle like a coward, had betrayed Artie and his friends. How Tiberius had frozen Kynder in rock in an attempt to save his life, only for Tiberius to turn to stone himself. How Artie found Qwon and met Shallot and Bors. And then, fast-forwarding through this chain of unlikely events, how Artie and his knights brought the Seven Swords together, just as Morgaine was about to strike, which took them to . . .

"Avalon!" Artie exclaimed.

And then Artie heard something other than the ocean. A moan. A person!

Artie doubled back along the beach, following the sound. He had made it to Avalon—that was good. But before the next moon rose he would have to open the granddaddy of all crossovers, those magical portals that linked the Otherworld to his world.

He would have to open the King's Gate.

Artie remembered Merlin's words as if the wizard were right there, whispering them in his ear: *If the next new moon rises before you open the King's Gate, then all crossovers will be sealed for a thousand years. . . . And you will not become king. . . .*

There was no way he was going to let that happen now. Not after all the battles they had fought. Not after Bors. Not after Kynder and Tiberius. There was no frigging way.

Artie heard the moan again, closer now. It was a girl and it sounded familiar. His heart lifted as a smile broke over his face.

"Kay!"

"W-what's going on?" Kay asked in a woozy voice. Artie skidded to a stop and fell to his knees next to his sister. She was sitting, her legs out straight. Something about the muted light of the mist made her red hair look as though it was glowing, and her mismatched eyes, blinking to wake up, were as bright as crown jewels.

"Kay," Artie said a little desperately. "Are you all right?"

She ran her hands over her legs. "I-I think so. Nothing feels broken. Are you?"

"I am now." Without another word Artie flung himself at Kay and wrapped her in a huge hug, his arms clasping the top of the infinite backpack, their magical bag that could hold nearly anything. Kay returned the embrace. "Nice to see you, too, Art. . . . Where are we?"

"Avalon, Sis. We made it. The swords worked."

"Seriously?"

"Seriously."

They released each other and sat back, Kay eyeing the beach and fog. "Doesn't look like much."

"Yeah, well, hopefully there's more to it. This King's Gate thing is supposed to be around here somewhere."

"Right . . . the King's Gate. Hey—where's everyone else?"

Artie shrugged. "Dunno. You're the first one I've found. The gate that brought us here must have been a doozy. Knocked us all out and scattered us everywhere."

"Oh," she said, still recovering. They sat in silence for a few moments, and then Kay asked solemnly, "What about Dad?"

Artie shook his head slowly. "I haven't seen him yet, but I guess he's still frozen in stone," Artie said angrily. He couldn't believe what Merlin had done to Kynder and that now his dad lay encased in stone, hovering between life and death.

Kay fought back her own feelings about Merlin and said, "Well, let's find that rock, then. As long as we have it we still have a shot at saving him, right?" Kay asked desperately.

"Yes. We have to," Artie said. And then, as if to convince himself that they truly did have a shot at saving their dad, he repeated emphatically, "*We have to.*"

"We *will* save him, Kingfishers," a deep voice said. Artie and Kay spun and saw the inchoate green figure of Numinae, tree lord of Sylvan, arriving through the mist. "I swear it to you."

"Noomy!" Artie and Kay said together. Another reunion followed, with hugs and congratulations and back slaps. Numinae said that Kynder's rock had safely made the trip, and it was just to the east on the other side of a low dune.

Artie and Kay breathed a sigh of relief. "I am so glad we made it, sire," Numinae said. "It may sound silly, but I'm proud of you."

Artie blushed a little. It wasn't silly at all. Numinae, as strange as he was with his moss for skin and his branchlike extremities and his freaky green eyes, was the closest thing they had to a father figure now. "We couldn't have done it without you, Numinae," Artie said. "And please, don't call me 'sire.'"

Numinae put a large green hand on Artie's shoulder. "My lord, this is Avalon. You brought us here. Only the king of the Otherworld can do that. Like it or not, you are no longer just Artie Kingfisher. You are a Pendragon, the Uniter of Worlds, Arthur the Second. You are my king . . . *sire*."

Artie was filled with so many different feelings that he couldn't put up a fight. "Okay, whatever, Numinae. . . . Have you seen any of the others?"

"Yes. Lance is near your father. And that was why I was looking for you. He needs our help."

"Well, what are we waiting for?" Kay disappeared into the mist in the direction Numinae pointed. Artie and Numinae followed. As they jogged, Artie asked, "To save our dad we need to get the—"

"The Grail, sire."

"The *Holy* Grail."

"Yes, sire."

"Any idea how to do that?"

"None at all."

"Great."

"Here he is!" Kay called, kneeling next to Lance. "Artie, he's burning!"

"*What?*" Artie knelt next to Kay, unslinging the scabbard.

Sure enough, the outside of Lance's right leg was seared to a smoking crisp. He was definitely alive, though, and he turned to face them, his eyes shut, his breath shallow and quick.

"Morgaine's dragon nicked him, remember?" Numinae said, also kneeling over Lance.

"Right, I forgot." Artie pushed Excalibur's scabbard onto Lance's leg. As soon as the leather made contact, a few blisters on Lance's skin withered and disappeared. Lance's lips twitched and he frowned as the wound began to magically heal.

"I can help as well, sire." Numinae pressed his hands together and hummed quietly. After a few moments he pulled his hands apart, a sheet of moss forming between them like a cat's cradle. He smoothed this over Lance's wounds. "This will ease his pain. Still, we need to get him someplace safe to rest. And fresh water to drink."

As Lance stabilized, Artie lifted Lance's sword, Orgulus, from the sand and handed it to Numinae. "Keep this until he's back on his feet, will you?"

Numinae took the rapier and slid it into his leg as if he had a sheath built into his hip. "It would be my honor."

Kay looked at the ornate hilt sticking out of Numinae's side. "That doesn't hurt?"

"A little, but you know me."

"Do I, you big weirdo."

Numinae smiled one of his creepy smiles as Kay punched him playfully in the arm.

Artie stood. "Let's find the others."

They fanned out across the beach and within fifteen minutes had located most everyone. To their great relief, none had more than a bump on his or her head. Thumb literally jumped for joy when he heard that they'd made it to Avalon. Qwon, more baffled than elated, held Artie hard by the arm and asked, "*Where* are we now?" Sami and Erik were both pretty casual about the whole thing, although Erik asked, "If this is Avalon where's the castle? There *is* a castle here, right?" Thumb and Numinae assured him there was. Shallot le Fey was the outlier. She wasn't happy or nonchalant.

She was sad.

After coming around she stayed seated in the sand, The Anguish laying across her legs. Artie sat next to her and asked if she was okay. Her answer was one small word: "Bors."

Artie squeezed her shoulder reassuringly. "I'm sorry."

Shallot shook her head, trying to rid her mind of the image of Bors's death. He had been whisked into the air by Morgaine's magic and torn in two, his body turning to golden dust and blowing over the Fenlandian beach. Shallot steeled herself and said, "I'm sorry also. But I *am* glad we made it."

"Me too, Shallot. And thank you for bringing Qwon to me."

Shallot forced a smile. Her sharpened teeth glowed in the dull light. Forgetting about Qwon, she said, "I will avenge his death."

Artie clasped a hand over hers. "No. *We* will."

They joined the others, who talked excitedly about Avalon. Numinae, however, was quiet and frowning. "We're missing—"

"Dred!" Qwon blurted. She sounded a little too desperate to Artie's ear, but his jealousy took an automatic backseat to his relief. He was, above everything, just happy that Qwon was back and safe.

"Over here, lads," Thumb called. The group rushed over and Artie plopped next to Dred, who was lying in a little depression and still unconscious. Artie touched Dred's arm and said, "Hey, wake up. It's Artie. Your . . . brother."

My brother, Artie thought. He could still hardly believe it.

Dred's lips moved and he slowly opened his eyes. "I'm here," he said hoarsely.

But before Artie could respond, Qwon dropped between them. "Are you okay?" she asked, taking Dred's hand.

Dred stared at Qwon and smiled. Artie watched them, his heart beating hard. Somehow, in spite of all they'd been through, Qwon's straight black hair was perfect. The skin of her rounded features was marred here and there with dirt, but she looked really, well, cute.

Artie turned his gaze to Dred. His brother had the same ruddy hair (though a little longer than Artie's), the same hazel eyes, the same straight nose, the same thin lips.

"I-I'm so sorry, Artie," Dred muttered.

"About what?" Kay asked. "You returned Excalibur to Artie! If you hadn't we'd all be toast."

"True. But my mother . . . Morgaine." His eyes darted around the beach. "I'm sorry she kidnapped you, Qwon. And that she imprisoned you, Shallot."

"You *should* be sorry for that, Fenlandian," Shallot snapped. But then she smiled a little and said, "Though for my part, I'm sorry I wanted to kill you when we began our escape from Castel Deorc Wæters."

Dred chuckled. "Looking back, I wouldn't blame you if you had."

Shallot pointed her chin at Qwon. "She stopped me. She and Bors . . . ," Shallot said, trailing off.

"I'm sorry we lost him," Dred said. "If I could have, I'd—"

Shallot tried to put on a brave face. "It will be all right. He died for a reason."

"And we lived for one," Numinae said in his deep voice.

Artie stuck out a hand, and with Qwon's help they pulled Dred to his feet. "That's right, everybody. We *did* live for a reason. Right now that reason is to get Lance into a bed, find this King's Gate thing, and then start on our next quest—for the Holy Grail."

"Darn right," Kay said weakly. She took a half step back and brought her hand to her forehead. Something felt different to Kay. Something felt off.

Artie leaned close to her. "You all right?"

"It's our link, Artie," Kay said just loudly enough that he could hear. "All of a sudden I can't feel it anymore!"

Artie took her hand. She was right! Their peculiar connection was gone, or at least in Artie's case, altered. Because he could feel *someone*—just not Kay. Artie frowned, searching his feelings, and then it hit him. Kay had been replaced by Dred. Artie could feel his breath and his arms and legs as they moved. This new sensation was not as intense as it had been with Kay, but it *was* there. Whether Dred had similar sensations, Artie couldn't tell.

"Don't worry, Sis. Maybe once we go home it'll come back."

Kay straightened. "I hope so."

"Everything okay, lads?" Thumb asked.

"Uh, yeah, Tom. Just having a brother-sister moment," Artie said.

"We're fine, Tommy. Thanks," Kay said without a trace of her trademark sarcasm.

"Peachy, lads."

Just then Dred clapped Artie on the back. "So—is there more to Avalon than this beach?"

"Certainly, lad," Thumb answered. "Castle Tintagel. I used to visit it in the olden days. . . ." He trailed off, lost in memories.

"Is it close?" Shallot asked.

"Avalon is not large, lady fairy," Thumb answered. "It won't be hard to find."

"Good," Artie announced. "Numinae, will you carry Lance?"

"Yes, sire."

"And Sami—can you grab Kynder?"

"Of course. You know a little thing like crushing weight can't stop me."

"I sure do." Artie looked over his friends—his *knights!*—and said, "The rest of us should check the beach for our things. When we're done, we'll head inland and find this Tintagel."

"Sounds like a plan, lad," Thumb said. "I'll go check over—"

But Numinae slid a finger over Thumb's lips and cut him off. The forest lord cocked an ear toward the mist as the others froze, their hands tightening around the hilts of their weapons. The only noise any of them could hear was that of the waves lapping at the unseen shoreline.

"Ready, friends," Numinae warned in a fierce whisper. "Something approaches."

𝕹uminae, all seven-plus feet of him, stepped toward the noise. "What is it, Noomy?" Kay whispered.

Numinae didn't answer. His right hand began to glow with a spell.

Then the knights made out a faint, high-pitched squeak. Artie pointed Excalibur at the sound and peered into the mist. "Clear!" Artie ordered quietly.

An invisible jolt of energy leaped from the sword's blood channels, wending around Numinae like a will-o'-the-wisp, and parted the mist.

After a few moments the mist revealed a grizzled old man, with a huge round nose like a turnip, dressed in a light cotton shirt and a heavy leather vest. Or it was half a man, anyway. He had a head and shoulders and arms and a chest and a stomach, giving him all the essential parts of a person, but he had no legs. His abdomen was strapped into a contraption that consisted of a single brass wheel, about two feet in diameter, covered with a black rubber tire. He propelled himself with a pair of weathered wooden sticks that attached to his wrists at right angles, leaving his hands free. In his right hand was a flare-muzzled musket like a pirate's.

"Who's that?" the man demanded, the black metal of the gun shaking like a leaf in a gale.

His eyes were open but they were as white as golf balls. He was blind.

"I am Numinae, lord of Sylvan."

The man stopped. "No, you are not. You cannot be here. It is not permitted."

"I am not alone."

The man's blank eyes darted in their sockets as if he could see. "Who brings you here?"

Artie stepped forward. "Me."

The man turned his ear toward Artie. "You sound a boy!" he exclaimed nervously. The man's gun hand shook more. Numinae held up his spell, ready to let loose.

Artie said, "So was the first Arthur, when he found out who he was."

The wheel squeaked as the legless man backed up a little. "Marvel! So you *are*—"

"Yes. I'm King Arthur Pendragon the Second. And I'm here to—"

In a startling burst the musket went off, blowing a cloud into the air. Numinae let his spell fly, but Artie stayed cool. He yanked Excalibur across his body and deflected the ball flying from the pistol at hundreds of feet per second. As the gray slug careened away harmlessly, Numinae's spell exploded in a flurry of leaves and sticks and knocked the man onto the ground.

Artie held up a hand. "Wait!" He lowered Excalibur and approached the man. "Are you all right?"

"I-I . . ."

"You weren't expecting me, were you, Bran?"

"How is it that you know my name?"

Artie knew because of Excalibur, but he didn't see the need to reveal this. "I know because I'm king."

Bran blinked. "I am sorry. It has been so long. I did not intend to fire. I am merely a decrepit guardian who has not been 'proximate to another living person for as long as I can recall. . . ."

Artie bent to help Bran get upright.

"It's okay, Bran," Artie said. "We're a little shocked ourselves."

"How came you here?"

"That's a long story," Kay said.

"Who is the lady?"

Kay blushed. "Kay Kingfisher. I'm the, uh, king's sister."

"Ah! A countess!"

She blushed some more. "Not exactly . . ."

Artie patted Bran on a shoulder. "There're more here too."

"Yes. I can hear them. And who might they be?"

One by one Artie introduced everyone, mentioning each of the Seven Swords when appropriate. Thumb was last.

"Thumb, did you say? *Tom* Thumb?" Bran asked excitedly.

Tom scrambled back onto the little dune. "That's right, Sir Bran. Do you remember me?"

"Of course I do! All of the castle knights called you friend. 'Cept Lady Guinivere as I recall. She was not accepting of so little and amusing a person as yourself."

"That's right, Sir Bran." Tom chuckled, lost in old memories.

"So there *is* a castle here?" Erik asked.

"Assuredly, Sir Erik, bearer of Gram. It is just yon, beyond the dunes, attendant—though it has been surrendering to gravity and the elements for many a century. A blind, legless caretaker is not always an adequate caretaker, if you follow."

"We don't care, Bran," Artie said. "Are there beds? Is there water?"

"Yes. The inside of the castle remains in pristine condition, that much I have managed. And the larders are full of medicines and potions and food and—"

"Food?" several asked at once, and at the same time they all realized how hungry they were.

Bran smiled. "Yes, food. Fruit, butter, bread—"

"Mac and cheese?" Erik asked.

"Um . . ." Bran hesitated.

"Popsicles?" Kay wondered.

"I'm not sure I—"

"French fries?" Qwon asked, who, along with Shallot, was probably the hungriest of all of them.

"I do not know of these things, but I can guarantee you will be sated," Bran answered.

This was great news, and the group immediately went nuts over the idea of eating. Artie moved to the front of the pack and wrapped an arm over Bran's shoulders. "Lead the way, buddy," he said, and they filed out.

As they left the beach, the sand gave way to an earthy loam covered in grass and wildflowers. The sun began to break through the mist, revealing a rolling, treeless countryside. The party walked uphill for nearly a mile following a winding gravel path. Aside from this, there was no sign of any people.

As they walked, Artie told Bran how they'd fought Morgaine and arrived at Avalon. Kay told of retrieving

Kusanagi, and Erik of pulling Gram from the tree, and Sami of being tricked by the trio of kids who'd infiltrated his camp and changed the course of his life. Thumb gloomily recounted Merlin's betrayal. Qwon, unable to forget for even a second all the grub Bran had promised, pined out loud for a cheeseburger and pickles and a Coke.

"Again, m'lady, I haven't the slightest idea what you speak of," Bran said apologetically.

"Good food, Bran," Qwon tried to explain. "Not good *for* you, but man, *good,* you know? I haven't had a burger in weeks." She paused. "What I really want is Red Lobster."

"Preach, Q!" Erik exclaimed. "I love the salad bar there."

"Mmm," Kay hummed. "Bacon bits."

"As promised, I will treat your appetites duly, my knights," Bran said comfortingly. "I can conjure or cook anything your heart desires at the castle. Speaking of which . . ."

The gravel path took a steep turn and just like that, as if it had been shrouded by some kind of magical veil, a modest stone fortress appeared in front of them. Bran announced, "Welcome, good knights. Welcome to Tintagel."

While there was no doubt it was a castle, it was nothing like Mont-Saint-Michel—either the lovely French version or the terrifying Otherworld one—where Artie and his knights had to go to retrieve Orgulus from the den of that horrible giant. Tintagel was smaller and tumbledown and neglected—in parts more ruin than stronghold. "Wow," Kay said sarcastically. "Nice."

"It was, once upon a time," Bran murmured. "Come."

He led the way down the path and over a rickety bridge, passing through the wall under a gateless arch and into a wide courtyard. At the far end stood a tall stone building with a peaked roof framed by a pair of towers. A tattered flag of indeterminate color wafted on the breeze at the apex of the building's gable. Scattered around the yard were outbuildings and storehouses, all in various states of decay. As the knights crossed the yard, Bran explained how the castle had been relocated rock by rock via crossover gate directly from Cornwall, England. Fairies and sprites, men and knights, had all lent a hand. "Arthur the First decreed that it be moved," Bran said over the squeak of his wheel. "It was the place of his birth and the home of his parents, Uther Pendragon and Lady Igraine. He wished it preserved for posterity, by sooth, from the destructive hands of the Saxons, who were nothing less than a blood-rotten scourge in those days."

Artie didn't care about Saxons. But he was curious about the parents. It occurred to him then that maybe Thumb had met them. "Did you know them at all, Tom?" Artie asked. "My biological parents?"

Dred raised his eyebrows. "*Our* biological parents."

Artie shot Dred a look. "Yeah. Sorry."

"All I know of your parents, lads, is that Igraine died not long after the birth of Arthur, and that Uther subsequently succumbed to a lonely heart." He paused. "Did you know them, Sir Bran?"

Bran grunted. "Not formally. On occasion I have seen their apparitions, though. They sometimes wander the parapet walls in the nighttime, holding hands. Even in death their love has endured." Everyone looked at the jagged castle walls, half expecting to see a pair of blue ghosts. "I cannot recall when I saw them last. Time is not one of my, er, specialties. I have spent too many days here to understand time's passage anymore."

"My parents are *ghosts*?" Artie blurted.

Qwon said, "Maybe we should have a séance. You'd like that, right, Dred?"

Dred was more serious. He shook his head. Thinking of Uther and Igraine only made him remember the finger bone and the lock of hair hidden under Castel Deorc Wæters—those same parental relics from which Morgaine had extracted Artie's and Dred's DNA so that she could biologically engineer the twins in that horrifying subterranean lab. "No," Dred said to Qwon. "They are dead as far as I'm concerned."

"That's the spirit," Shallot said coolly. "No pun intended, of course."

"Whatever," Artie said. He didn't want to admit it, but he was a little disappointed he probably wouldn't be seeing his parents floating around Castle Tintagel's halls. "Maybe now that me and Dred are around, they'll show up and we can ask for some ghost stories."

"Maybe," Dred said quietly.

"Regardless," Bran said, "I have not seen the Pendragons in decades." He stopped before a huge set of double doors. "Or perhaps centuries. But lo, here we are. Time for you to see what this castle keeps."

"The King's Gate?" Kay asked eagerly.

"But maybe we could eat first?" Qwon asked quietly. All this talk of food had set her imagination—and her taste buds—on fire.

"Seriously—I'm starving," added Erik.

"Of course," Kay said, punching Erik in the shoulder and making his pale cheeks blush. "But Artie here needs to make it official. That's one of the things we've been fighting toward, remember—making Artie king."

Much less eagerly, Artie said, "Kay's right. As soon as we're full of food and have gotten some rest, I need to find this King's Gate, Bran. And then, we need to figure out how to bring our dad back."

"Do not fret, sire. The King's Gate is not hard to find. Let's inside." Bran pointed one of his sticks at a spot on the wall and, with exact precision, pressed an inconspicuous button. He brought his stick down, and the doors, which were painted with King Arthur's seal—a red field with three yellow crowns—swung inward.

A pitch-black hall appeared before them. Bran entered first, followed by Artie, who drew Excalibur and asked for some light. The blade began to glow, and the inside of Tintagel was revealed.

As promised, this part was not tumbledown at all. The floor was covered with an ornate rug that ran the length of the hall, and the stone walls were hung with tapestries showing all manner of woodland scenes and battle motifs. Bran wheeled farther in, sweeping his hand through the air. "Down there to the left is a staircase that leads to the bedrooms. There is one for each of you and more to spare. You can put your ailing friend in the nearest one to rest."

"If you'll open me a moongate, sire, I'll go to Sylvan to get what I need to help Lance recover more quickly," Numinae said, referring to the moongates that Excalibur's pommel stone could open for Artie and his knights to get around both worlds.

"Consider it done," Artie said.

Bran continued, "Past the staircase are halls leading to various storerooms that you will find not at all interesting, but at the end of the hall is a special room that you must visit."

"The King's Gate?" Artie asked.

"I cannot say, sire. It is for you—all of you—to see first-hand."

Just then they reached the staircase, and Artie stopped. He eyed Lance, who moaned in Numinae's arms. "Numinae—you and I'll go upstairs and help Lance. The rest of you get some snacks. Bran, when we're done, we'll go together into this surprise room of yours. Is there a place to sit in there?"

"Assuredly, sire," Bran said with a smirk.

"Then we'll be eating dinner there too."

"I will start on your meal posthaste."

Kay nudged her brother and whispered, "So authoritative."

Artie winked at her and said, "All right, see you guys in a few." And then he strutted up the stairs, Numinae following.

As the others watched them, Artie heard Qwon whisper to Kay, "Hope this king thing doesn't go to his head."

Kay paused a second and said, "Yeah, me too."

An hour later, after stuffing themselves with bread and cheese and almonds and dried fruit, the knights reconvened in front of a heavy metal door at the end of a long hallway.

"Have at it, Bran," Artie said.

The caretaker nodded and reached into the contraption attaching his body to the wheel. His hand clanked around in the metal innards and came free holding a long spike with a series of holes bored through it. "The key," he explained. "The key to the Royal Chamber."

"Sweet," Erik whispered from the back.

The rest were silent as Bran inserted the spike into a small circle set in the middle of the door. Sounds of locks being thrown came from within and it began to open. It was not a normal door, though. Not at all. It didn't swing in or out, but instead it sort of came apart as an intricate series of interwoven metal bars slid into the wall at all angles. It took thirty seconds for it to finish opening, and when it was done Artie stepped into the dark and cavernous room. As soon as he crossed the threshold a host of lights beamed on, and a huge fire leaped to life in a stone hearth so big even Numinae could have walked into it without ducking. It was as if the chamber was a living thing that knew they were there.

"Cool," Qwon breathed.

"Morgaine used to do tricks like that all the time," Dred mused.

Qwon leaned on Dred a little and said, "Lucky for us, there's no Morgaine around here."

"You can say that again," Shallot said from behind them.

Kay pushed past her brother and walked into the chamber. "C'mon, guys, let's check it out."

The Royal Chamber was a round room seventy feet in diameter with a high domed ceiling. The floor was covered in thick animal pelts. The air inside was cool and fresh. The walls were hung with the banners of the old Knights of the Round Table—those heraldic signs emblazoned on their shields or sewed to the tunics covering their armor. In front of each banner was a chair—and between the chairs was a massive round table.

The party filed in. "Far out," Erik commented, scanning the impressive room. All of them stared, their mouths hanging open.

Artie pointed across the room to a red banner with three crowns on it. "That one's King Arthur's," he said proudly.

"And there's Sir Kay's!" Kay exclaimed excitedly. "And there's yours, Tommy!"

"Aye, lass."

"And that one was the first Mordred's," Dred said, pointing the Peace Sword at a banner with a double-headed eagle stitched over a field of purple and white.

"Who are those for?" Qwon asked, sweeping a finger across a series of unclaimed emblems.

"Perceval and Gawain," Artie said.

"And Tristram and Lancelot," Shallot added.

"And Galahad," Thumb said reverently.

They turned circles, taking it all in. The high ceiling and the banners were impressive enough, but what was most jaw-dropping was the table. It was so big that it looked as if the tree that produced it had been felled on the spot, and the room then built around the stump.

At forty feet across, it simply dominated the room. Artie walked right to it and laid a hand on the smooth, worn surface. The wood was strangely warm to the touch, and as his fingers felt the grain, his mind filled with sounds that only he could hear: the banter of countless men, and a few women, talking over one another; the clank and bang of metal; the thump of boots on the floor; laughter and music and revelry. Here was where King Arthur the First had discussed his problems with his knights. Here was where they strategized tactics and undertook new quests. Here was where they feasted and relaxed and told their stories. Here, at this table, Arthur was safe, with his friends and confidants.

And Artie would be too.

Artie spun on his heel to look at his friends. "I . . . I don't know what to say. Guys, this is it. I can't thank you enough. Each of you has saved my life at some point, some more than once. You've all been nice to me, and encouraging, and, well, not freaked out. Or not *too* freaked out, anyway. But guys"—he waved his hand behind him—"this is it! This is where King Arthur—*King Arthur!*—went about his business. It's where the Knights of the Round Table decided what was right and what was wrong, and figured out how and where to fight for what they believed in. And now . . ." He trailed off.

"It's where we will do the same, Brother!" Dred said excitedly.

"Darn right!" Kay seconded, pulling Cleomede from its sheath and holding it overhead. Then all of the knights drew their weapons and pointed them at the ceiling and called out Artie's name.

Artie smiled and his heart filled. He'd never felt like this. Never. Not back home in Shadyside, not in battle, not even when he'd put that school bully, Frankie Finkelstein, in his place.

"That's right, guys," Artie said. "Welcome home. Welcome, New Knights of the Round Table!"

There was more cheering and backslapping and hugs and smiles, as all of them were infected with the joy of having achieved a goal that not five months earlier had been unimaginable. As the noise died down, Kay found herself next to Artie and said, "We did it, Bro. We freaking did it."

"Yeah, we did." He turned to the group. "We need to talk about what's next. We've got to help Kynder, and we need to deal with Merlin, as much as I don't want to."

"Aye, lad."

"And we need to open this King's Gate thing, wherever it is."

"That we do, Artie," Numinae said quietly, holding out a hand to guide Artie to his throne.

"Great," Artie said, following Numinae's direction. "Everyone, let's grab some Round Table pine and talk things over."

They sheathed their weapons and made their way around the table. As Artie walked to his throne he passed a simple stone chair pushed against the wall. It was so small and out of the way that he didn't give it a second thought. But Numinae, who walked alongside him, said quietly, "Remind me later to tell you something important about that chair."

"Roger that," Artie said.

Finally he reached his throne. It was large but also very plain. Its rough finish was reddish brown and it had two simple flourishes: a blue velvet seat cushion and a plate-size circle cut out of the apex of the chair back. Inside this cut-out was a lens of pale glass that caught the room's meager light.

Artie scooted between the table and the throne. He placed Excalibur on the table with a clunk. He grabbed the armrests and lowered himself onto the cushion.

His heart filled even more. This was it. They were now King Artie Kingfisher and the *New* Knights of the Round Table.

But as soon as his full weight rested on that ancient

chair, the hall filled with the sound of a tempest and Artie's banner whipped up and battered the air. The others gasped and had to catch their breath as a wind swirled through the room. What was happening? A high-pitched howl pierced their ears. It came from behind Artie, and he spun to look, half expecting to see the ghostly bodies of his long-gone parents staring down at him. Instead, he saw an opening in the wall behind his banner. Before he could say anything, a bright-green flash blinded all of the knights. Some raised their weapons, others their hands. But not Artie. Instead, Artie was being whisked into the air on invisible strings and dragged into an unknown portal.

Artie reached out to try and grab something—anything—that would stop him. But nothing was there. He heard his friends calling out in desperation and caught sight of Sami bounding over the Round Table, his massive arms outstretched. The light grew very bright, and Artie yelled, but no sound came.

And then, just like that, the world was dark.

𝕭𝖑𝖆𝖈𝖐𝖓𝖊𝖘𝖘. 𝖀𝖙𝖙𝖊𝖗 𝖆𝖓𝖉 𝖈𝖔𝖒𝖕𝖑𝖊𝖙𝖊. 𝕬𝖗𝖙𝖎𝖊'𝖘 body was suddenly weightless. It was like he was in a dream. . . .

He tumbled through this featureless abyss, the *thump-thump* of his pounding heart the only sound he could hear. But he was not afraid. Because Artie knew with total certainty that he had just passed through the King's Gate.

He didn't know *how* he knew; he just did. Like so much that had happened to him, it was magic.

He drifted for an indeterminate amount of time.

Then a loud noise came like a thousand doors opening all at once. Artie blinked as images appeared before him. A tree. A car. A television. A sword. An Xbox controller. A bird. A dragon. A waterfall. A thin blue line. A white stag.

His sister's red hair when it was still long. The Seven Swords. The many-tailed fox from Japan. Twrch Trwyth. Lavery. Cassie and her crazy eyes. All of it. Everyone he and Kay had seen and met on their adventures in the Otherworld. He saw creatures: dire wolves, a giant vulture, a pigeon, a saber-toothed tiger, an aurochs, all manner of dragons.

Then he saw one final thing: the Serpent Mound in faraway Ohio, where little Thumb had opened the first crossover point between the worlds; the moon hung in the sky like an ornament. It was a scene from a fairy tale. And then Artie thought, *I* am a thing from a fairy tale.

And that was when Artie realized that *all* of earth's crossover points had just been opened—triggered by the opening of the King's Gate. It seemed that in this strange abyss, he was passing each of these portals that linked the Otherworld to the normal world Artie had grown up in.

The worlds had finally been rejoined.

From now on it would be just like the old days when fairies and men interacted; when spirits visited the likes of Qwon's ancestors in Japan; and when lucky children would be able to play in fields or attics with little people like Tom Thumb. As Artie passed through this void, he understood that this was the way the worlds were meant to be, and it made him feel great. They shouldn't be separate. There were not two worlds but one. Everything was connected, and everything was wondrous. Everybody—every kid or grown-up from every age of man—wanted to believe in some kind of magic, and now they would have that chance again. Moreover, Artie understood that if he could just find enough sangrealite to bring to his side, then he could get started on giving his world a completely clean source of energy.

Maybe, just maybe, Artie could *literally* save the world.

Which was pretty nuts.

Then the images disappeared, replaced by total darkness. Whether Artie drifted through this black place for days or for a split second, he couldn't say. Time was immaterial. Would he die there? Would he get out? He didn't know. A pit of anxiety began to grow in his belly, but when it reached his lungs, causing his breath to quicken, a face formed in the middle distance. It belonged to a man with ruddy hair, thin lips, and hazel eyes. The face got closer. There were his neck and shoulders. Artie could see that his nose was so crooked, it looked as if it had been broken in about a thousand fights with a thousand bullies. The man was older than Artie, perhaps by thirty years. There was a long scar over one of his cheeks. Stubble roughed the skin like sandpaper. His hair was long and swept into a ponytail. A shirt came into view. It was . . . silver.

The man smiled.

Artie frowned. Who wore a silver shirt?

And then Artie saw that it wasn't a shirt at all. It was the edge of a breastplate. Across the top of the breastplate, over the collarbone, were three small crowns, a stripe of red painted behind them.

Artie stopped drifting and realized that he was face-to-face with King Arthur I.

"Hi," Artie mouthed, the void swallowing all sound.

King Arthur sat atop a massive speckled horse. Both wore full plate armor like you'd see in any half-decent medieval RPG video game (like *Otherworld*, for instance). Arthur raised his hand. The old king wanted to show the new king something.

Arthur pointed.

Artie squinted. It was hard to make out, but at the end of all the darkness there was a simple black door, and in its center was a little hole shaped like a crown.

A keyhole.

Arthur gave Artie a stern look. He jabbed his finger at the door, then at himself, and then, finally, at Artie.

Arthur was saying that he had once gone through that door and that Artie would have to go through it as well.

All he had to do was find a crown-shaped key.

The ancient king spurred his horse and it launched forward, barreling toward Artie, who couldn't move out of the way. He brought his hands to his face and ducked, preparing for impact. There was no sound, but he could feel the horse's hot breath on the crown of his head just before it hit. Artie was terrified, certain that he was about to be trampled to death in some weird dreamscape.

Only he wasn't. There was no pain. In fact, he didn't feel a thing. The horse had passed right through him.

But the dreamscape had changed. Artie *could* hear again. And what he heard was the wind blowing.

He opened his eyes. No. The wind wasn't blowing. *He was falling through the sky!*

He cartwheeled violently and saw purplish clouds, a sprawling forest, and a hill in the distance. The wind squealed. A flock of pigeons flew past him. Then he caught sight of the horizon and looked down. He was falling over a lake—*the* Lake—and it was getting closer, fast.

He scrambled in the air, trying frantically to control his body. He didn't have a parachute—he was going to die!

But as Artie approached the glassy surface, another unexpected face appeared, this one just below the water. Was it . . . ? Yes, it was! The Lady of the Lake smiled placidly, as if to say, "Relax. You'll be fine."

Here goes nothing, Artie thought. At the last moment he righted his body so that his feet were straight down. Just before impact he brought both hands to his face, took a huge breath, and clamped his nose shut.

Splash!

Artie slowed quickly but had to hang on to his nose and

clench his jaw to prevent his entire head from filling with water. As he regained his sense of direction, he kicked and paddled, hoping to get to the surface and take a full breath of air.

But no matter how hard he tried to swim, he went nowhere.

No. Worse than that—no matter how hard he tried to swim, he went deeper!

He looked down. His heart was full of fear and his lungs were stinging. Beneath him was the blue form of the Lady of the Lake. She had wrapped her watery tendrils around his feet and was dragging him to the depths.

"Dash your fear," her calm voice echoed in his ears. "I am helping you."

He wanted to scream, "By drowning me?" but didn't dare open his mouth.

She dragged him farther and farther down. His ears wailed and popped painfully three, four, five times. The light from the day faded. The water pushed all around him.

There was no avoiding it. He was going to drown. And then he did.

𝕺𝖓𝖑𝖞 𝖍𝖊 𝖉𝖎𝖉𝖓'𝖙 𝖉𝖗𝖔𝖜𝖓. 𝕳𝖊 was shocked to find that he was still breathing—*breathing water*!

He began to panic, but the Lady wrapped him in a big hug. "Stay, friend; you are alive and well."

Artie willed his body to stop moving. He stared into the dark eyes before him. He could see them perfectly, as if there were no water to blur his vision.

The Lady—who still had the face of a girl of five or six, and whose skin and hair were still tinted blue—retreated a little. "Try to breathe easy."

Easy for her to say, Artie thought. His face must have contained some indication of his discomfort, for the Lady said, "It is all right. Your body will accept it. Stay," she repeated. "Calm your heart."

Artie did as he was told. He found himself barely breathing at all, yet he was very conscious and very much alive. The water must have contained a high concentration of oxygen; either that or the Lady was simply keeping him alive with some kind of aquatic magic.

They were in an underwater cul-de-sac with a high wall of rock on three sides. All around, the water was lit by an ethereal glow. As Artie's senses adjusted he realized that the source of light was the Lady herself; she shone in blues and greens and the ends of her hair trailed light like a luminescent sea creature. Behind the water fairy was a stand of tall plants that shimmied on unseen currents. Artie understood that she was right: if there was any danger in the world above, then he *was* safe here. Artie felt like this might have been the safest place in either of the worlds.

He tried to talk, but the Lady held up a hand. "I regret to say that you will be unable to speak. I will attempt to answer your queries, though. I am Nyneve. The Lake is me, and I am the Lake. . . ."

You mean you can hear my thoughts? Artie wondered, realizing that if she really was the water, then she was literally inside his head. Not to mention a lot of other places.

He blushed a little, and the Lady gave him a comforting smile.

"Not perfectly, but I can comprehend the direction of them."

Artie's thoughts swung helplessly to Kynder and Kay and all of his friends. Then he thought: I need the Grail, Nyneve. I need the Grail to save my dad.

"Yes, I will tell you about the Grail in good time. But first I must warn you of the wizard."

Merlin?

"There is a thing you must know about him, Arthur." She paused and retreated a little on the currents. "The sword wants him dead."

Artie knew it was crazy to think that a sword could want something, but this was Excalibur they were talking about—and Excalibur was anything but a typical sword.

I kind of want him dead too, Artie admitted halfheartedly. Merlin had given Artie strength and self-confidence and even purpose, which was a tall order for a twelve-year-old boy. But he'd also taken a lot from Artie. He'd lied throughout this whole thing, and he'd practically killed Kynder. The thought of that alone filled Artie with rage.

Nyneve smiled. Her teeth were as white as pearls. Her eyes twinkled with something between satisfaction and desire. "Good that you wish him dead too, for the only hand that can wield Excalibur in slaying the wizard belongs to you. Arthur, you alone must strike down Merlin Ambrosius with Excalibur!"

Artie's body shook. He'd seen what Merlin could do in

battle; Artie did not dig the idea of fighting Merlin up close and personal. He wondered, Why me?

But he knew the answer.

"You are the king," she said matter-of-factly. "Pray, Arthur, has Numinae told you of Merlin's soul?"

Artie frowned. Huh?

"It is part demon. This, in sum, is why the firebrand wishes him dead."

A demon! Artie thought, his head spinning. Really? If true, that could explain a heck of a lot.

"It is true. Confronting the wizard will be unavoidable, Arthur. Excalibur is risen for this purpose. Do you understand?"

Artie nodded unenthusiastically. Yeah. I get it. Me versus a sorcerer. A sorcerer who, not that long ago, I looked up to. . . .

Great.

He shook his head and thought, But the Grail . . .

Nyneve held out both hands. "If you must have the Grail, start with the witch. She knows things I do not."

What? Artie had just defeated Morgaine—now he had to ask her for help?

Nyneve didn't offer an answer. "The magic sustaining you is weakening, sire. Before you leave, I ask you to receive a gift. The king of the Otherworld is due one last tool. This is exceedingly powerful, one of the most potent items the worlds have ever seen. Few know of it. Arthur the First possessed it, and in all his years never found occasion to use it. Wait here."

Where else would I go? Artie wondered.

Nyneve drifted away. As her glimmering body drew closer to the wall, it revealed a cutout in the stone. It was lined with a silvery metal, throwing Nyneve's luminescence in all directions. She reached in and worked out a small something that Artie couldn't see.

She returned, her hands cupped together. In them was a thin metal tube, no longer or wider than a finger.

"This is Scarffern."

Artie looked at it dubiously. That was one of the most powerful things ever? What was he supposed to do with it?

"Blow it, sire. You must discover its spell for yourself. Excalibur is the symbol of your power, Arthur Pendragon the Second, and it is a swift and cunning blade. But Scarffern is the *secret* of your power. Properly wielded, Scarffern will make the lords and lordesses of the Otherworld respect you, even if they despise you."

Morgaine, Artie thought.

"Yes, sire."

Artie held out his hand, and Nyneve dropped the little tube into it.

"Keep it safe."

Artie looked into Nyneve's eyes. Thanks, Nyneve, for watching over this. Excalibur too.

"It is my duty, my liege. Now, our time is up. Since you haven't Excalibur with you, I've opened a moongate by the chestnut tree. It will return you to Tintagel."

In that instant Nyneve disappeared and the grotto went completely dark. And then Artie started to rise—fast. He clenched Scarffern in his fist as the water rushed around his body. As he rose, he found that he could no longer breathe. His heart quickened, his chest tightened, and within ten seconds he broke above the surface like a submarine blowing out its bellows.

Red-faced, Artie gasped and got control of himself.

He was treading water in the middle of the Lake, close to the buoy he'd visited with Kay and Thumb back when they were first there to get Excalibur. Moored to the buoy was the red canoe.

Artie swam to the boat. He climbed in and collapsed, catching his breath and gathering his thoughts. He stared up at the Otherworld sky. Every now and then a pigeon flew by. He wasn't sure, but he thought he saw the angular silhouette of a red-tufted jaybird—one of those Fenlandian creatures loyal to Morgaine—as well.

The sun was fading and the air was starting to cool. He was still wet. He needed to get back to the castle.

He pushed the mysterious Scarffern into a front pocket of his jeans. He untied the canoe's line, positioned himself in the rear seat, and began to paddle. He easily sighted the chestnut tree and navigated toward it.

He paddled hard, and it felt good. His heart rate rose, his chest warmed. Sweat gleamed on his forehead. As the boat glided through the water, he watched the shore grow closer and closer. Then he caught sight of the shimmering light of a moongate. He was nearly there. He was nearly back with his friends.

But what Artie didn't know was that just above the moongate, perched on a large branch, was his old friend and new enemy, the wizard Merlin.

IN WHICH MERLIN GETS HEATED

𝕿𝖍𝖊 𝖈𝖆𝖓𝖔𝖊'𝖘 𝖐𝖊𝖊𝖑 𝖈𝖚𝖙 𝖎𝖓𝖙𝖔 the sandy shore and stopped. Artie threw the paddle onto the ground and clambered out. He walked to the bow and pulled the red boat clear of the water. Then he stopped and looked over the Lake.

It was a beautiful scene. In a way, the Lake was the source of his power. It was where Excalibur lived, and this Scarffern thing too, whatever it was. He was a little scared to put it to his lips. What could it possibly do that would make Morgaine respect him? Would it weaken her in some way, or bind her, or make her really small, like Thumb was back on Artie's side?

What *was* its secret?

Artie shrugged. He'd find out eventually.

He watched as a black swan swooped in the distance and

slid onto the water. He stuck his hands in his pockets and pushed down, locking his elbows. "Thank you, Nyneve."

"Don't thank her yet, my boy."

Artie wheeled. Could it be? "Merlin?"

"Yes, child."

Artie's palms clammed up. Fear grabbed his stomach and wouldn't let go. Here he was, exposed—no sword, no friends, no magic—against Merlin, the greatest (and now craziest) wizard ever.

Artie couldn't show his fear. He swallowed hard and forced his voice to be steady, saying defiantly, "Don't call me 'child,' wizard."

It was hard not to be afraid, though. Merlin had changed. Artie was nearly mesmerized by the metamorphosis: Merlin's dark skin, the red eyes, the vitriol rising off his shoulders like steam. It was as if his demon half had merely been waiting to reveal itself.

Merlin smiled. His teeth, white as puffy clouds, stood out against his charcoal gums and lips. "Where is Excalibur? You should not be traipsing around without it."

Artie fought his fear again and latched on to the next available emotion. This was anger, laced with impatience. He was the king now, and Merlin, in spite of his power, was being impertinent.

And then Artie realized *exactly* what he was feeling. Hate. He would have to be careful that it didn't betray him.

"Is that a threat?" Artie asked, trying to feature his impatience over naked ire.

Merlin shrugged and said menacingly, "It is a fact, young king."

Artie raised his eyebrows. "Excalibur's in Avalon." He shifted his eyes to the moongate. "Go and fetch it for me if you're so concerned about my safety."

Merlin laughed. "Is that an invitation, boy?"

"No." Both of them knew that the only way for anyone outside of Artie's group of knights to get to Avalon was to be invited by the king himself. "I wouldn't invite you there in your wildest dreams."

Merlin tut-tutted and said, "I thought not."

"Merlin, what do you want?" Artie demanded.

"What I've always wanted. To punish Morgaine for imprisoning me."

"But you also want Excalibur."

Merlin cocked his head. "Nyneve told you things, did she? Meddlesome things?"

"Maybe." The impatience grew in Artie, and his fear subsided. He liked the way he felt. He liked that Merlin was talking to him as an equal.

"Did Nyneve say that the sword wants something from me, perhaps?"

"You could say that."

Merlin drew a few feet closer, and Artie felt the heat

pulsing from the wizard's body. Melrin's eyes burned like embers. "Don't toy with me, Artie Kingfisher. I made you; you owe me the truth."

Artie spat on the ground. Suddenly, his nerves were gone. The power of the Otherworld ran through his feet and into his body. He might need Excalibur to defeat Merlin but not to stand up to him. "Uh, technically, Morgaine made me. And I don't 'owe' you squat, Merlin. In fact, I think you're the one who owes me. . . . You *definitely* owe Kynder."

Merlin's body shook with rage. "Pshaw! Enough." He raised his cane. "I should kill you now."

Calmly, Artie took a slow step toward the moongate. "So you *are* threatening me."

"Apparently."

It was time for Artie to leave. This fight would have to happen another day. And Artie thought he'd just figured out a way to make sure that it did. "You know what, Merlin? You probably should kill me. But if you do, you'll have a major problem on your hands. Which is that you'll *never* get Excalibur. It will stay in Avalon, since no one but me has the authority to invite you there. You'd have to go through this whole exercise again, engineer another king and everything, just to see the sword."

Merlin snapped his wooden cane, carved with the head of an owl, to his side in annoyance.

He doesn't know! Artie realized. He doesn't know that I am the one who has to strike him down.

Artie smelled a small advantage, but he didn't want to get cocky so he changed the subject. "Nyneve told me you were half demon. Is that true?"

"Nyneve! That watery tart. She should mind her own business."

"As guardian of Excalibur, this *is* her business."

Disgusted, Merlin didn't say anything.

Artie chanced another step toward the gate, pushing the toes of one of his feet under the discarded paddle lying on the sandy shore.

Fifteen feet lay between Artie and the portal. The wind picked up and Artie's hair pushed off to the side. "Honestly, Merlin, I'd rather not argue with you," he said, trying to sound less confrontational. "I sure as heck don't want to fight you. Don't get me wrong, I'm *really* pissed about what you did to Kynder, but if I thought you'd leave me alone, I'd be happy to let you have it out with Morgaine, regardless of what Excalibur wants."

Merlin scowled. "I don't believe you. Why would you let me be? Surely there must be a price?"

"Well, now that you mention it . . . do you know anything about a crown-shaped key?"

Artie knew this was a great risk, but he wanted to see

Merlin's reaction. Maybe the wizard had a copy, or maybe he knew where the door hidden in the King's Gate led. Maybe he would slip up and reveal something unexpected.

Instead, Merlin's eyes narrowed. He didn't just look bad, he looked wicked. "What key is this?"

A brisk wind blew off the water and Artie trembled. "For a door I saw in a dream."

"Imagine that." The wizard straightened, his eyes opening wide. "No, I don't know about a key, sputtering kingling."

"Disguising lies with insults is bush league, Merlin." Artie risked picking up the paddle, holding it like a staff. He took two methodical steps toward the moongate. "I'll be leaving now, if you don't mind."

Merlin didn't move. "Actually, I do."

Fear returned as the hairs on Artie's neck raised. Maybe he'd messed up. Maybe Merlin *did* know that Artie was the only one who could kill him. "What happened to you, Merlin?"

It was a genuine question—not one that was asked to gain position, hide a fact, or glean a weakness. Artie truly just wanted to know.

And Merlin seemed content to answer. "Freedom, Artie. Liberty has wakened my darker tendencies. These, combined with the wits of my human side, have made me what I am to the core."

"And that is . . . ?"

Merlin looked as if the answer was obvious. "Why, the greatest wizard the world has ever known!"

Artie shook his head vehemently. "You'll never be that. I don't understand it. You were a cool old dude back at the Invisible Tower. But now . . ."

Merlin started to chuckle, and this grew to a full-throated laugh. He craned his head toward the sky. Artie slid closer to the moongate—one more step to escape—but then Merlin went quiet. Quickly, he flew in front of Artie, blocking his escape.

Artie raised the paddle defensively as a bolt flew from the eyes of the owl carved on top of Merlin's cane. It hit Artie squarely in the chest, lifting him off his feet. He sailed through the air and landed hard in the bottom of the canoe.

But Artie was alive, saved by the filthy armor he still wore, including one of Merlin's impenetrable graphene shirts. He writhed and coughed. He thrust his hand into his pocket and wrapped his fingers around Scarffern, pulling it out before Merlin was on him. Should Artie blow it? What else could he do? Merlin wouldn't be so careless the next time. The next shot would be directed at his head, which was completely unprotected.

Merlin drifted over the bow of the boat. "Ah, I'd forgotten about all of your protective gear."

The wind screamed. Artie brought his fist just over his mouth, reflexively covering another coughing fit. He was ready to blow Scarffern. Nyneve might not be happy, but he didn't seem to have a choice.

But then, just as Artie prepared to blow, a massive, ocean-size wave crested over the stern of the beached canoe. Nyneve's blue-green glow was plainly evident in the wave's leading edge, her hair tossed in the foam and her dark eyes bearing hard on the wizard. The wall of water was at least thirty feet tall and it crashed down at once. Artie crooked an arm around the boat's yoke and held on tight. As the boat spun and jerked on the water, Artie slipped, and the whistle came out of his hand and rattled into the bottom of the canoe.

He frantically searched all around but could not find the mysterious whistle.

As Artie searched, Merlin sloughed off water and gathered himself. "Nyneve!" he screamed in anger.

On cue the sprite rose from the water. She no longer looked like a child. She now appeared as a woman in the prime of life. Her muscles were sinewy and powerful, her face determined.

A crackling sound like a barn on fire erupted from the shore as Merlin encased himself in a ward of flames, burning the ancient chestnut tree in many places, singeing the ground and causing the water's edge to boil and steam. Nyneve cried out in pain. Merlin laughed.

"Hold on tight, my king," Nyneve exclaimed. She let out a warbling cry, and Artie could hear something on the other side of the Lake awaken and take to the sky.

The water beneath the boat churned, and before Artie knew it the canoe was rising on top of another wave. Merlin's flames burned in a rainbow of colors, and the chestnut tree popped and hissed. The canoe was aimed straight at the moongate. Artie crossed his fingers, hoping the wave would push him through it to safety.

The boat hurtled toward its target, but Merlin floated in front of it and blocked the way once more.

Artie wasn't going to make it.

Just then the sky darkened. Artie's heart lifted as the old wizard's face went blank. Bearing down on him was a huge flock of passenger pigeons, arranged in the shape of an arrow.

"Now!" Nyneve cried. Merlin raised his hands, and thousands of birds shot down like darts. They plowed into him, pecking his body all over, and threw him clear of the moongate.

Then Nyneve's wave catapulted forward and launched the canoe. Artie held on. The Lady of the Lake receded into the water as the pigeons spun in the air like a great school of fish and shot over the burning chestnut tree. Artie shut his eyes at the last moment, Merlin screaming, "Go home! See what you have wrought! See what gift I have left in your precious Shadyside!"

𝕿𝖍𝖊 𝖈𝖆𝖓𝖔𝖊 𝖋𝖑𝖊𝖜 𝖙𝖍𝖗𝖔𝖚𝖌𝖍 𝖙𝖍𝖊 air and landed loudly, scraping along and finally coming to a stop. Artie opened his eyes and crawled desperately around the bottom of the boat, looking for the little whistle, but it was nowhere to be found.

He sat up, a knot tying his stomach. He was in the Royal Chamber, the canoe resting on top of the Round Table. No one else was there. He could still smell the remnants of the food from the meal his friends must have eaten while he was gone, but they had all cleared out.

He slapped his forehead. I'm such a klutz! he thought. How could I lose the most powerful thing in all the worlds?

"Artie, is that you?" His heart lifted as Qwon called from behind him. "Guys, guys! It's Artie! He's back!"

He turned. Qwon jumped onto the Round Table and ran across it, her cheeks lifted in a smile. But before she reached him she stopped short, bent, and picked something up. She held a long silver tube. "Artie, did you—"

"Omigod, Qwon! You found it!"

She resumed walking toward him, a puzzled look on her face.

"I thought I lost it."

Qwon handed Scarffern to Artie, who stuffed it deep into one of his pockets. "What is it?"

"Not sure exactly. I'll tell you what I know later. Just don't tell the others, all right? Not yet?"

Qwon shrugged. "Whatever you say, Artie." Then she held out her arms and they hugged. Artie lost his balance, since he was still standing in the boat, and he awkwardly leaned on Qwon. She kept him from falling over and helped him onto surer footing.

"I'm glad you're back. We were starting to get worried. We didn't know where that portal had taken you. It *was* the King's Gate, right?"

"Yeah, it was crazy." They walked over the table toward the throne. "How long was I gone?"

"Just a couple hours."

"Where're the others?"

"They're here. Kay was really worried about you, so she started bossing everyone around."

"Ha. Maybe she should be the king. . . ."

They reached the edge of the table and jumped to the floor. "Naw. You're better at it. Oh, the Green Knight dude and the kid with one arm and a prosthetic leg are here, too."

Bercilak and Bedevere. "Great. We're all together. Let's go. I got things I need to tell you guys."

Together, he and Qwon went to the others, and there was much rejoicing.

The knights reassembled in the Royal Chamber, now joined by Bercilak and the too-long-absent Bedevere. Numinae was back as well, and Lance was up and at 'em enough to sit in his chair—the one situated before the banner of none other than Sir Lancelot. Sami, however, had left. Kay had taken a moongate coin out of the infinite backpack—the same coins they had used to gate around before Artie had mastered Excalibur's pommel stone—and opened a portal back to Sweden.

"He missed his camp too much," Erik said.

Artie understood perfectly. "Will he come back if we need him?"

"Yep, all we have to do is ask," Erik answered with a grin.

That made Artie feel better. Everyone sat and Artie told them about the trip through the void, going underwater to talk with Nyneve, and confronting Merlin. Bercilak broke out a twelve-pack of ice-cold Mountain Dews, and the knights enjoyed some well-earned soda pop as Artie broke the news that if they wanted more info on the Grail, they'd have to pay a visit to Morgaine. This was not a popular idea. Artie also described Merlin's appearance. "He's definitely gone over to the dark side. Very Darth Vader. Creepy." He took a sip from a frosty can and sighed.

"It's the sangrealite," Thumb said quietly.

"What do you mean?"

"It's a long story, lad, but the gist is that Merlin rubs liquid sangrealite on his skin."

Bedevere, Numinae, and Bercilak gasped as Shallot exclaimed, "*Liquid* sangrealite? But no one knows how to liquefy sangrealite. It is ancient knowledge, forgotten, impossible."

Thumb shook his head. "Not for Merlin. It nearly drove him mad figuring it out, but he did. He had a small key of pure sangrealite at the Invisible Tower, and he changed it, like an alchemist, into a dark tincture. That's where all the tattoos came from. That's why no one but people and creatures from the Otherworld could see them."

"But I could see them," Kay said.

"That is because you're special, lass. Surely you know that by now."

Kay looked down, trying not to let the others see that she was blushing. She loved Tom Thumb, even if he was a shrimp, and it was a nice thing to hear.

"Anyway," Thumb continued, "Merlin ran out of the stuff when he sent the three of us to retrieve Excalibur from the Lake. Now he must have more. Much more. It is what makes him so powerful—but it also corrupts him."

"As if being half demon weren't enough," Qwon observed.

Kay rolled her eyes. "Seriously."

Dred clapped his hands. "It's the sangrealite he stole from Fenland, isn't it? That's what he's using now?"

"I'd wager, lad," Thumb said.

Lance leaned forward, his blue eyes bright and clear. "Where does he keep it, Tom? Where's he holed up?"

Thumb shook his head. "I knew once, but I've forgotten—although I'm certain it was on your side, sire."

"My side?"

"Yes. It wouldn't be safe for him anywhere in the Otherworld—not with you as the king and Morgaine still trying to figure out where he is."

"C'mon, Tommy. Try to remember!" Kay pleaded.

But Thumb shook his head. "I don't know. . . . I'm sorry. It's like a hole in my memory. . . ."

"A hole the wizard put there, no doubt," Bedevere said, the thick scar drawn over his cheek wrinkling as he spoke.

"No doubt," Thumb confirmed.

Artie clapped his hands. "Well, on that point maybe

I have some good news. The last thing Merlin said at the Lake was, 'Go home! See what you have wrought! See what gift I have left in your precious Shadyside!'"

"Could be a trap," Qwon said.

"Yes, it sounds squirrelly, sire," Bercilak added, his giant suit of green armor clattering.

"Maybe—but what choice do we have? If Merlin left something there—anything—maybe it'll have some clue that will help us track him down."

"Makes sense to me," Shallot said. "But there is no way you will convince me to visit your side, sire. I'm sorry. I am a fairy, and I belong in the Otherworld."

"That's all right, Shallot. Believe me, half the time I don't think I belong over here."

"You're doing fine, sire," Shallot said with a wry smile.

Artie shrugged. "Thanks. But who *does* want to pay a visit to the old crib?"

"I do," Erik said eagerly.

"I'll go with you," Bedevere said. "It may sound crazy, but the only thing I hate about my injuries is that they've kept me out of the mix. You're stuck with me, sire. I don't plan on missing any more action."

"I should probably stay here, kiddos." Lance looked wistfully at his still-healing leg. "Numinae says I'll be back in shooting form in a couple days, but at the moment I'm plowed. Speaking of shooting—while you're there can you grab my spare bow? It's in the trunk of my cab, which I left parked in your driveway."

"You got it, Lance," Artie said.

Kay stood. "You know I'm in, Bro. A shower in our bathroom sounds like winning the lottery at this point."

"Ditto," Artie said.

"Yeah, you do kind of reek, Artie," Erik observed.

There was a pause, then Qwon said quietly, "I'd like to go home too, Artie."

They fell silent as Artie looked at Qwon. Of course she wanted to go home! Hadn't that been what he'd wanted too until this whole Avalon whirlwind? "I know. I promised your mom I'd bring you back, and I will." He looked from knight to knight. "Well, what are we waiting for?"

Bercilak shot his arm into the air. "Ooh, sire! Can I come too?"

Lance turned to the Green Knight. "Uh, I'm not sure that'd be such a hot idea. A walking, talking, empty suit of plate mail isn't exactly *normal*, sorry to say."

Bercilak lowered his hand tentatively. "But . . ."

"He's right, Bercy. Let us check it out first," Kay said. "Then we'll bring you over for a nice meal of Mountain Dew and Big Macs. Real American junk food. You'll love it."

Bercilak shook off his disappointment and said, "I've waited this long, what's a little longer?"

"That's the spirit," Kay said.

Artie turned to Dred. "What about you?"

Dred beamed. "Of course I want to come to your side! You *are* my brother."

"While you're in Shadyside, I'll go to the Library," Numinae said, "and do some of my own research on the Grail."

Thumb jerked his head. "I'll join you, mate."

"Splendid."

Kay clapped, "Well, let's do this!"

Artie pulled Excalibur from his scabbard and led them to the yard and, finally, back to Shadyside.

Artie opened a moongate that deposited them smack in the middle of the Kingfishers' backyard, and he, Kay, Dred, Qwon, Bedevere, and Erik crossed over. It was a dark night in Pennsylvania—no moon, no stars. Barely visible over their fence's edge, a streetlamp flickered weakly, as if the bulb was dying.

Artie drew a breath through his nostrils. The air was crisp and fresh, but also tinged with an acrid waft of garbage. It must be pickup day tomorrow, he thought. People here were going about their daily lives.

He didn't say it, but he was jealous. He wanted a daily life, too. One that wasn't so dang nuts.

He looked to his house. "Well, here we are. Castle Kingfisher."

"What time is it?" Kay asked.

Qwon illuminated the face of her pink digital watch. "Two seventeen a.m."

Dred spun in a circle. He took in the tall trees of the suburbs, the Kingfishers' nice but modest home, the large yard, and Kynder's neglected vegetable garden. "It doesn't look *that* much different from the Otherworld."

"It is," Bedevere assured him. "Cars, planes, too many people. Food is better though. And they have this thing called TV, which is like a sangrealitic picture machine. It's pretty—what do you say, Kay?—dope."

"Sure is, Bedevere. We'll make a regular teenager out of you yet." Kay shivered. "But let's go inside. It's *chilly*."

Kay kicked along the grass toward the patio, fallen leaves crunching underfoot. The others followed; Artie and Dred brought up the rear. As Kay crossed the deck, Dred stopped and put a hand on Artie's arm.

Artie stopped too. "What is it?"

"Artie, if we have to go to Castel Deorc Wæters to see Morgaine, you should know that the place we were born is . . . well, it's pretty messed up."

Artie frowned. "More messed up than riding a dragon, or being dragged underwater to chat with an aquatic fairy, or fighting an army of dudes on bears?"

Dred smiled. "Maybe not. But the experiments Morgaine did to make us . . . they're pretty gruesome."

"Don't worry about it, Dred. It takes a lot to surprise me these days."

Kay opened the back door with a key from under the mat, and she and the others went inside. From the corner of his eye Artie noticed the light in the kitchen go on, and then the one in the den.

Dred continued, "The lab where we were made is horrible. Full of these glass canisters with *things* in them. Dead things. Babies, kids, and men who look just like you and me except that they're missing limbs, or they have no eyes, or their skin is turned inside out." Dred thought for a second. "I guess those ones don't look anything like us."

"Gross."

"Yeah. I just thought you should be prepared. I sure wasn't. If someone could have warned me, I would have appreciated it."

"I do. Thanks, Dred."

"No prob—"

They were interrupted by a scream. Artie felt Dred's nerves jostle, and vice versa. The brothers drew their swords and rushed headlong from the dark into the Kingfisher house, and toward trouble.

𝕬rtie burst through the door, Excalibur tingling in his hands. Bedevere had leaped onto the kitchen island and Qwon was behind it, her back to the fridge. Artie could hear Kay yelling from the hallway that led to the front door but he couldn't see her.

Blocking her was Erik in full berserker mode, bouncing off the walls. He was attacking a very large creature that appeared to have the front end of a saber-toothed tiger and the powerful back half of a rhino.

Surely, this was Merlin's "gift."

As soon as Artie was through the door, the creature charged. Artie held Excalibur across his face as the saber-tooth/rhino raked a massive paw through the air. Artie's blade cut deep but it didn't make the creature stop, and the force of its blow knocked Artie over. He slid across the small kitchen table, upended it, and banged his head into the wall, the table collapsing on top of him.

Dred stepped into the breach, jabbing the Peace Sword at the creature's head. The creature swung its haunches to the right and Dred thrust the Peace Sword forward. It sank deep into the creature's furry shoulder. So deep that it became stuck.

"Ack!" Dred exclaimed, trying to work the sword free.

Artie untangled himself from the table and knelt. "Qwon, use Kusanagi to call the wind!" Artie could feel each sword in the room as if he were attached to it with invisible thread.

"What?" Qwon yelled.

"Call the wind! Kusanagi can—"

But Artie was struck speechless by a sudden change in air pressure. Windows cracked and shattered. Loose things were sucked into the middle of the room. It grew dark, and then came a low rumble followed by a high-pitched wail. Erik—who had just stuck Gram halfway into the right thigh of the beast—was blown hard into Dred's chest. Together they were thrown into the den, over the couch, and onto the coffee table. Artie struggled to stay on his knees as he squinted across the kitchen. Qwon stood there, fighting with the power in her hands, her eyes shut and her knuckles white. Bedevere stood next to her, his remaining arm drawn over his face.

The storm cascaded from Kusanagi in visible waves. It was like Qwon was holding an artillery cannon. Viewed from the outside, the Kingfisher house looked like the scariest, most evil haunted house the world had ever seen. There were flashes of lightning in the windows and billows of mist, and the wind blew so hard that the clapboard siding of the house trembled.

In the midst of all this, the sabertooth/rhino lowered its head and dug its claws deep into the floor. The wind passed over it, tearing at its fur, making it look like a field of wheat undulating in a summer squall.

Artie drew Excalibur in front of him again, intent on striking the creature's undefended backside—but just before he could act he had to duck a large, bulky object that soared over his head.

It was the microwave.

"Enough!" Artie shouted, though no one could hear him. "ENOUGH!" he screamed, to no avail.

He peered across the room. He could barely make Qwon out—the air was so thick with debris—but Artie could tell that she had lost control of her sword's tempestuous power.

Bedevere and Artie momentarily locked eyes. Artie pointed Excalibur at Bedevere's inactive phantom arm and then at Kusanagi. Artie watched as Bedevere's lips made the word *Phantoma!* and the ghostly and magical appendage that Merlin had made for him grew from his stump in an instant. He reached down and grabbed Kusanagi around the blade just above the circular handguard. He yanked it quickly, breaking Qwon's grip. The look on her face was one of shock but also relief.

The storm died, and the sabertooth/rhino wasted no time. It swiped a huge paw at Erik, who barely dodged it, and then it spun and tried to bite Kay. She backpedaled, holding out Cleomede, and her sword caught the beast across the jaw, drawing a deep cut. Dred and Artie pounced on the wounded animal. Bedevere dropped Kusanagi, launched over the kitchen island, and landed on the thing's head, trying to draw its attention from Kay. It worked, but now Bedevere was in trouble. The animal was just about to dig its knifelike teeth into Bedevere's good leg when Dred swung the Peace Sword and sliced off its left front paw. The creature cried out and Bedevere jumped to safety. Then Kay stepped forward and drove Cleomede deep into its side.

That was it.

The knights panted and regrouped and finally Artie asked, "Why would Merlin put this poor creature here?" He was not happy that they'd had to kill it.

"A test maybe," Bedevere said.

"And why a sabertooth and a rhino?" Kay wondered. "Does this mean he's going to attack us with some crazy horde of hybrid animals?"

"Who knows," Dred said. "But I wouldn't put it past—" He made a start as the doorbell rang. "What's that?"

Qwon, who looked like she still couldn't believe she'd made that huge storm, said, "Easy, Dred. Someone's at the front door. That's all."

Kay ran down the hall, calling over her shoulder, "I'll see who it is." She checked the hall clock on her way. It was 2:32 a.m. Who rang the doorbell at 2:32 a.m.?

She reached the door and opened it halfway.

Two officers stood on the threshold. The older one—short, bald, stocky—had a hand on the grip of his holstered gun and a concerned look on his face. "Good evening, ma'am—er, miss—is everything all right in there?"

Kay, still panting from the fight, moved so that she blocked the view into the house. Being six feet tall helped. The taller officer craned his neck, trying to get a look inside. "Oh yeah, officers, everything's fine. The, um, we had a gas leak. Pilot light went out, I guess. The, uh, whatchamacallit"—Kay snapped her fingers a few times—"the compressor on the fridge must have ignited the gas." She'd seen this in a movie somewhere, and while she had no idea if it was plausible, it sounded good. "We were all upstairs. Kind of a mess, but everyone's fine."

"If there's a gas leak, we need to call the utility company, miss," the closest cop said.

"Oh, don't bother. Like I said, everything's fine."

The taller cop took a few steps away from the door and bobbed back and forth. "Hey, Ed, isn't this the Kingfisher residence?"

The short one squinted. "Yeah. It is." He turned back to Kay. "Are you Kay Kingfisher?"

Kay frowned. "That's right."

The shorter one said, "You've been reported to the truancy board. You haven't been in school for weeks."

"And your father, Kynder, has been reported missing," the taller one said.

Kay's eyes widened. "Missing? Truant? All due respect, Officer Ed, but that's crazy." Wasn't Merlin supposed to take care of all that with those magical letters?

"It's Officer Schwartz, miss." He tapped the badge on his chest. "And you haven't been to school since September thirtieth. Neither has your brother—what's his name?"

"Arthur," the other officer said.

"Yeah, Arthur. And if I got my dates right, your dad has not been seen since October fourth. It is now"—he spoke over his shoulder without taking his eyes off Kay—"What time is it, Carl?"

"Precisely two thirty-five a.m., twentieth of October," Officer Carl announced.

"Two thirty-five on October the twentieth," Officer Ed repeated.

Kay resisted the urge to make a sarcastic remark and said, "Look, officers, my dad's not missing, he's just booked solid." Which was *sort* of true, right? Since he was frozen in rock and sitting in the middle of the yard back at Tintagel?

Just then, Artie appeared at Kay's side. He took the door from her and opened it wide. "Hey, Kay. Everything all right?"

"You Arthur?"

"That's right."

"Your dad around?"

"Uh, no. He had to go to Cincinnati for a funeral. Terrible. Best friend from college just dropped dead. Brain aneurism, I think."

Officer Carl shuddered. "Ugh. My uncle died of one of those. Nothing you can do."

"That's what Kynder said." Kay shook her head sadly.

Officer Carl took a step back. He seemed to be coming around.

Officer Ed, however, looked unconvinced. "Miss Kingfisher, does the name Erik Erikssen mean anything to you?"

Kay paused. This was not good. "Kind of. He's some twerp I go to school with." *Merlin* was *supposed to take care of this!*

"That's right. He's also been missing since October the fourth. His family is worried sick."

"He's in my class," Artie said. "I was wondering where he went."

Kay shot Artie an unbelieving look. When did he become a world-class liar? "You were?" she asked.

"Sure I was." Artie took a step toward the cops and tilted his head toward Kay. "She doesn't pay any attention to Erik because, you know, he has a crush on her."

Man, he's good, Kay thought.

"Ah, I remember what that was like." Ed gave Carl a look and shrugged. "Listen, kids, we're going to call the gas company and have them come out tomorrow. And we'd like to talk to Mr. Kingfisher when he becomes available." He held out a business card. "Please, have your father call us. You got a nice place here, in a nice neighborhood. I can't imagine your dad would like a visit from Child Services. This kind of truancy is a big deal, miss. Get back to school, understood?"

"Understood! Thanks!" Then she stepped back and shut the door.

She and Artie stared at each other for several moments in silence. They heard the police talking but couldn't make out their words. Artie cupped a hand over the peephole, held it there for a few seconds, and then looked through it. Erik came into the hall. "Who was th—"

Without turning from the door Artie held up a finger and cut him off.

Several more moments passed. Finally, Artie turned from the door, a concerned look on his face. "They're gone."

"Well, who was it?" Erik whispered. "I heard you talking about me."

Bedevere and Qwon were framed in the weak light at the end of the hallway, equally curious. Dred was in the living room peeking through a crack in the drapes.

Kay stepped forward. "It was the cops, Erik. They know we've been missing. *Everyone* does."

The lights of the squad car shifted through the windows as it turned around and drove off.

"What?" Erik asked.

Artie nodded. "They know Kynder's not around too."

"Those magical letters Merlin wrote aren't working," Kay said.

"Or never did," Artie said ominously.

Erik turned a tight circle. "Oh, man. I am *so* dead. I could get grounded for . . . forever!"

Kay nodded. "Seriously. Sorry."

Artie rubbed his hand over his mouth. He was preoccupied with Merlin. "Or he made it so the letters *stopped* working."

"Ugh . . . my parents . . . school . . . ," Erik sputtered.

"Erik, get a grip. We've been through a lot worse," Qwon said.

"True," Erik managed.

Kay squeezed his shoulder. "Don't worry. Once you show up, your folks will be so psyched they'll forget all about how you went missing."

"But what'll I tell them?"

"We'll worry about that later," Artie said. "Let's deal with that poor thing Merlin sent us." He pointed at the dead creature. "While we're working, we'll figure out what to do next."

𝕿𝖍𝖊 𝕶𝖎𝖓𝖌𝖋𝖎𝖘𝖍𝖊𝖗 𝖍𝖔𝖚𝖘𝖊 𝖜𝖆𝖘 𝖆 wreck. The sabertooth/ rhino must have been there for at least a few days. It had commandeered the living room for a bedroom and Kynder's bed for a litter box, and had completely destroyed the dining room. If they hadn't shown up when they did, it might have destroyed the whole inside of the house.

Still, it did yield a clue. Strung around its neck was a tight cord, and on this cord was a gold disc the size of a half dollar. One side was smooth and blank. The other had an inscription. It read, *Dim mwy o gemau.*

"What is that gobbledygook?" Qwon asked when Artie read it out loud.

"Welsh," he answered.

"It means, 'No more games,'" Dred continued.

"That's right," Artie confirmed.

"Since when do you speak Welsh, Artie?" Qwon asked. "Dred I get. He grew up with that crazy witch. But you . . . you barely passed English last year!"

Artie winked. "Excalibur taught me. Kingly perk."

Qwon whistled. "I'll say."

"What do you think it means?" Erik asked.

Artie shrugged. "I guess it means we're in this mess for real, Erik."

Kay huffed. "As if that weren't, like, painfully obvious."

"You can say that again," Bedevere said, leaning on the bulk of the slain animal.

"All right, listen. You three"—Artie pointed at Bedevere, Erik, and Dred—"why don't you go back to Tintagel and sleep there. I'm sorry, Erik, but I have to ask you to stay in Avalon for now. If you went home, you could get wrapped up in family, plus we have no good explanation for where you've been. You're too important. We need you. *I* need you."

Erik shuffled his feet and ran a hand through his close-cropped blond hair. "All right."

"Good. The three of us will stay here and take Qwon home first thing in the morning. When we get back, we'll talk about visiting *your* house, Dred—which is probably going to be a ton of fun."

They laughed uneasily but agreed to the plan. Bedevere

used his superstrong arm to drag the animal out back and shove it through the gate to Tintagel, where Bercilak would get to work with his ax and a bonfire; meanwhile, the others cleaned the kitchen as best as they could. It was a bloody and unfulfilling task, but they did it.

Just before sunup everyone but Artie, Kay, and Qwon crossed back to the Otherworld. Artie went out to the driveway to Lance's cab—which had been loitering there since their disappearance—and grabbed Lance's spare bow. He stashed this, along with Excalibur, Cleomede, and Kusanagi, in the back of the cabinet where they hid their Mountain Dew and then sat down to a quick breakfast of Honey Nut Cheerios with Kay and Qwon. When they were finished, Artie turned to Qwon. "Ready to go see your mom?"

"Heck yeah."

As the sun was rising, Artie, Kay, and Qwon stole into the backyard, completely unarmed. They grabbed three bikes from the shed and went to the back gate. Artie cracked it open and peeked into the alley. No police, no garbage trucks. Just the old, familiar alley.

He pushed his Schwinn onto the pavement and got on. "Lead the way, Q," he said with a smile.

Qwon took off. Artie had forgotten how fast Qwon liked to ride. They zipped down the alleyway, leaves twirling in their wake. Qwon slammed the brakes and skidded onto the sidewalk, putting a foot down and pivoting. Then she stood on the pedals and turned them as fast as she could.

Artie kept up as Kay's competitive spirit took over. She pedaled like a crazy person and surged in front of Qwon, laughing the whole way. The nippy morning air filled their lungs. Artie stood too and jogged his bike back and forth with his hands—tilting it left, right, left, right—with every pedal stroke.

Sunlight broke over the treetops as they rounded the corner of Qwon's street. Artie's face hurt, he was smiling so hard. *This* was freedom. *This* was what he was supposed to be doing. *This* was where he belonged.

It was plain that Kay and Qwon felt the same way. Qwon had been kidnapped and imprisoned and basically pressed into Artie's makeshift army. They had *all* been pressed. Artie watched as the girls rode down a cut in the curb, Qwon following on Kay's wheel, into the empty street. They slalomed back and forth in wide arcs past one another. Artie kept to the sidewalk, blasting through piles of leaves and taking little jumps off the crooked, root-raised sections of pavement.

As they got closer to Qwon's house, Kay eased up and let Qwon get in front. Qwon turned wide out of the street and launched up her driveway before clamping the brakes. She let the bike slide out from under her and clatter onto its side as she vaulted forward and ran to her home. Kay and Artie screeched to a halt and watched. Qwon picked up speed as she sprinted to her door, but before she got there it swung inward, and Pammy Onakea stood on the threshold, her arms outstretched, her eyes glossy and bright.

Artie and Kay had never seen a more intense hug. Not in movies or video games or the school yard or even in their dreams. Qwon and Pammy embraced for a whole two or three minutes before speaking. As they pulled apart, Artie realized that he was crying too.

Kay leaned into Artie's shoulder and said, "I miss Kynder so bad, Art."

Artie looked at his sister. They didn't need words. He put an arm around her and pulled her tight.

They watched silently for a few more moments before Pammy held out her arms and said, "Come here, you two!"

Artie and Kay rushed over, and the four of them wrapped together in a huge, tight hug.

When they were done, Pammy asked, "Kay, what did you do to your hair?"

Kay ran a hand through her short locks. "Do you like it? It was either my hair or my head, so . . ."

"Ah, good choice," Pammy said uneasily. "Why don't we go inside?"

They followed Pammy to the kitchen, where she poured them full glasses of orange juice and started cooking. "Have the police been coming around here too?" Artie asked as bacon sizzled in the pan.

"Not too much." She looked at Qwon. "I told school that your dad's favorite uncle died in Hawaii and that you had to go there with him." Qwon's parents were divorced, so that seemed believable.

"Oh," Qwon said. "Sorry I've missed so much school, Mom."

"It's okay, honey." Although by the look on her face it clearly wasn't. "But you're probably going to have to repeat the seventh grade, or at least work your butt off catching up."

Qwon rolled her eyes. "Great."

"You two, too."

"Sweet," Kay said drily.

"I figured," Artie said. "To be honest, if Merlin wasn't being such a . . . a . . ." Artie hesitated. He wanted to use a bad word.

Pammy winked at him. "I know what you're thinking. No need to say it."

"Yeah, if he wasn't being such a one of those, then we'd *all* be back in school right now."

While they ate they told Pammy everything. *Everything.* Talking to her while eating a normal breakfast in a normal kitchen in a normal house they all knew well (not to mention Pammy let them have ice cream for dessert!) opened the floodgates. Qwon's mom was a great listener, and she took their weird news really well. She pushed back tears when she heard about Kynder but was relieved to hear Artie and Kay vow to bring him back. Artie even told them about the Scarffern whistle and showed it to them.

"What's it do?" Kay asked.

"I have no idea. I nearly blew it when Merlin was trying to kill me, and then I thought I lost it, which would have sucked. Luckily, Q found it right after I shot through that emergency moongate."

"Why would it have been so bad to lose it, Artie?" Pammy asked.

"Because Nyneve said it was the most powerful thing in either of the worlds! More powerful than Excalibur, even." Artie snapped his fingers a few times, trying to remember exactly what Nyneve had told him. "She said something like, Excalibur is the symbol of my power and this thing is the secret of it. She also said not to use it unless absolutely necessary, so . . ."

"So we save it for when we see our friend Merlin again," Kay said.

"Or Morgaine," Qwon added.

"Or whatever hellish thing is sure to be guarding the Holy Grail," Artie said glumly.

Kay stared into her juice glass. "Yeah, or that."

Pammy sighed. "You kids have really been through the wringer." It took every ounce of her will not to forbid them to ever go back to this place that was so dangerous and unknown.

"We have," Artie said. They were quiet for a little while. Artie started thinking about his trip through the King's Gate and how all the crossovers were open now. Finally, he asked, "Pammy—has weird stuff been happening on this side? Anything at all?"

"Not that I'm aware of. Should there be?"

"I don't know. The worlds are rejoined now, like they had been for a long time until Morgaine closed up the Otherworld. I guess I was just curious if anything magical was happening over here. And I mean that literally."

"No, not yet," Pammy said. "But this whole thing *has* had a weird effect on me. Obviously, when your daughter gets kidnapped to another world by a kid dressed in moss, you've got to come to terms with some things."

"I can imagine," Artie said. Qwon reached out and squeezed her mom's hand.

"It also jogs some memories." Pammy leaned forward, warming her free hand on her cup of tea. "Qwon, you know how your great-grandparents, Ojiichan and Obaachan, were devout believers in the spirit world? The *Otherworld*?" Qwon nodded. "Ghosts and fairies and gnomes were every-where for them, and for me too when I was a little girl. When I was young I heard of Kusanagi from old Tetsuo, just like you. And when my great-aunt, all one hundred and four years of her, gave me that monocle on my wedding day—the one you used to look between the worlds, Artie— she told me never to lose it for any reason. 'Why?' I asked. 'It is powerful, dear.' 'How?' She didn't know, or if she did, she wouldn't tell me—it was like your whistle. But what reason did I have to doubt her, and what would have been the point if I had? I kept it safe. If I hadn't, you wouldn't have found Kusanagi. If you hadn't found Kusanagi, then you wouldn't have been able to bring Qwon back to me." She took a sip of her tea. "I guess I'm a believer now, Artie, like my grandparents used to be." Another sip. "And there's one more thing. Something I'd completely forgotten until Qwon was back in my arms just today."

To everyone's surprise, she turned to Kay and gave her a deeply sympathetic look.

Kay shifted in her seat. "What is it, Mrs. Onakea?"

"It's about Cassie."

Kay's heart skipped a beat. "My mom?"

"Yes."

"What about her?"

"We used to be pretty good friends before she, well, went crazy. And as far as I know, I was the last person on this side to see her before she disappeared. She came here in the middle of the night. She was a babbling mess. She couldn't stop talking about how you"—she shifted her eyes to Artie—"weren't supposed to be here. How you were not even human, which was clearly ridiculous."

Pammy paused. The kids were silent, riveted.

"I tried to calm her down, but nothing worked. That is, until I mentioned you, Kay, and how it wouldn't be fair to you for her to leave."

"You can say that again," Kay said weakly.

"Kay . . . before she left, your mom gave me something. She said, 'Keep this. When the time is right, give it to my daughter. You'll know when the time is right.'"

Kay's eyes widened. "That time is now, isn't it?"

Pammy let go of her daughter's hand and stood. "Yes. Yes it is."

𝔐erlin stood in front of a trio of full-length mirrors, wearing a simple loincloth and inspecting every inch of his body. He was searching for another spot on which to apply a drop of sangrealite. He'd liquefied as much as he'd ever need since returning to his cave in western Wales, and so long as he could continue to administer the stuff, he would be the most powerful wizard who had ever lived.

But there simply was nowhere else to put it. His body was completely covered in the inky sangrealitic tattoos. His ears, his eyelids, his lips, the spaces between his fingers and toes—every inch of his skin was now a dark blue color like that of a moonless night sky.

He raised his chin and stared at his reflection. His eyes were very red. Not as bright as a fire engine or a maraschino cherry, but definitely approaching apple territory.

He blew into his hands as goose bumps prickled over his dark skin, then he held up his arms and, magically, a cloak fell from above and draped over his body.

He left the mirrors and walked through a rocky hall cut from the earth, passing several cavelike recesses. He passed one room that was closed with a large glass-and-metal door. Beyond it, computer mainframes, constellated with blinking lights, hummed for as far as the eye could see. Merlin paused to observe the data center, a sinister smile on his lips. Beyond that door, numbers were being crunched and processed. The computers were all hacked into the game servers that hosted *Otherworld* the video game. The same game he'd developed in his cave under Cincinnati and then sold at auction to a major distributor. The same game he'd seeded with actual magic. The same game that had helped to draw the hapless Artie Kingfisher to the Invisible Tower. And the same game that would soon help him defeat this upstart king.

He rubbed his teeth with a blue finger. Beyond that door, he thought, my army is being prepared. Soon I will inject the circuitry with the power of sangrealite, and the switch will be thrown. . . .

The ghost in the machine would awaken.

Merlin resumed walking. The sounds of the sea could be heard in the distance. He turned a corner and entered a huge room with a large cage at the far end. It looked empty, but it most definitely was not.

Something was in there—a hybrid animal like the one he had sent to the house in Shadyside, but bigger and stranger. A thing that, when he was done with it, would be better than any dragon.

He walked to an oaken counter. He stopped in front of a finely crafted bowl made of polished bone and wrapped his fingers around it. The dark liquid inside was neither cold nor hot. He raised the bowl to his nose. There was no odor. He put the bowl back down and dipped a finger into it.

The liquid sangrealite inside—about eight fluid ounces—did not adhere to his skin in any way. When he withdrew his finger the sangrealite fell from it like water droplets shedding from a duck's plumage.

Merlin brooded for a long time. The tide from the sea outside his subterranean complex was rising, and the cave whooshed and moaned as water poured into the lower sections, forcing air through them like they were tubes of a pipe organ. The smell of the ocean filled his nostrils. Every now and then a noise came from the dark cage. A hiss, a low grunt, a whine or whimper.

Finally, Merlin reached out and grabbed the bowl and lifted it high overhead. He chanted, asking for guidance. He wanted to know where his enemies were—Morgaine; Excalibur; the king. Artie had said he would consider leaving Merlin alone, but they both knew that was not going to happen.

Jealous, silly sword, Merlin thought. Excalibur belongs back under the water. Or better, to be destroyed. To be melted and used, just like this.

He brought the bowl to his chest and stared into it. He took a deep breath. He closed his eyes. His hands shook slightly. And then he greedily pressed the bowl to his lips and drank.

He took less than a quarter teaspoon—less than a thimble would hold. He placed the bowl back on the table and held the liquid in his mouth, sloshing it around. Its taste—coppery yet sweet—was unexpected. As he let the liquid run over his teeth and gums, under and around his tongue, the flavor coated his mouth and rose into his head like a strong drink.

He swallowed.

The sensation was like having a star ignite inside his chest, its light radiating in every direction, filling him from the inside out. It started in his stomach and lungs, then moved to his heart, his ribs, his abdomen, and up to his neck and shoulders. The feeling was bright and overwhelming. Every finger and toe, every strand of hair on his head, each of his long eyebrows, his muttonchop sideburns, his teeth, his eyes—they all tingled and pulsed. He began to shake pleasantly, and his brain lit on fire. This fire cascaded over the top of his head and fell, like a waterfall, corkscrewing around his spinal cord and zipping along every nerve and back again. Then his body went ramrod straight, and he teetered on his heels and fell backward like a board. He hit his head hard on the ground.

Which hurt, but pain was nothing now. It subsided quickly, and then he saw:

Morgaine in Castel Deorc Wæters, in her cathedral-like boudoir, searching frantically for something. Then, *znip*, like a channel changing: Artie and his pesky knights slaying Merlin's test subject in the Kingfishers' kitchen. *Znip*: Artie and Kay and the girl, Qwon, appearing well rested and clean at the Onakea house in Shadyside. *Znip*: less certain things—a crumble of rocks; a high-pitched whistling; flashing steel and exploding clouds over the barracks of Castel Deorc Wæters.

Merlin stirred. These last things were yet to happen. Future sight was always blurry like that.

It appeared, however, that Artie and some of his twits of friends were off to Morgaine's palace for some foolish, unfathomable reason. A confrontation was inevitable.

He smiled. Why not take a few friends and join the fun? Yes. Why not.

He stood as a drawn-out whine wended from the cage.

Merlin turned his attention to the unseen thing within. "Wait, love. You are perfect, but not ready. Patience. Your time will come. Your time to eat is near."

Merlin rose from the ground and floated out of the room and through the cave, passing the side rooms and the data center. He turned into another passageway and passed over a narrow natural arch, a river of water beneath it, and finally arrived at a low opening sealed by a heavy steel portcullis.

"Agorwch," Merlin growled.

His order was answered by the sound of bars dragging as the portcullis lowered into a gap in the floor, stopping with a clang and echo. Merlin drifted into the pitch-dark chamber and stopped in the middle of the room.

He held out his right hand, palm side up. A blue flame ignited in a jet and cast a sickly light over the room.

A harsh buzzing sound came from a large cage to Merlin's left as the blue flame rose in the air like a little balloon, five, ten, fifteen feet, and stopped.

Merlin grinned. His teeth were gray. "Hello, my little monstrosity. I hope you are angry. A witch and king are out there, waiting for us to pay them a visit."

𝔓ammy returned holding a small metal box. "Here you are, Kay. The box your mom gave me."

"What's in it?"

"I don't know. I've never looked."

Kay took it uneasily. The box fit in the palm of her hand. It had small legs on it, like a desk or a chest, that looked like an animal's legs. Other than that, there was nothing remarkable about it. No etchings or carvings. There was a tiny latch and a set of hinges.

Kay turned the box over.

"Well, are you gonna open it?" Qwon asked.

"Sweetie," Pammy gently chided.

"Sorry. I'm just—"

Quickly, Kay flipped the latch and pried the box open.

She peered inside. Her expression was blank.

"Tell us what it is!" Artie demanded breathlessly.

Kay gave him a hard look. She tried to joke, "Don't order me around, Your Highness. I'm still your big sister."

Artie tilted his head. "Kay . . . what is it?"

"I don't know. Looks like a key, maybe. On top of a folded piece of paper."

Artie's palms went cold as he considered the very unlikely prospect that this key was the crown-shaped one that could open the black door at the end of the King's Gate. "What's it look like?"

"What do you mean? It's a piece of paper, Art."

"No—the key."

"Oh. Here." Kay reached into the box and pulled out a silver skeleton key, the handle in the shape of a galloping horse.

Artie took it. No way was that the key that fit in the King's Gate door. There was nothing crown-shaped about it, and it was way too small.

"What's the note say?" Qwon asked.

Kay didn't answer. She stared into the box, holding it by the sides with both hands. Then she abruptly lifted her fingers and snapped it shut.

Qwon started to speak, but Pammy held up a hand. "Read it when the time is right, Kay."

Kay looked into Pammy's eyes. "Thanks, Mrs. Onakea.

It's just that with everything else—with Kynder frozen in a darn rock, and Merlin, and Morgaine, and the fact that we're going to have to find the Holy frigging Grail—sorry for the language—"

"It's okay."

"With all that, I don't think I can handle an eleven-year-old note from my mom."

Pammy nodded. Artie wanted to reach out and take his sister's hand, but it just felt too weird.

Kay turned to Artie. "Do you think we'll ever see her again?"

"I don't know, Kay." They were quiet for a few moments. Artie returned the key to Kay, and she slipped it into her jeans pocket.

After a few moments Artie asked, "Mrs. Onakea—Pammy—can we hang here until tomorrow morning? I just want to feel normal for a few hours."

Pammy smiled. "Of course. Honestly, I do too."

They played in the yard and ate more food and took naps, but later that day they made the ill-fated decision to watch the news.

And the news was not normal at all.

There were reports from around the world about the appearance of all sorts of extinct animals. There were passenger pigeons and giant sloths and saber-toothed tigers and huge vultures. There were dire wolves and dodo birds and short-faced bears. People were shocked and scared. Many of the larger creatures were shot on sight, and many more escaped into the wilderness. No one had any idea where they were coming from or had any explanation as to why they were here.

But they were.

And, as every report pointed out, it had happened before. On the slopes of northern Sweden, when a few aurochs happened to be found wandering over the northern plains.

"Crossovers," Artie said as soon as he saw the first report. "The worlds have mended, and this is the result."

All four of them sat in front of the TV like zombies. After a few hours Qwon suggested that they should take notes. "Maybe there's some kind of pattern or something," she said. "Maybe there'll be some clue that will help us figure out where Merlin is."

Artie thought it was a great idea. They wrote down everything they could think of. What kind of animal was turning up where; how many there were; did anyone see them appear? No one had, thankfully. And as far as Artie and the others could tell, there were no reports of people going missing.

In the midafternoon Artie said, "People from this side can't cross. Excalibur let me know. Only people like us can go over there—people with some connection to the Otherworld.

But any creatures from the Otherworld can come over here."

"Why?" Pammy asked.

"It was always like that. Think about it. The Otherworld is the fairy world. Pretend for a moment that every fairy tale you heard was true. Fairies would always poke their heads into the world of humans to have some fun, but did humans ever go to the fairy world? No. We were always stuck here."

"But that's not true, Art," Kay interjected as some CNN reporter gave a breathless play-by-play of a wolf the size of a bear loping across a Montana interstate. "A lot of those stories are about one person going over. Jack and the beanstalk, that Gulliver guy, even King Arthur himself."

"They were the special ones—just like we are now."

They were silent for a few moments. Finally, Pammy said, "Well, I hope it stays that way. If folks start disappearing like your mom did—if the world truly learns of the Otherworld—then it's going to scare the you-know-what out of a lot of folks."

Kay huffed. "You know what'll scare the you-know-what out of a lot of folks? If Bercilak decides to cross over in search of Mount Pepsi, asking everyone all over for Mountain Dew." The four of them laughed uneasily. And then Kay said, "Oh, man. But for reals, no dragons better come over here."

Artie went white. "No. That would be a major problem."

They turned back to the TV and watched it dutifully,

continuing to take notes. Just before dinner, Qwon gathered their work, put the major details into an Excel doc, and printed it out. When they sat down to eat they pored over the pages, trying to figure out if there was any information hidden in them that they might be able to use.

Toward the end of a mostly silent meal, Artie said, "I don't see anything that would help us find Merlin—do you guys?"

"It's all over the map," Kay added. "Animals are showing up *every*where."

Pammy served dessert—hot fudge sundaes—and for a while they ate in more silence.

"Wait—that's it!" Qwon exclaimed, standing quickly, a dribble of chocolate running down the corner of her mouth.

"What, honey?" Pammy asked, pointing at Qwon's chin.

Qwon wiped it with her napkin. "'All over the map!' Mom, do we still have that big fold-out *National Geographic* map?"

Pammy nodded. "Let me check." She got up and left the dining room.

"What is it, Q?" Artie asked.

"It's something about *where* the animals have been turning up."

"But they're everywhere. There must be a million crossovers out there," Kay said.

"Actually, there's a thousand and one," Artie said. "Don't ask me how I know that; I just do."

Kay said, "All right, a thousand and one. Still, the things aren't being picky."

"Here it is, sweetie," Pammy said, returning to the dining room and unfolding a huge sheet of glossy paper.

"Thanks, Mom." Qwon grabbed the map, plopped onto the floor, and began working feverishly. "Let me know if I miss something." Using a Sharpie, she circled places where animals had been reported: Ohio and Pennsylvania, of course, but also the rest of North and South America, Iceland, Western Europe, Eurasia, the Middle East, the Far East, Africa, Australia, New Zealand. The others stood over her, watching in amazement.

When she was done, she was practically sweating. She sat back and admired her work. "Notice anything?"

"That you're some kind of human supercomputer?" Kay said.

Pammy, however, was used to this kind of thing from Qwon. She pointed at a spot on the map. "There."

Artie leaned forward. "Is that right?"

"Whoa," Kay said.

Qwon nodded. "Yep. Unless they're not reporting it, there haven't been any signs of animals showing up in southwestern Britain."

Artie knelt next to Qwon. "Which is pretty weird, since

a flock of those jaybirds was seen in London—"

"And one of those huge vultures was seen flying over Mont-Saint-Michel," Qwon added.

"So something's going on in Wales or Cornwall," Pammy said.

"Like something is being hidden there," Qwon mused.

"But what? And hidden how?" Pammy wondered.

"Merlin!" Artie and Kay exclaimed in unison.

Artie jabbed a finger on the map. "His hideout must be there somewhere, and he's using some kind of magical smokescreen to keep it secret. Tom said it was on our side, and it makes total sense that it would be in that part of Britain, since that's where Arthur the First was king." Artie grabbed Qwon by a shoulder. "Do you think you might be able to narrow it down at all?"

"I'd have to do more research, but I could try."

Artie stood. "Great. Qwon . . . would you consider staying here to do this? Instead of coming back with me and Kay?"

"Well, I—"

"It's important, Q. Almost as important as figuring out how to get the Grail." Artie looked at Kay. "Which is what we are going to start doing right away."

"Cool," Kay said.

Qwon stood, too. "But, Artie, you worked so hard to bring the Seven Swords together, don't you think they should stay that way? Especially if you're going back to Fenland?"

Pammy shifted her weight. She hated thinking about her daughter being in a life-or-death sword fight. "Please, sweetie, stay here with me."

Qwon spun to Pammy. "Oh, Mom. I *want* to stay here! More than anything, I want to. But don't you think Artie wants to stay too? And Kay?" Pammy looked at all three of the children with sad eyes. "Only they *can't*, Mom. They have to save Kynder and deal with Merlin. I need to help them. It wouldn't be right if I stayed!"

"Qwon, you *would* be helping us do these things," Artie insisted. "We really need to know where Merlin's hideout is. You can meet us back in Otherworld when you're done."

"We're still going to spend the night here, though, right?" Kay asked.

"Absolutely, Kay. I want a regular bed and a fluffy pillow more than just about anything right now. We'll leave in the morning, first light."

"Great."

"Awesome," Artie said, clapping his hands. "Starting tomorrow, we're gonna get our quest back on!"

CONCERNING ERIK ERIKSSEN'S NIGHTTIME GAMING HABIT

They woke at five a.m., finished showering and eating by five thirty, and were out the door by a quarter of six.

They rode their bikes to the Kingfisher house while Pammy jogged along a different route. If the cops or the utility company were still poking around, they didn't want to draw any attention by parking Pammy's car in the driveway.

A few minutes after the kids had dropped the bikes into the backyard shed, they heard Pammy's footfalls in the alleyway. She pushed the gate open and they convened near the crossover that had joined the Kingfishers' yard with the yard at Tintagel. Pammy took a few minutes to inspect the crossover up close. "So this is what one looks like?" she asked in awe, waving her hand over the shimmering surface.

"Yep." Artie stood in front of the portal and held out an arm. "Want to see the other side?"

Pammy shivered with anticipation. "But can I? I thought you said people from this side can't cross."

Artie smirked. "True. But I'm the king. If you're with me, you can. C'mon."

Pammy stepped next to him, and together they leaned forward, their top halves completely disappearing.

Pammy faltered. "Oh my goodness!" she exclaimed. Bercilak was standing guard next to the portal, and he spun around.

"Hey, Bercilak," Artie said.

The Green Knight held up his gigantic ax in salute and said, "Hello, sire! And greetings, Qwon elder. You are related to our esteemed Sir Qwon, no?"

"Y-yes," Pammy managed to say. "They told me about you, but, well—you're still kind of a shock!"

"A shock? I don't know any lightning magic, if that's what you mean. But I am full of other surprises! Or, I guess I should say, I am empty of them!" He lowered his ax and guffawed, his armor clanking.

"We'll be back soon, Bercy. Just have to tie up a few loose ends."

"Understood. Make sure they are tied down tight, m'lord!"

"Will do." Artie and Pammy leaned back through the crossover. "He's pretty literal," Artie explained.

"I could tell," Pammy said with a chuckle.

They turned from the crossover to the house. The sky was just beginning to brighten as they walked up the back steps and onto the patio.

Artie knelt at the welcome mat to get the key when Kay said quietly, "Artie, the door's open!"

It was open! "But you locked it, didn't you?"

"Yeah, double positive."

"Dang it." Artie peered through the nearest window into the kitchen. It looked the same as before—a total wreck—but at least empty of a dead saber-tooth/rhino.

"You think it's another one of those things?"

"Only one way to find out." And before Kay could stop him, Artie stole into the house.

There was no sign of anything in the kitchen. No sign of anything in the den. He tiptoed in farther and hit a creaky floorboard. He froze and listened. No sound. He shifted his weight off the board and it creaked some more. Listened again. Nothing. A few more steps, and he'd reached the cabinet where the swords were hidden. He opened it carefully, leaned in, and emerged holding Excalibur. He pulled out the blade and slung the scabbard over his shoulder. Then he peeked at Kay and gave her the all clear.

The others crept in. Artie handed Kay and Qwon their swords, and the girls drew their weapons immediately. Artie passed his dagger, Carnwennan, to Pammy. "You keep that," he whispered. "And stay put."

Pammy slid the knife from its sheath and winked at Artie.

Artie, Kay, and Qwon fanned into the house. They cleared the dining room and the living room and then returned to the entryway. Then they went up the stairs, keeping to the left and skipping the third, seventh, and eleventh steps since he knew they were as noisy as noisy steps came. Snaking along the upper hallway, they arrived at Kynder's room: clear. Guest room: clear. Kay's room: clear.

Artie's room: locked.

Artie and Kay exchanged wild looks. Neither Artie nor Kay had any idea where the keys to the upstairs rooms were kept, or if they even existed. The Kingfishers simply didn't lock their doors.

Artie took a step back and pantomimed kicking the door in. Kay and Qwon nodded in agreement. "On three," Artie mouthed.

"One.

"Two.

"Three."

He kicked hard. It flew inward and Artie did too, but the door rebounded and its edge hit him across the knuckles. It only hurt for a second, but the shock was enough to cause him to drop Excalibur.

As he skidded to a stop, a form rose from the bed. A glint of metal caught what little light filtered into the room, the metal coming fast for Artie's head. His reflexes kicked in and his fists crossed in front of him, like a prizefighter protecting his face. This was it: he was about to put the scabbard to the deathblow test.

But before the weapon could split his head like a coconut, someone said, "No!" which was followed by the grating of metal on metal on metal.

Half a second passed and then a breathless voice said, "By the fens! I'm sorry, Brother!"

Artie opened his eyes. Three of the Seven Swords were crossed in front of him in a tangle of steel. Kay and Qwon had jumped to either side of Artie, crossing Cleomede and Kusanagi in defense of Artie's noggin, the Peace Sword caught in their crook.

"Dred!" Qwon exclaimed.

"I'm so sorry! I was just having the strangest dream, and you startled me!" Dred stepped down from Artie's bed and offered Artie the hilt of his weapon. "Please, Arthur, forgive me."

Pammy called from downstairs, "Everything all right?"

"Yeah, Mom. We're fine."

"Okay!" Pammy said.

Artie straightened. "Please, Dred. Keep your sword. It was a mistake. But why're you here?"

"Yeah, Semibro, why are you in Art's bed?" Kay asked.

"I came with Erik," Dred explained, wiping sleep from his eyes with the back of a hand. "After we reached Tintagel, he got really homesick. He insisted on coming back here, even if only for the night. I decided to keep him company. Just made sense to stay in your bed, Artie. I locked the door out of habit—and, er, I was a little afraid, to be honest. I'm new to your side. I hope you don't mind."

Artie shook his head. "Not at all. But where *is* Erik?" Artie was seized with the sudden fear that Erik had gone home to his parents, who would ask a *lot* of questions.

"Downstairs, I think. In the game room."

Artie sighed. "Oh, good." He turned to Kay. "C'mon."

They sheathed their weapons and returned to Pammy.

"My goodness again," Pammy said, seeing Dred for the first time. "You really *do* look like Artie."

"Mom, this is Dred. My, uh, kidnapper and friend."

Dred held out his hand, and when Pammy took it he bowed and kissed the back of it. "Oh my," Pammy said, blushing. Artie rolled his eyes.

Dred stood and let Pammy's hand go. "It's a pleasure to meet you, Lady Onakea. Your daughter is a wonderful person."

"Thank you, Dred. I think so, too."

Kay pushed past them, saying, "Yeah, yeah. We're all wonderful people, really and truly. But let's go see Erik." She disappeared down the stairs.

Artie followed his sister. "We'll be right back."

When they got to the game room, Erik was sitting cross-legged in the middle of the carpet, the VR goggles strapped to his head. The TV was not on and the only light in the room was the flickering green and blue shafts leaking from the sides of the glasses. Erik was completely still. The golden Xbox controller sat idle in his hands. His back slumped. Artie walked around him. Erik's mouth hung open, a thin string of drool falling from it.

"Erik," Artie said, but Erik didn't move.

The lights in the goggles, however, went dark.

"What's he, asleep?" Kay wondered, clicking on a lamp in the corner.

Artie shrugged. "Erik!" he called more loudly.

Still nothing. The drool came free and landed on one of his knees, which was soaked.

"Erikssen," Kay said, pushing him lightly on the back.

"Wha'?" Erik blurted. He let go of the controller and fumbled with the glasses. "Who's there?"

"It's us." Artie wrinkled his eyebrows. "Did you fall asleep playing video games? Sitting like that in the middle of the room?"

"Huh, no. I, uh . . ." He finally got the glasses off and blinked as he looked at Artie and Kay.

"What's with you? You look like you've been hypnotized or something."

"What? No. I was just playing *Otherworld*."

"Or getting a lobotomy," Artie said.

Kay rapped her knuckles on the side of her head. "You all there?"

"Yeah, I'm fine, guys," Erik insisted. He jumped up and bounded over to Gram, which leaned against the wall near the game console. "Totally fine."

"Why are you down here?" Artie asked.

Erik sighed. "I wanted to go home but I knew I shouldn't, so I just started playing *Otherworld*. Hope you don't mind that I played with your character, Artie."

Artie felt a little uneasy—something about the situation bugged him. "Course not." He moved back to the stairway. "Come on. We're going back to the real Otherworld. There's a lot to do."

Erik nodded. "Great."

As they left Artie said, "And, Erik, I promise to get you home as soon as I can. I'm so sorry you can't go there yet."

"It's okay," Erik said quietly. "I did write my mom a letter, just to let her know I'm all right. I didn't tell her anything about all of this. She wouldn't believe it anyway. Can I send it to her?"

"Definitely. We'll have Pammy drop it in the mail."

"Cool, thanks."

They shut off the Xbox and the VR goggles and met the others in the kitchen. Artie gave Pammy Erik's letter while Kay went into the pantry and pulled a twelve pack of Mountain Dew from behind a case of canned beets that had been there for as long as they could remember. It was one of their best hiding spots.

They said their good-byes and wished one another good luck. Artie and Kay watched the Onakeas leave while Dred and Erik got some snacks in the kitchen.

"You read Cassie's letter yet?" Artie asked.

Kay shook her head. "Couldn't work up the nerve."

Artie resisted the urge to make a joke about how Kay never hesitated to do anything, and instead said, "You will. Soon."

"I hope so." She faced Artie. "We've got to bring our dad back. Like, ASAP."

"I know." Artie spun on his heel. Dred and Erik stood a few feet away, munching on trail mix. "We're out, guys. Hope you're ready, Dred. Because we're headed to Fenland. We have some unfinished business with Morgaine."

𝔅ack at 𝔗intagel, they loaded up on swords, armor, arrows, helmets, bucklers. Kay filled the infinite backpack with water and snacks, and made sure there was rope in it. They double knotted their shoelaces and tucked in their shirts. No loose ends.

The knights going to Fenland were Artie, Kay, Dred, Erik, Bedevere, Shallot, and last, Lance, who was fully recovered. Thumb and Numinae were still at the Library in Sylvan doing research, and Bercilak was content to stay at Tintagel and stand guard.

Before crossing to Fenland, Kay gave them a once-over like a drill sergeant. "All right, ragged Knights of the Round Table! Game time!"

Shallot tested her scentlock; Lance twanged his

bowstring; Erik spoke some Swedish to Gram.

Using Excalibur's pommel and Dred's knowledge of Castel Deorc Wæters, Artie opened a moongate into a side passage near Morgaine's bedroom. Dred snuck through to check if the coast was clear. It was. Artie went next, and the others followed.

The moongate snapped shut. Since all of Castel Deorc Wæters's sangrealite had been stolen by Merlin, the lights were still out. Kay fished a headlamp out of the backpack and flicked it on.

They huddled in a circle, their weapons drawn. Lance already had two arrows nocked in his bow—which looked exactly like his original bow, painted with stars and stripes and bald eagles and everything. Orgulus, reclaimed from Numinae, hung from his belt.

Dred leaned forward. "Most likely she'll be in her room, plotting away."

Artie ran a hand over his jeans pocket. Scarffern, his secret and mysterious weapon, was waiting and ready. If he needed it on this trip, he wouldn't hesitate to use it. "We go right to her," he said. "Confront her here and now and demand to know about the Grail."

"Numinae should be here," Shallot lamented. "We're going to need his magic."

"We'll be fine," Artie said resolutely. "She'll hear us out."

Lance raised his eyebrows. "I hope you're right."

Artie turned to his brother. "Dred, lead the way."

Dred moved into the hallway. Torches, set in iron sconces, burned at regular intervals. Dred walked up a flight of stairs, turned again, and stopped. In front of him were the huge double doors that led to Morgaine's bedroom.

Dred held up a fist to knock, but Artie raised Excalibur. "I'll do it."

He knocked three times, but there was no answer. No evil, sickly sweet voice that Dred knew all too well. Artie knocked again. Nothing.

"Maybe she's running some errands," Kay said.

"Or maybe she jumped into that fetid moat of hers," Shallot hissed.

"I doubt it," Dred said. "You guys ready?" They nodded, and Dred pushed the doors open.

Shoulder to shoulder, Artie and Dred entered. The room was illuminated all around with torches and many-fingered candelabras dripping with wax. These rose toward the ceiling on magical cords, going as far as the stained glass windows in the upper reaches of the chamber. Artie asked Excalibur for some light, and it began to glow. The others followed cautiously.

"Where is she?" Artie whispered, his stomach suddenly full of butterflies.

"I don't know," Dred said, searching for any sign of Morgaine.

"Could she be invisible?" Kay wondered.

"No. I would see her," Shallot answered, which made sense since she could turn invisible herself.

They took a few more steps, and Dred straightened. "She's not here." And then, as he was about to sheathe his weapon, he caught sight of Eekan, his mother's red-tufted jaybird, sleeping on a pedestal stand on Morgaine's vanity.

Dred turned to Shallot. "If you'd be so kind as to get that bird, mistress fairy."

She sheathed The Anguish, pirouetted, and disappeared. A few seconds later Eekan was screeching and flapping helplessly in Shallot's invisible hands. She twirled and was visible once more. The bird was not happy.

Dred approached, followed by the others. "Where is she?" he asked. The bird struggled and squawked. "Don't lie, Eekan. You know I'll be able to tell." The bird tried to bite Shallot's hand, but she adjusted her grip and caught the bird around the throat. He whimpered. "Last chance," Dred said. "If you don't tell me, the fairy will turn you into dust. You don't want that, do you?" Shallot smiled, and the bird finally began to chitter and click in a language only Dred could comprehend.

When Eekan was finished, Dred said, "Son of a witch."

"What is it?" Artie asked.

"She's downstairs."

"So?" Kay said.

Dred sighed. "She's in the place where you and I were made, Brother. The place I told you about." He paused dramatically, then whispered, "Her lab."

"Oh." Artie was a little unsure about going there, but they had no choice. "Well, lead the way, Dred."

Before leaving, Shallot asked, "What about the bird?"

"Keep it hostage," Dred said. "Mum loves that bird more than anything." Shallot snickered, tightening her grip around the feathery neck. And then they filed out of the room and through the darkened Castel.

Down, down, down they went, retracing the same path that Qwon and Shallot had taken when they'd escaped from Castel Deorc Wæters with poor Bors. They met no resistance. Morgaine's minions had either been decimated in the battle with Artie, Merlin, and the knights; or, as was more likely, had simply deserted after Morgaine had failed to capture Artie Kingfisher.

Finally they reached the subterranean tunnel containing the secret door that led to the lab. Dred ran his hands over the wall until he found the hidden stone that Bors had shown him. He pushed it, and the door swung open.

Dred continued to lead the way. Lance and Shallot brought up the rear.

Many small footprints could be seen in the dirt on the floor. "She's definitely been down here," Dred said.

They reached the end of the passage. The door there was open. Inside they could hear the clink of drinking glasses and a woman's distant voice.

Artie looked at his knights. "Here goes, guys."

They went in, this time with Artie in the lead. Just like Dred had before them, they gawked at the abominations set in endless rows of glass canisters lining the room. Unfortunately for everyone but Artie, they had not been warned.

"What *is* this place?" Kay asked, her voice quavering.

"Looks like a mad scientist's lab," Lance mused.

Shallot just hissed, and Bedevere steeled himself silently.

"It's where Artie and I were born," Dred said solemnly.

"Far out." Erik clearly wasn't as freaked out as the others.

They drew closer to the end of the room, and the things in the tubes got more and more recognizable.

"Gross, that one looks just like you!" Kay cried out before clasping a hand over her mouth, sure she'd given them away.

Which she had. A loud whoosh came from the back of the lab, and before they knew it Morgaine floated before them. With arms outstretched, she cooed, "Hello, my liege!" Her voice was dangerously sweet and tinged with sarcasm. "Come and meet your faithful servant, your vanquished foe, your besotted tribute, the Lordess of Fenland!"

Artie stepped forward. "Morgaine," he said confidently.

"King." She swept her arms through the air. "What do you think of your nursery? I slaved in here for longer than you can imagine."

"It's great," Artie said insincerely. "And thanks. Really. If it weren't for you, I'd be a finger bone and a lock of hair."

"So true!" She came closer and into better view. Her auburn hair was twisted atop her head like a pile of icing on a cupcake. Her war dress was gone, replaced by the kind of clothing Dred was more familiar with: a loose pantsuit and silver shoes and a yoke of tacky necklaces that jingled whenever she spoke. The sangrealitic bracelets she'd worn on her forearms in battle, though, were still there.

"So, Arthur Kingfisher-Pendragon, et cetera, et cetera. How goes the kingdom?"

Artie walked to within seven feet of Morgaine and stopped. Her necklaces tinkled. "Tell me about the Grail," he stated flatly.

"Ha! Cutting right to it, aren't you?"

"Hey!" Kay said. "Don't talk to him like—"

"Please, Lady Kingfisher, I am speaking to the liege, not you."

"I'm no lady."

"No kidding."

"Watch it, Mum," Dred warned.

Morgaine didn't even look at Dred. "I shall address whomever I like, however I like." Her voice was full of hate. "Thanks to you and that foul wizard, we have no power on Fenland—but I did keep some for myself."

"Your bracelets," Shallot said.

"Your dagger," Dred added.

"Yes, those, my dears."

Dred stepped next to Artie. "Mum, listen—"

Morgaine rushed to Dred in a blur and waved a hand in front of his face. "Enough! I will *not* listen to you, traitorous boy!" And before Dred could respond, a web of skin-colored string wove across his mouth and laced it shut.

Dred brought a hand to his face, his eyes wide, and made a muffled sound in protest.

Shallot slid to one side of the room and disappeared, jaybird and all.

"Don't bother with your parlor trick, sprite," the witch said. "I can see you. I was always able to see you."

She's lying, Artie thought. Shallot has the bird. If Morgaine cares about it as much as Dred says, then she'd be scared for it.

Artie took a chance. "And don't bother with your attitude, Lordess Morgaine. I need to know about—"

Morgaine waved a hand dismissively. "Yes, yes. The Grail."

"You *will* tell me about it," Artie commanded.

Morgaine pointed a crooked finger at the young king. "Aha! So forceful, so determined. See, Dred? This is what I wished for from you. But answer me, Arthur—why would I tell *you* anything?"

Artie gathered himself and said, "I'm the king of the Otherworld. You *have* to answer my questions."

Morgaine tut-tutted. "My boy, it's going to your head."

"It's not." Artie pointed at Dred's mouth. "Release my brother and help us. Now."

"Your brother? What do you know of your brother?"

"That he saved us."

"That's right! By abandoning his dear mum. That doesn't bode well for you, king. Once a traitor, always a traitor."

Artie turned. "Come on, guys, this is a waste of time. We'll have to find out about the Grail some other way." Dred moaned in protest, but Artie started to walk away. "Don't worry, Dred. Numinae'll fix your mouth."

Morgaine rose into the air a few feet. "What if I were to stop you from leaving?"

Artie paused as Lance strung two arrows and got ready to fire. Bedevere held up his stump, ready to activate his phantom arm. Erik started to vibrate with rage.

"You *can't* stop us," Artie said. He thought of blowing Scarffern right then just to shut this annoying woman up.

"I can if I want to. Especially if I stop using my power to hold on to certain things . . ."

With that, Morgaine spread a hand over her face. Artie turned back to her as she moved her hand away, and with it came . . . *her youth*! Suddenly the witch appeared wrinkled and half wasted. Dred, recognizing this version of his mum from when he saw her during one of the sangrealitic blackouts, gasped through his nose.

Lance was startled as something unseen jostled his wrist, causing the pair of arrows to inadvertently take off in Morgaine's direction. As soon as Artie heard the string release, he jumped and swung Excalibur. With one swipe he cut the projectiles clean in half, and they clattered to the floor.

"Shallot!" Lance yelled. "Don't ever do that again!"

Morgaine laughed. Artie let a few beats pass and announced, "I saw Nyneve recently. She told me some things."

"Such as?"

"That Excalibur also wants Merlin dead. And that I am the only one who can strike him down!"

"You think I didn't know that? I can work around that constraint, fool king. I could hypnotize you. I could take your friends and torture them. I could—"

Artie took two big steps toward Morgaine. "You'll do *none* of that! Because I also realized that I could just give Excalibur back to Nyneve." The witch frowned. "You know she'd have to take it. It's her duty. And no one but me could get it back from her. Not you, not Merlin, not Dred, not Numinae. Her underwater grotto is the safest place in the entire Otherworld. I know it, and you do, too."

Morgaine was momentarily speechless. "You wouldn't."

"Why not? The worlds are rejoined. When Merlin finds you, he'll take care of you in a jiffy. If I were to give Excalibur back to Nyneve, Merlin wouldn't have any reason to come after me. No, Morgaine. If you still want Merlin dead, then you need me *more* than I need you. Much more."

Artie tried not to sound too proud of himself, but he was. He'd beaten her, and he hadn't needed Excalibur or Scarffern. That's how kings rolled—good ones anyway.

Morgaine's face struggled to stay calm. After a few seconds she descended to the ground. When she touched down, a jeweled staff grew from her hand and met the floor with a light tap. Her baggy pants fluttered as she walked across the floor, her gait erect and graceful. Artie fought his nerves as she approached, the weak light of the lab flickering on her cat-eye glasses. She was shorter than Artie by a few inches, and old, but still strong. "Very well," she said quietly, coming to a stop just in front of Artie. "But first the sprite must release my bird."

Artie nodded at Shallot. Reluctantly, Shallot held out her arm and let Eekan out of the choke hold. The bird flapped to Morgaine, clicking and cawing its hatred for the fairy, and perched on Morgaine's shoulder. Morgaine cooed at the bird and stroked its beak. "Come," she said. "Follow me and I'll tell you what you need to know to find the grail."

𝔐orgaine pushed past 𝔄rtie and the Knights of the Round Table and walked down the room of botched Arties and Dreds. As she passed her erstwhile son, she waved a hand and the strings on his mouth unlaced and dropped away.

Dred stretched his jaw as Artie hurried forward to walk alongside the witch.

"Much misinformation was spread on both sides about the Grail after Arthur's death," Morgaine explained as she led them through the castle. "By the high Middle Ages it was rumored to be in no less than a dozen places. It was in Roman-era ruins in Spain and prehistoric mounds in Ireland; it was in France, it was in Glastonbury; in subterranean sangreal pits in the land of Jag and frozen temples in northernmost Surmik. All were lies. The misinformation continued, on your side especially, where the Grail took on its freighted religious meaning. The Knights Templar had it, the Cathars, the Rosicrucian Order. It was in the Louvre in Paris; it was in the ancient city of Petra in Jordan; it had been sent into outer space during the Cold War. Blah, blah, blah. All nonsense."

At the top of a flight of stairs she ducked under a low archway and tapped her staff on the ground. It made an awful noise, and the jagged jewels set in it threw off a cool light. The wall opened in front of them as if it were some kind of wild 3-D puzzle, revealing a narrow hall. She glanced over her shoulder at Artie. "Shortcut," she explained. Then she took off at a brisk pace. Artie followed, the other knights in tow. Shallot remained invisible.

Morgaine continued. "Galahad was the last person from your side to hold the Grail. He was an insufferable knight. More full of himself than Merlin and Arthur put together. After he died, the Grail went back to the Fisher Kings, those woeful creatures missing limbs or sight or both"—Artie immediately thought of Bran—"and they took it through the King's Gate. They were allowed to use the gate since they held the Grail. Where they put it in there, I have no idea. As you know, the King's Gate is for the king. . . ."

Morgaine stopped before a closed door and placed her hand on it.

Of course! Artie thought. That was what Arthur's ghost was trying to show him in the void of the King's Gate. The Grail was somewhere behind that dark door that Arthur had pointed to—it *had* to be.

Artie took another chance. "Do you know anything about a crown-shaped key, Lordess Morgaine?"

The witch paused. "A key . . . ? No. Not one like that." She pushed the door open, and daylight poured into the narrow passageway. "But I have something else to show you. It's just across the yard, on the other side of the barracks."

She moved into the light, and Artie followed her, but then Dred yelled, "Stop, it's a trap!"

Artie spun as Dred smacked hard into an invisible barrier sealing the passageway from the yard. He looked really worried, and Kay, who was right behind Dred, did too.

"Now!" Morgaine yelled. And then, right before their eyes, the witch disappeared.

Dred banged on the invisible door as Artie pushed his free hand into his pocket. Time to see what the most powerful thing in the Otherworld could do.

But before Artie could get his fingers around Scarffern, something snaked over his wrist. It was one of those silver ropes that had wrapped him up on the slopes of Surmik!

The line pulled taut and his hand was yanked from his pocket, turning it inside out. The whistle flew free and hit the ground, rolling out of sight under a nearby hay bale.

He'd lost it again!

He slashed at the rope with Excalibur, cutting his hand free, and searched all around for Morgaine, but she was nowhere to be seen. Instead, a dozen of her knights were approaching from all sides. They were well over six feet tall and each wore a suit of purple-hued plate mail. There was something off about them, but Artie couldn't quite put his finger on it.

Then he realized they were floating about a foot off the ground, which was pretty weird. Were they *ghost* knights?

Artie wrapped both hands around Excalibur and turned back to the doorway. But instead of seeing his friends struggling to escape, he was face-to-face with a huge knight rushing toward him with a gigantic rectangular shield.

Artie reacted. Excalibur caught the top of the shield, shearing a section off, but the full weight of the bash knocked Artie onto his butt. He caught something in his peripheral vision and another rope wrapped around his arm. And then another. And then two on an ankle, and then his other ankle, and then around his waist, and then, at last, his sword hand.

Excalibur fell to the ground with a thud.

"Fool king! I don't *really* need you!" Morgaine's voice boomed from every direction. "I will kill your friends, including your brother, enslave you, and take your hallowed weapon. Then I will draw the wizard to me. And when he comes, my dragon and I will strike him down, and then at the last moment, you will be brought forth in chains to finish him off with Excalibur. You will do this because you will have no reason not to. You will be but a shell, thanks to me. A dragon, my king—do you understand? Merlin may be powerful but he doesn't count the power of a dragon on his side! That, my liege, is where he—*and you*—fall short."

Artie whipped his head in all directions, trying to figure out where she was. As he searched, he realized that it didn't matter if she was right or wrong—so long as she believed it, she was still a menace.

As Artie struggled he was pulled into the air like a rag doll, his limbs stretched to their limits.

And that's when he finally saw Morgaine. She was perched on the thatched roof of the barracks, hunkered over the gable like a beggar and laughing like a madwoman.

She was silenced by a shattering sound. Artie could barely see the doorway, now on his left, as Lance barreled through it, Orgulus's ornate hand guard leading the way. He had used the sword that could punch through anything to smash the invisible barrier holding back Artie's friends!

Artie's knights spilled into the courtyard. An arrow shot past Artie's head and into the narrow eye slit of one of the purple knights. His arms fell to his side and he gurgled and fell over backward, completely dead.

Bedevere launched into the circle. "Phantoma!" he yelled, his stump sprouting its magical arm. He faced the nearest knight, who dropped his rope and held up his empty hand. He flicked his wrist and a blade like a bayonet grew out of his forearm. He stabbed at Bedevere, but Bedevere simply grabbed the blade midthrust with his phantom arm and twisted. The knight did a cartwheel and landed hard on his side. Before the knight could gather himself, Bedevere reached down and with his superstrong hand crushed the thick purple plate mail around the collar. The neck inside was very much crushed as well.

Another rope fell from Artie, and another and another. The purple knights drew swords and engaged their nearest adversaries. And Artie found that he was free to move and fight.

"Kill them all!" Morgaine shouted from atop the barracks. "All but the king!"

Something flashed on Artie's left. He held up his buckler as a whip wrapped around it. The other end of the whip was yanked hard, and Artie crumpled to the ground.

"Flixith, Artie!" Erik yelled from behind him.

Of course!

Artie pulled Flixith from its curved sheath and sliced his arm free of the whip. A purple knight was bearing down on him with a club. Artie spun his blade, and thanks to Flixith's magic, his arms seemed to multiply. The purple knight swung wildly as Artie brought the real blade across the knight's leg, catching a gap in the armor, taking his leg clean off at the knee. The knight fell and made a zombielike sound—gurgling and angry, not desperate at all. And that's when Artie understood: Morgaine's purple knights were not living men at all, but undead ones. Big and strong and determined, but undead all the same.

Which made the idea of cutting them to pieces a lot easier to swallow.

The newly legless zombie knight was about to smack Artie across the chest when Kay appeared and promptly drove Cleomede halfway through the knight's back.

"Hey, Bro!"

"Hey!"

"These brain eaters are nasty, huh?"

"Sure are. Let's rid the world of 'em."

"Done!"

Just then Shallot's sweet smell whisked by them, and Artie suddenly found himself holding Excalibur once more.

"Thanks," Artie said. But the fairy was gone.

"Morgaine!" Dred warned from somewhere.

Artie looked to the witch as a gray jab of magic flew from her cane. Artie planted Excalibur's pommel in Kay's shoulder and pushed her away. She scooted across the ground and plowed into the hay bales where Scarffern had fallen.

Artie was not as quick. The spell caught Excalibur on the crossguard, and the sword was momentarily charged with electricity. The sangrealite in the metal conducted the power harmlessly through Artie's hands and body and down his legs and into the ground.

Thanks to Excalibur's scabbard, Artie was able to weather this attack. He sprinted across the yard as more bolts of magic exploded at his heels. He saw Erik, who was a blur, Gram glinting here and there, as he took on two of the zombie knights at once. Bedevere had his claymore out and was fighting the big one who'd shield-rushed Artie. Judging by Bedevere's yellow-toothed smile, he was enjoying himself. It didn't matter that he had a parabolic prosthetic leg or a phantom arm: Bedevere was in it to win it.

Lance stood on top of the breastplate of a felled zombie, shooting arrows at Morgaine at a furious pace. This was one reason she wasn't able to land a good hit on Artie—with her off hand she was catching the arrows and throwing them onto the roof as fast as she could.

Artie ran straight for the only unengaged enemy. The knight bent forward eagerly, his visor guard up, and readied his long mace. His eyes were green and clouded, and skin peeled from the bridge of his nose. He was ugly, but he was still dangerous.

When Artie got in striking distance he swerved, and the knight's mace came straight down into the ground. The zombie released the mace and slapped at Artie's face, but Artie ducked under the strike like a boxer and came up quick. He was right next to the knight now. Artie pulled Excalibur hard and fast, aiming for the middle of the knight's chest, and as the blade passed in front of Artie's eyes, he caught the reflection of Morgaine parrying the close-quarter strikes of The Anguish, as wielded by Shallot le Fey.

Excalibur was on its way to cutting the zombie knight in half like butter—except that the knight somehow used his right hand, which was farthest away, to grab Excalibur by the blade and stop it in its tracks.

Artie looked into the knight's milky, undead eyes. The zombie pushed down hard on Excalibur, and Artie's knees buckled. All of a sudden, he found himself on the ground.

The knight moaned, his metal gauntlet prepared to punch Artie square in the face and crush it like a grape.

"Artie, catch!" Kay said. Artie could momentarily feel her, just as he had all his life until recently. He knew exactly where she was and what she was throwing. Without looking, he reached up and caught it.

Scarffern.

The zombie punched. Artie dodged the strike by leaning in so close that his cheek pushed against the cold metal of his opponent's purple breastplate. Artie looked up and, holding Scarffern like a tiny knife, drove it hard into one of the knight's eyes.

Without so much as a zombie peep, the knight fell onto all fours. Artie let go of Scarffern and in one motion stood, pirouetted, and brought Excalibur down across the thing's neck.

Its head dropped to Artie's feet and rolled away. Artie put a foot on the zombie's shoulder and pushed the body onto its side.

"Sire!" Bedevere yelled. "The witch!"

Morgaine floated above the roof now, out of Shallot's

reach, as Shallot jumped like a kitten chasing a toy. Artie did a quick scan of the yard. Erik was flushed and panting but calm. Dred coiled a silver rope that he'd taken from one of the zombies. Bedevere leaned on his claymore like nothing had happened. Kay was still near the hay bales. The undead purple knights were defeated—no longer undead, but actually dead.

"Morgaine, give up!" Artie announced. "If you still help us, I'll forget this ever happened."

Her eyes burned. For an answer she put both hands on her staff and pointed its business end at Artie. She let everything she had fly. So much for not killing the king.

Kay and Dred shouted, "No!"

The spell was on Artie instantaneously. It hit Excalibur, and light and dark exploded off the blade, swirling along the blood channels. The Latin inscriptions—*Iacta me* and *Tolle me*—twinkled with golden light. Then the sword gathered all the energy into its metal. Artie pointed it at Morgaine, and the spell flew back at her, multiplied in strength by the purity of the blade.

It hit her full in the chest and exploded in red and green sparks. Morgaine's staff splintered into a million little pieces. She spun and fell. In the sudden silence they could hear her loose clothing flapping as she cut through the air.

She landed on the side of the roof with a thump. Dred was closest. He ran to the eave and waited. Her body rolled down the pitch and over the edge and fell into his arms. He placed her on the ground and stepped back, feeling sad and angry and relieved all at once.

The witch moaned as Artie jogged over. Dred secured her sangrealitic dagger. When Artie reached her, he ran Excalibur's tip over the bracelets on her arms. Effortlessly, the blade cut through them, and they came free.

She'd been stripped of her power.

"That's it, Morgaine," Artie said. "You're done. I—"

"Oh no."

It was Erik. The red in his cheeks was gone. He was as white as a sheet.

"What is it?" Kay asked.

"There!" Erik strained toward the sky.

Shallot, still on the roof, said, "I don't see anything."

"Are you guys blind?"

"Erikssen, there's nothing—" but then Kay was struck dumb.

There *was* something.

"What is *that*?" Bedevere asked.

A billowing cloud in the sky grew from a speck into a large ball. It got bigger and bigger and bigger.

Morgaine rolled onto her back. "You're right, sire. I

am defeated. We all are."

"Kid, is that who I think it is?" Lance asked, readying a handful of arrows.

Artie's shoulders slumped. "Yeah . . . it's Merlin."

IN WHICH MERLIN REARS HIS UGLY HEAD

A spike of fire shot from the cloud, scattering Artie and his knights in all directions. But Morgaine couldn't scatter. The fire hit her directly in the side and drove through her torso. She tried to scream, but no noise came.

Artie ran as fast as he could back to the zombie head he'd cut off. He fought back nausea as he fumbled to get his fingers around the bloodied Scarffern. He pulled the whistle out of the eye socket with a pop and wiped it hurriedly on his jeans. He looked over his shoulder as more flaming spears shot from Merlin's cloud. These were random, hitting the yard and Castel Deorc Wæters all over the place.

"Artie, over here!" Dred called from the cover of a stone

arch. Artie got to his feet and, as he ran, blew Scarffern as hard as he could.

The sensation was odd: it was as if Artie's tongue had become as narrow as a worm as his breath wound its way through the convoluted passageway within the tube. What a journey! Scarffern seemed to go on and on and on, tumbling this way and that and turning back on itself before emerging from the far end. Perhaps most strangely, the whistle made no sound at all.

He blew and blew and blew, and as he did, nothing happened.

What the heck? Artie thought.

He had nearly reached Dred when three flaming bolts landed in the earth, blocking his way. He skidded to a halt.

"King!" a voice boomed, as if spoken through a bullhorn.

Artie turned. High above was Merlin. He rode in a tall saddle strapped to the back of a black housefly as big as, well, a house.

"Merlin," Artie called.

The wizard slapped the fly with his owl-headed cane, and the insect zigged and zagged as it came closer. It stopped and hovered, its wings audibly buzzing, about a hundred feet away.

They were just close enough that Artie could make out

Merlin's face. His eyes had grown even redder. His mouth had turned completely black, teeth included, as if Merlin had been eating mud since their last meeting.

They watched each other like gunslingers in an old western.

A few moments passed before Merlin simply said, "Good-bye, Artie Kingfisher."

A flurry of fiery spikes shot from Merlin's hand, headed right for the king.

Excalibur shook and then, as it had before on two critical occasions, time slowed. Artie slid twenty feet to his left, and as soon as he reached relative safety, time ramped back up.

Merlin bellowed, "Two can play at that."

A shock wave rolled off Merlin. This was Merlin's own time-slowing spell, and it affected everything but Artie and the wizard.

Artie's stomach turned as he held up Excalibur.

"Darkness!" Artie ordered. But Merlin reached out a single finger, and the blackness coming off Artie's sword frittered and fell to the ground like ashes. "Light!" Artie commanded, but the blinding flash he expected sparkled weakly and failed.

Artie was, after everything, really, really scared.

"As I said: good-bye, Artie Kingfisher." A ball of energy gathered over Merlin and shot forward. The end was coming.

Artie shut his eyes.

But then the sky lit up in oranges and reds, and the sound of an explosion came as Artie's face grew hot.

He heard a pair of wings cutting the air and looked: flying toward them was a black dragon of Fenland! Its flammable, oily breath had hit Merlin's bolts and caused them to explode before they could kill Artie.

If this is Scarm's replacement, shouldn't it be helping Morgaine? Artie wondered. Why did it save me?

And then it dawned on him: Wait a minute, what if Scarffern *had* worked? What if, somehow, it had called this dragon to help *him*?

Artie watched as Merlin turned his attentions to the dragon, shooting a wild flurry of bolts at Artie's unexpected ally. The dragon dodged most of them, sliding through the air like a fighter jet, and ignited others with its breath. The black dragon wheeled and momentarily turned its back to Merlin, and the wizard let out a quick strike that clipped the creature and sent it reeling.

Artie fell to his knees. Merlin was too strong.

But then, from the far end of the yard, Kay screamed a name Artie thought he'd never hear again.

"Tiberius!"

Artie craned his neck—there was *another* dragon! He squinted. Was Kay right? Could it be?

And then the black smoky breath they were so familiar

with met Merlin's attack, turning his bolts of fire into small shards of black rock just as they were about to finish off the Fenlandian serpent.

It was! Tiberius! His green iridescent skin, his great horns, his small wings, his rainbow eyes! He snaked through the air toward Merlin, as the black dragon cartwheeled and came to Tiberius's side. Together these two concentrated their attacks on Merlin, and in seconds Merlin had switched to defense.

Lance emerged from behind a building. "Look!" He pointed away from the action with his bow.

The other knights came out of hiding. A third dragon was arriving!

It zoomed into place and flanked Merlin. His giant fly turned this way and that, confused and frightened. Merlin stood in the saddle, and, just as the three dragons converged on him, he leaped off his mount and disappeared in a puff of smoke. "Another day!" he said, his voice booming through the air. He had escaped, though not his poor fly. The dragons made quick work of it, tearing it to pieces and flinging its chunks to the ground.

The knights jumped up and down, yelling and screaming.

When the dragons were done, Tiberius dived to the ground, a smile on his face. The other two saviors stayed airborne, making sure there weren't any more wayward wizards who needed to be dealt with.

Tiberius settled in the yard, taking up more than half of it. "Hmmph. Young king. Hello."

Kay couldn't help herself. She dropped Cleomede and ran full tilt to Tiberius. She slammed into his scaly neck and dug her fingers into his skin. Tears spilled from her eyes, and Tiberius's too. A big drop hit the top of her head, soaking her short red hair.

"Hmmmmmmph. Mistress Kay."

"Oh, Tiberius. How? How are you here?"

"The call wakened me. We dragons are susceptible. Strong'n' hard otherwise, but weak to the call . . ."

"Scarffern . . . ," Artie said quietly.

"Hmmmph. The Dragon Horn."

"The Dragon Horn . . . I thought it was a myth," Shallot said reverently.

"The words *Dragon Horn* haven't been spoken in a king's age, fairy Shallot. Hmmmph. Might as'll be myth."

"Can it bring back Fallown?" Shallot asked eagerly.

"Hmmmph. No. I was not quite dead. That is the only reason I am here. Fallown and Scarm—they're gone."

There was a brief silence before Lance asked, "What *is* this Dragon Horn?"

"It calls us, archer, and compels us to the king. Anywhere'n' any time. Breaks bonds. No matter who the dragon calls lord." Tiberius pointed his tail to the sky. "That black one—Snoll—is in place of dead Scarm. Loyal to the witch, but once Scarffern rings, it must obey. The lords and lordesses of the Otherworld have been served. Now, the dragons serve the king, and the king alone."

"Cool!" Kay shouted.

"Can they cross over, Tiberius?" Lance asked.

"Hmmmph. In direst need, yes."

"*Really* cool!" Kay said even louder.

Tiberius smiled. "Yes, mistress Kay."

Artie turned the whistle in his hand. Such a small thing. In that moment he understood more about the Otherworld than ever before. Fairies and trolls and elves were its people, and sangrealite was its lifeblood, but the dragons were its beating heart.

Control the dragons and you controlled the Otherworld.

Just like Nyneve had said: this was the secret to his power.

"Oh, Tiberius, I'm so glad you're back," Kay said, still gushing. Seeing him gave her hope that she would see her father soon, too.

"Me also. Hmmmmph." He paused. "The wizard has turned."

"Yeah, you could say that," Artie said.

"And what of Kynder?" A heavy silence fell. Kay shook her head. "Still's frozen?"

Neither Artie nor Kay could bear to answer. Dred stepped forward. "Yes, master Tiberius."

Tiberius tilted his head at Artie's twin. "You are Mordred."

"Yes. Call me Dred, if you please."

"Dred. You came and helped the king."

"I did. He helped me, too."

"Hmmmph." Tiberius looked back to Artie. "For Kynder, you'll be needing the Grail cup."

Artie nodded and thought, Dragons are always so direct. "That's right," Artie said. "Can you help us get it?"

"Hmmmmmmmph." Tiberius let his head settle onto the ground. "This thing isn't dragonly. It is for men and the dreams of men."

And then, from the far end of the yard, Morgaine moaned.

Tiberius looked. "The witch. She is defeated."

"Yes," Dred said bitterly.

Artie patted Tiberius. "Come on. Let's go talk to her before . . ." He led the way, and when he reached the witch knelt next to her.

Dred knelt too. "Mum, why? Why did you betray us?"

"Oh, Mordred," she said weakly before coughing uncontrollably for a few seconds.

And then, as her body shuddered, Artie did something unexpected. He took her by the hand. "Please, Morgaine. The Grail."

"I had nothing to show you. It was a trap. Only a trap."

"So that's it? You're just a liar?" Kay barked.

Artie shook his head. "Kay, please. She's dying."

Kay shuffled. "Sorry."

Artie ran a hand over Morgaine's forehead. "Morgaine, if you want us to beat Merlin, tell me if you know anything about the Grail."

Morgaine's pupils narrowed. "Yes. There was a key, shaped like a crown. Like the one you asked after."

"I have seen the door that key opens. I think it leads to the Grail. I need to find it," Artie said breathlessly.

"Hmmmph," Tiberius cooed.

Morgaine then grabbed Dred by the hand and dug her fingernails into his skin. "The Grail! If you get it, please, do not use it on me. Let me die now. I will help you—" Her voice faltered and she fell into coughing again.

Dred, breathing fast, repeated over and over, "Okay, I promise. Okay, I promise." But she didn't seem to hear.

Artie stroked her back and she stopped hacking. "If that's what you want, Morgaine, I swear to honor it."

"Thanks. I'm old. And tired . . ." She trailed off as her face grew paler. "Yes . . . I did lie before. I knew the crown key, long ago. And it will lead to the Grail. Merlin . . . Merlin . . ." Her head lolled to the side and, though still conscious, she lost her train of thought.

Dred fought back tears. Some love still lived in his heart for the Lordess of Fenland. "Go on, Mum," he said.

She came back to them and said, "Merlin had it."

"Where?" Artie asked eagerly.

"I don't—" The coughing resumed, this time worse. When she was finished, blood dripped from the corner of her mouth. "I borrowed it once . . . a copy. Made copy."

"What copy?" Artie asked.

"Mordred. Mordred, I . . ."

"Where is it, Morgaine? Tell me, and I promise to defeat Merlin. I have the Dragon Horn."

"Scarffern?" she whispered, her eyes filling with tears. "Truly?"

"Yes."

"King!" she said weakly, and finally turned her eyes to Artie. "Forgive . . . please."

"I will. I do. Now tell me."

She struggled to breathe as she said, "The copy . . . carved . . . ironwood . . . hidden. Merlin stole the container. He didn't know what was in it. Couldn't open it. There was another key. Different. An heirloom. Passed down. I gave it to—" She seized for a moment. Artie squeezed her hand harder. "It opened an obsidian chest. Big. A desk. With legs like . . ." Her eyes rolled into her head.

"Mum!" Dred called.

Artie unslung Excalibur's scabbard and pressed it into her chest.

"Legs like what?" Kay pleaded.

The knights surrounded Morgaine as her body went limp.

Dred stroked her cheek. "Like what, Mum?"

Her irises spun back into view, one brown, one purple. She was close to passing out. It took every ounce of energy for her to say, "Legs like a horse's. The key for the door. The door for the king . . ." All color drained from her face and fear flooded her eyes. "Please, my children, my sons . . . Let me be. . . ."

And then she faded.

Artie snagged the scabbard and stood quickly. "Tiberius, stone her."

"Hmmmph. Are you certain?"

"Yes. We'll do what she asked, but we can't leave her like this—Merlin might come back for her body. If you stone her we can bring her to Tintagel and keep her safe."

They formed a circle around Morgaine. Tiberius lowered his head over the witch and let out a thin stream of smoke. The black basalt unfolded around her waist, moving over her stomach and back.

Dred looked at his mother, full of confusion. "Artie, how are we going to find this chest?"

"Don't worry, Brother. I know where it is."

"*What?*" Erik asked.

"The Invisible Tower," Kay said quietly.

"Yep, the Invisible Tower," Artie confirmed.

"But I don't understand, kid," Lance said. "The Grail was right under Merlin's nose that whole time?"

"No. But if Morgaine is right, the crown-shaped key was. And that will open the door that will lead us to the Grail. I'm sure of it."

Tiberius stopped breathing smoke as the witch was finally encased. Artie turned to his dragon. "Tiberius, I invite you to Avalon. Can you get there?"

"Yes, lord king."

"I invite all of the dragons to Avalon. Can you gather them?"

"Hmmmph. You have blown the Horn. So yes, lord king."

"Go. Tell Numinae and Tom—they're in Sylvan. Meet us as soon as you can at Castle Tintagel. Take Morgaine as well, and put her with Kynder. Bercilak will show you where."

"Yes, lord king."

Artie looked over his friends. "Knights—time for us to return to lovely Cincinnati, Ohio. To the Invisible Tower. Where all this nuttiness began."

Snap, through one of Excalibur's moongates, and they were there.

The store was pitch-dark and musty and smelled like broken rocks. It had been several weeks since the actual invisible tower had crumbled around the old Vine Street Cable Railway Building that housed the store, the Invisible Tower, which was still closed for business.

"What time is it?" Bedevere asked.

Kay consulted her watch. "Two in the afternoon."

"Sure is dark in here for the afternoon," Bedevere said.

"Merlin liked it that way," Lance said. "He couldn't see outside, so he didn't want anyone who came in here to be able to see outside, either."

"Jealous and spiteful then too, huh?" Bedevere remarked.

"I hadn't thought of it that way, but yeah." Artie said. He leaned into the darkness and whispered, "Light!" Excalibur burned with a blue glow. A film of dust coated the books and comics and action figures and, well, everything.

"This is where the wizard *lived*?" asked Shallot, who was not happy to have been transported to Artie's side, where fairies did not belong.

"He lived downstairs," Kay answered. "In a giant basement."

A scurrying sound came from nearby and Shallot spun, stabbing her blade through a rack of comic books. A high-pitched squeal followed amid a flurry of paper. When she brought The Anguish into the light, a gray rat hung by its front paws from the blade's wavy steel. The rat's eyes went wide as its hind legs bicycled the air.

Shallot flicked her weapon and sent the rodent to the floor. It scurried under a bookshelf, but then darted back out and ran up Shallot's leg.

Shallot slapped at the rat, but it was nimble, and within a few seconds Shallot held it in front of her by the tail.

Dred chuckled. "It likes you."

"Apparently," Shallot said.

"It's your fairy blood, isn't it?" Bedevere wondered as he scratched the long scar over his cheek.

"Hmm," was all Shallot could manage.

"So that's why you didn't want to be over here—you're a vermin magnet!" Kay observed.

Everyone but Shallot laughed. Artie opened a glass case containing a collection of Stormtrooper helmets and random *Star Wars* action figures. "Put the little guy in here." Shallot did, and Artie shut the case quickly. The rat pushed its paws against the glass like a prisoner and tracked the fairy with its eyes and nose.

Shallot dusted off her hands. "Where is this chest, sire? I would like to make this trip quick, if possible."

Artie pointed to the rear of the store. "This way."

As they walked, Artie remembered vividly the last time he'd been there—it was after the tower had fallen. He was surveying the damage with Thumb and Kynder. Pammy sat on the desk in a daze—Kynder had given her a mild sedative to combat her anxiety over Qwon's kidnapping. The sedative was like a much milder version of the spell Merlin had cast on Kynder when they first met: a spell that kept the Kingfisher dad ignorant of what was going on and agreeable to the fact that Artie and Kay had swords, among other things, and were going off on adventures in some place called the Otherworld.

Artie slowed as an idea struck him. Did Merlin cast a spell on me, too? And Kay? Is that why we went along with everything?

He knew the answer: yes. His stomach turned inside

out as Kay pointed over his shoulder.

"There!" she exclaimed. Artie looked. The hulking thing sat where Artie had first seen it, where, in fact, he had first met Merlin. The ancient cash register still sat on top of it, along with a ledger and a couple of empty water bottles.

But Artie couldn't think about the desk just yet.

"What is it, Art?" Kay asked, placing a hand on his back. She didn't need their special connection to see that something wasn't right.

Artie leaned on Excalibur, both hands tight around the grip. The blade vibrated. "Nothing," he managed.

"You sure—"

"Hey, Erik! You coming?" Bedevere interrupted from the back of the line.

No answer came.

"Hey, kid! Wake up!" Lance said.

Erik hadn't moved since they arrived. It occurred to Artie that Erik hadn't said so much as a peep since Merlin had shown up back at Morgaine's place.

"Hey, berserker," Shallot called. She picked up a nearby paperback and flung it, striking Erik in the side of the head.

"Ow!" he said, coming to. "What was that for?"

"You were all la-la land, Erikssen," Kay said. "Like the other night, back in the game room. You okay?"

"I'm fine, Kingfisher. You?" He came to a stop next to Bedevere.

"We're fine, but—" A loud crash and a jangle of ringing bells cut Kay off. The knights turned to the commotion. "The desk!" Kay exclaimed. It was gone. In its place was the ancient cash register that had sat atop it, lying on its side like a boat thrown ashore by a tempest.

"Where'd it go?" Dred asked.

"Light!" Artie ordered, and Excalibur glowed brightly. "There!" He pointed at the velvet curtain at the rear of the store. Something had just passed through it.

Artie stumbled forward, his stomach still churning from the realization that Merlin had enchanted him and Kay, and pushed through the curtain. He could hear the clop-clop of hooves going down the stairs.

Artie spun to his sister with wild eyes.

"Mrs. Thresher!" Kay exclaimed, remembering the doorway at the end of Merlin's basement.

Artie nodded fiercely. "We can't let it reach that door! It could go through it and right to Merlin!" Artie pushed forward, down the stairs, his knights in tow.

They spilled into the first room with the sink and the robes and the walking sticks. Artie sprinted to the archway at the other end and peered through. The desk was a few rooms ahead. Walking was clearly not its thing. The legs in the front faced forward, those in the back faced backward. It was forced to crab-walk through the rooms, but it was too wide to pass through the archways this way, so it had to fumble around at each juncture.

Dred pushed his way to the front. "This will be easy, Brother."

"Wait!" Artie exclaimed.

But Dred didn't. As soon as he stepped into the orchid room, the plants spit spikes at him and bit the air and writhed on their stems. They were mainly a nuisance, but then, as Dred neared the far end of the room, two very large orchids jumped from their pots and laced their roots across the next archway. As he cut these down they shot more roots at his arms and wrists, and then his ankles and thighs. Within seconds he was completely wrapped up.

"Dred!" Artie said.

"I'm all right."

"Step aside." Shallot moved to the front and turned invisible. She passed into the room unnoticed by the plants and freed Dred with a combination of blade work and a low humming song that seemed to placate and enrapture the wild orchids.

The desk had put more distance between them, but still struggled to make progress.

"Looks like we're going to have to run the wizard's gauntlet," Lance said unenthusiastically.

Artie snapped his fingers. "Kay, Dred gave you a coil of Morgaine's magic rope, right?"

"Yeah."

"Give it to me—please."

Kay flashed a smile, pulled the backpack from her shoulders, and dug into it.

"Erik, your head out of the clouds? You ready to turn it on?" Artie asked.

"You know it."

"Here's the plan: you, me, and Shallot go and stop that thing. Erik has the speed, Shallot's invisible, and I can deal with hits on account of the scabbard. Lance—"

"What's up?"

"Cover us. Be careful, though. It'll get tight fast."

"You know I'm deadeye. Don't worry."

"What about us?" Kay asked, tilting her head to Bedevere.

Artie took the coil of rope and slung it over his shoulder. "You two hang back." He held out a hand. "I'll need to borrow Cleomede, if you don't mind."

Kay shook her head. "Don't like it."

"No time to argue. We can't let that thing get to Mrs. Thresher." He reached for Kay's waist and drew Cleomede from its sheath as Dred returned to the first room. "You ready, Shallot?"

"Sire!" she affirmed from a few rooms ahead.

"Light it up, berserker!"

Erik brought Gram in front of his face and his eyes rolled into his head as his body jittered. His skin turned red and his feet began to dance and within seconds he was a cartoonish blur. Artie got as close to this ball of violent entropy as possible and said, "Go!"

Erik shot forward, Artie in his wake.

The orchid room was easy. The next room was freezing cold, the floor slippery. The dark-colored lichens that clung to the walls and ceiling curdled and moved. Foot-long spikes of ice shot at them from all directions. None of these shards touched Erik, though. And while Artie was hit by a couple on his chest and legs, they didn't slow him down. The scabbard was doing its thing.

The third room was as hot as an oven as flaming jets shot from the floor. Erik bounded along the wall and ceiling, out of reach, while Shallot slunk around, trailing her wonderful scent. Artie simply got burned. His clothing never caught fire, but his bare hands and wrists were hit twice with full blasts. They burned and oozed with pus, though thankfully the scabbard healed him quickly.

They ran through the next few rooms—a living room, a gym, a small kitchen—without any problems.

Shallot went first into the next room, which contained a menagerie of small and medium-size animals—rodents, birds, lizards, even a few giant spiders. She was invisible, but as soon as she was in, all the cages flew open and the animals went wild with excitement. A bird flapped from nowhere and managed to latch on to her head in the confusion. She wheeled just as one of Lance's arrows struck it through a wing. The bird fell to the ground as Shallot stepped quickly into the next room.

Artie moved into the doorway, holding Excalibur in front of him. "Darkness!" The blade threw off an inky pool of pitch black, filling the room. Artie could still see, though, just as he'd been able to see when he'd used this same trick to fill Qwon's room back in Shadyside when Dred was in the middle of kidnapping her. The animals didn't know what to do, and many of them immediately stopped going crazy.

Artie stepped forward. "C'mon, Erik! Move quickly!"

Erik didn't need much encouragement. He churned through the room, damaging a few of the animals—nothing major, just a few bumps here and there. Within seconds, all three of the knights were in the following room.

It was a kitchen, and as soon as they were together, knives began to fly from the wall. Artie very nearly got hit in the neck, but Lance knocked that knife out of the air with a well-placed arrow, while Erik suffered a good nick on the top of his right ear. Shallot pirouetted and dodged and emerged from the kitchen unscathed.

The next room was a science lab. Artie pushed past Erik and held out his arm. "Wait." He stuck Excalibur into the middle of the room, and the sword was immediately hit with a jolt of blue electricity. Artie shuddered as the current jostled through his body and into the ground. He readied Cleomede. "I've got this one."

He stepped into the room and was attacked by a quartet of arcing coils, but Excalibur kept him safe by sucking all the power to it, like a magnet. Artie's teeth chattered as he sliced each coil to pieces with Cleomede, blue sheets of electricity cascading over his body. He'd forgotten how subtle a blade Kay's sword was. He could feel the cold metal of the coils part and shatter. In a few seconds he was done.

"Go! We need to wrangle that desk!"

Shallot and Erik shot forward. Artie sheathed Excalibur, stuck Cleomede in the ground, and undid the magical rope. The desk was only twenty feet away. Holding tight to one end, he flung the rope toward it.

It snaked through the air between Shallot and Erik and caught the desk by one of the closer legs, wrapping it up like a lassoed rodeo calf. It didn't like this, and began to buck and kick to try to get free. Two arrows split the air and embedded into the desk's dark wood with a *tha-thwack* as Erik and Shallot tried to subdue the thing with Gram and The Anguish. As soon as they drew close, though, the desk reared and kicked them both square in the chest. They flew into the opposite wall and collapsed, heaving to catch their wind.

Artie pulled hard on the rope to try to hold the desk, but it was no use. It was too strong. I wish Sami were here, he thought.

Just then the desk planted its closest hooves in the

ground and knelt. It stopped pulling for a second. Artie hastily tried to tie the rope to an iron support column, when he was distracted by two loud cracks. He wheeled and watched in astonishment as the rear legs of the desk slowly turned around so that they were now facing the same direction as the other pair of legs! It was no longer working against itself. It reared again, knocking the upper end into the ceiling, came down, and took off at a thunderous gallop.

Artie wrapped the rope around his wrist and he held on tight. It was about to be rodeo time.

Within seconds Artie was yanked from his feet. He bounced painfully along the floor as more of Lance's arrows filled the air. He hit chairs, tables, pillars, sconces, bookshelves, cauldrons, weapon racks, and blew through a large beanbag, scattering little white pellets everywhere (which felt pretty nice, compared to everything else). The scabbard kept him in one piece, though, and after several rooms he managed to work his way up the rope to within ten feet of the desk. But he couldn't risk getting closer—the pounding hooves were too wild and would surely knock him back, if not clean out.

He squinted. Mrs. Thresher was only four or five rooms away. And to make matters worse, he could see that she was open!

During a nasty bounce that gave the rope a couple

feet of sudden slack, Artie turned another loop around his hand. With his free hand he drew Excalibur and held it out. "Darkness!"

The room he was in—full of colored flames that didn't give off heat—went completely black. At the same instant, the desk slammed its front hooves to the ground and skidded to a halt. Artie was thrown, the rope trailing behind him.

When his feet hit the floor, he found himself between the desk and Mrs. Thresher!

Artie threw the slackened rope, and it quickly lashed the desk's legs together in an uncomfortable-looking bundle. It wasn't going anywhere now, but it wouldn't give up. If anything, the fact that Artie had just lassoed it made it even more desperate. The hind legs drove forward, and the edge of the desk took out Artie's feet. Now he was lying flat on top of the thing as it made a last, desperate push toward Mrs. Thresher.

Artie peered over the rear end of the desk. His knights had regrouped and were only forty feet away. Kay had pulled Cleomede from the ground and was running hard with it at her side.

Artie looked back at Mrs. Thresher. His eyes wide, he did the unthinkable: he pulled his sword arm back and flung Excalibur end over end toward the door—if he did it just right, Excalibur would land point down in the floor and create a final barrier between the desk and Mrs. Thresher. If he did it wrong, Excalibur would fly right through to Merlin himself, and that would be that.

But it was a perfect throw. Excalibur hit the ground just in front of the door and drove halfway to the hilt. At the last moment the desk plowed into Excalibur and stopped short.

A sound like jingling pocket change came from Mrs. Thresher as the door shook violently on its hinges, egging the desk on just a little farther. It was so close.

"Eat this!" Artie heard Lance say as he loosed a fireballer. It passed through the doorway and disappeared in the void mere feet from Artie. The explosion on the other side couldn't be seen, but it clearly worked. The door that led directly to Merlin shut immediately, as if recoiling in pain.

Kay entered the room holding another coil of the magical rope, and Artie said, "Sis, hog-tie this thing!"

"Aye, aye!" With Erik's help, Kay secured the rear legs, and that was it. The desk continued to buck and shudder as if it contained the world's largest Mexican jumping bean, but it wasn't going anywhere.

"Nasty piece of work," Shallot observed.

Dred leaned on his sword. "You can say that again. Good work, Brother."

"Couldn't have done it without you guys," Artie pointed out. "Erik, Shallot—you guys cool? That was a big hit. You want some of the scabbard?"

Erik rubbed his chest. "I'm fine."

Shallot just spit on the floor.

Kay sheathed Cleomede. "Alrighty, then."

"Well, sire," Bedevere said, "should we open this thing up?"

Artie pulled Excalibur from the floor. "Absolutely."

On one side was a fist-size padlock. Emblazoned on its front was a silver galloping horse.

Artie pointed at the lock. "Kay—that's the same horse that's on the key Cassie left for you!"

Kay leaned in. "Holy hand grenades! You're right." She slid the key out of her pocket and tried the lock. It was a perfect fit. She turned it and the lock fell open. The desk immediately stopped moving, as if it had been mercifully put to rest.

Erik gaped. "Why do you have that, Kingfisher?"

"Long story." Kay looked to her brother. "I guess I better read that letter as soon as I have a chance."

"Uh, yeah, you should."

Shallot, who apparently didn't care where the key had come from, wedged the tip of her blade in the hairline crack that ran around the top. She pushed down and in. With a gasp of air, the desk's lid swung open.

They stared into it. "By the trees . . . ," Bedevere said breathlessly.

A narrow flight of steps descended before them, as if

into the floor itself, disappearing after several feet into an inky blackness.

Artie put one foot into the cavity then paused. "I guess next stop is a mystery staircase into another dimension. Then he walked down and disappeared.

𝕿𝖍𝖊 𝖐𝖓𝖎𝖌𝖍𝖙𝖘 𝖋𝖔𝖑𝖑𝖔𝖜𝖊𝖉, 𝕯𝖗𝖊𝖉 𝖌𝖔𝖎𝖓𝖌 last. He did so cautiously—he wasn't scared, but something about this chest made him uncomfortable.

He swallowed hard and then, one foot after the next, dropped into nothingness.

The world disappeared. Up ahead, Artie could see only the faint outline of his nose. He heard the others calling out behind him, but it was like they were hundreds of feet away. They sounded lost.

Walking carefully, Artie reached to either side to keep his balance as the stairway twisted and turned. After walking for several minutes he felt askew and uneasy. And that was when he realized that his body had turned in such a way that he was walking *on* the wall. "Guys!" he yelled into the blackness. But no answer came—just more muted calls from his companions.

After a short while a weak orange light appeared ahead. There was no choice but to move toward it. Artie reached a corner, turned, and found himself in a cube-shaped room, measuring about forty feet along every edge—a room with a very strange enchantment on it.

The others entered, and when Dred finally arrived, he exclaimed, "Whoa—*we're on the wall!*"

"Yes," Bedevere said. "Gravity is playing some funny tricks here. It takes a second to get used to."

It was doubly disorienting because, while they didn't feel like they were going to fall over, their hair and anything loose that was strapped to their bodies—swords, backpacks, necklaces, shoelaces—*did* fall to the side, obeying the usual laws of physics.

As the knights moved farther in, their feet raked through a bunch of things on the floor—er, wall. The entire surface was covered with keys hanging from rough metal hooks. Each key appeared completely identical to the others— about eight inches long, a skinny neck with a loop for a handle, and a toothy, crown-shaped blade. All were made of the same dark wood. Artie looked around, and that was when he realized that all six sides of the cube-shaped room were covered with keys!

"By the fens, there must be ten thousand keys in here!" Dred said.

"But only one will work, right?" Lance asked.

"According to Mum," Dred said.

Artie stared all around. "How do we find the right one?"

While the knights discussed what to do, Erik wandered toward the ceiling, where the keys hung like sleeping bats. He parted some with his hand and frowned. He placed a knee on the ceiling. Then the other. He crawled forward and stood. Then he was standing upside down! His hair hung below him, and his outermost shirt fell around his chest, but he stayed put. "Guys, check this out!"

Everyone gasped. Kay said, "Frigging cool."

Artie counted his knights. "There's seven of us. Let's each take a wall and look for this key. If you see one that's even *slightly* different from the others, grab it."

Moving to the other surfaces was surreal, but before long all the knights were in place, their bodies pointed toward the middle of the room. Bedevere and Lance worked their wall together, while the others searched on their own. Artie had taken the floor, moving along on hands and knees, which, on account of the hooks, was neither easy nor comfortable.

Why are there hooks on the floor? he wondered.

Finally he reached the center. Here was the lone blank

spot on the whole surface. It was only six or seven inches across. There was no hook, but in the middle was a square of dark-green glass. Artie leaned over and peered into it but could see nothing on the other side.

He craned his neck. Erik was above him, walking along and tapping each key with Gram's tip. Directly overhead was the same blank spot, though it appeared to be of a different hue. "Guys—is there a small glass square in the middle of your wall?" Artie asked.

The others checked. Yes, every wall had one.

"What do you think they're for?" Lance asked as Bedevere tapped their spot with his boot.

Artie stood. "No idea." He stepped onto his, keeping his feet together. Excalibur tingled. "Try standing on yours."

Each knight moved into position. Shallot was the last to do so, and as soon as she brought her feet together, the room turned!

Before Artie knew it, what had been the floor was now a wall, then another wall and another, and then the ceiling!

He stepped from his spot and the spinning stopped.

"Whoa!" Kay said, stepping from her spot too. "That was weird."

"Look!" Shallot shouted, pointing across the chamber.

"Great," Erik said drily. The doorway that had brought them there was gone.

"We probably just have to spin it back into place," Lance said.

"What does it matter? We still don't have this stupid key," Kay said. "We're going to have to open a moongate and take all of them, Art. You know that, right?"

Artie shook his head. "It's here somewhere. We just have to find it." He tapped one of the keys surrounding the glass with Excalibur. It made a pleasant sound. Curious, he tapped the one next to it. Even though it looked exactly the same, it made a different sound. He tapped each of the others, one after the other. He realized that if he started with the correct one and moved clockwise around the space, they made the notes of a major scale.

"Guys, you hear this?" He repeated the sequence. "Do yours do that too?" Each knight tried and found that theirs, too, produced a major scale. They all looked at one another in wonder.

"Keys can be used for doors—*and* for music. You think that's something?" Lance asked.

"Could be."

"Anyone have a good enough ear to know what scale this is?" Erik wondered.

"F major," Kay said decisively. "I knew those piano lessons would come in handy one day."

"So what—now we just each play a little ditty?" Erik asked. "How's that going to help?"

"Dunno," Kay said. "Wouldn't know where to start, anyway. I quit piano after a year. I was really good at the scales, but that was it. If there's one thing I'm bad at, it's playing actual music. I remember Kynder used to sing us lullabies, but he had the most awful singing voice. Right, Art?"

"Horrible," Artie confirmed.

"I do remember this, though," Kay said, playing "Mary Had a Little Lamb."

"We have that tune in Leagon as well," Shallot said as Kay hit the keys at her feet randomly.

"Wait, do that again," Dred said.

Artie peered at his brother. "'Mary Had a Little Lamb'?"

"No. The other one."

"I was just goofing," Kay said.

"But I've heard that tune before." Dred nicked a few of the keys at his feet. "Morgaine sang lullabies when I was little, too. One a lot. It went, '*Heno, Heno, hen blant bach . . .*'" Dred searched around the notes, fiddling with the melody—just a couple of bars before it repeated—and on the last go-around changed one note. When he was finished, the little glass spot glowed bright and a light shot from it like a laser into the middle of the room.

"Nice!" Kay shouted.

"Let's all do it," Artie said. "Dred, show us."

One at a time, the knights played the tune and activated

the spots at their feet. Each patch of glass shot the same light into the middle of the room. Artie went last, and when he was finished his light joined the others.

A blinding flash came from the intersection of lights as the room spun wildly, throwing the knights to their hands and knees.

Finally it stopped. Every key stood at attention, pointing directly at the center of the chamber. And there, rotating maniacally on invisible strings, was something small and black that hadn't been there before.

Dred thrust out the Peace Sword. "Look!"

"Is that it?" Erik asked.

"Can't tell," Artie said. "It's moving too fast."

"That has to be it," Kay said. "But how are we going to reach it? It's gotta be twenty feet from any of us."

"You have any of my mum's rope left?" Dred asked.

"Oh, yeah. One more coil, I think." Kay rummaged in the infinite backpack and pulled out the last piece of silver rope. She held on to one end, and tossed the other to the middle of the room.

It flew toward the thing like a magnet and wrapped it up. Kay gave the rope a hard yank and the thing came free. The rope swung through the air, and as it passed Dred, he reached up and grabbed it.

"Well, what is it?" Artie asked.

Dred had a huge smile on his face as he held out the

object. Sure enough, it was a key. It was nearly like all the others, except that the neck was a double helix, like a strand of DNA.

Artie clapped his hands. "Yes!"

"So that's it? That'll open the door inside the King's Gate?" Kay asked desperately, thinking of the Grail, and of Kynder.

Artie beamed. "Sis, there's only one way to find out."

"𝔇ragons!" 𝔐erlin yelled. "𝔇ragons, dragons, dragons! The temerity of that aquatic sprite! 'Oh, here's Scarffern, m'lord, use it well,' I bet she said. 'The lords and lordesses of the Otherworld will bow and kneel and scrape! They will sniff at your toes and give you flowers and honey and blood!' Ack! I would drain that Lake into hell itself if I could! Nyneve! Troublesome, tiresome Nyneve!"

Merlin reached into the huge cage standing next to him and snapped his fingers. A huffing sound came from within. "Dragons!" he spit.

Merlin grabbed a bloody hunk of meat from a nearby table and held it out. "*Agorwch*," he called, and the cage's door unclicked and swung wide. He tossed in the meat. "*Caewch*," he ordered. And the steel bars slammed shut.

"Soon, beast. Tomorrow or the day after. I will give you something so fresh to eat that the brain will still be fracturing with electricity."

From inside the cage came the chompings and gnashings of a ravenous thing. The snapping, crunching, and splintering of bones. The sucking of blood between teeth and gums. The licking of lips and jowls. The gulping of a long throat. The belch of a hastily consumed meal.

"Yes, pet beast. Soon you will see battle. You will slay many dragons! But not the king. No, the king is mine. . . ."

Merlin twirled from the cage and floated into the passageways of his cave. "Scarffern! The little interferer. Its vile echo rings in my ears even now." As he moved he dragged the butt end of his owl-headed cane along the rock. *Click-clack-a-tat, click-click-tick.* He arrived at the room that hummed with computer mainframes. He held his hand over a scanner and winced as the light traveled up and down his palm, reading the ancient lines of his skin, still there in spite of all the sangrealitic tattoos. The door hissed open, and Merlin went inside.

The room was warm. He glided to a desktop computer with a flat-screen monitor and pounded on a keyboard. Terminal windows opened and closed and opened and closed as streams of code flew from his fingertips. He was an evil master of magic and of programming. The total package. A five-tool player. A wizard and a nerd extraordinaire.

He peered into the computer screen. Peering back was the reflection of his eyes, so red now that there was no difference between the iris and what had been the white. The pupil was no longer black but purple and clouded. His eyes were less like a demon's than those of a deepwater fish.

"More surprises, pet," he said, even though the creature was still in its cage in a far-off room. Merlin scratched his left temple manically. His eyes twitched. "So many more surprises. That unwitting boy has no idea that I looked through his eyes and saw that Artie has the key that will lead him to the Grail. Gram's ragged keeper, we will make a traitor of you yet."

Merlin lifted his hands from the keyboard dramatically. The screen went completely black before filling with images. Images of children, slumped in couches and overstuffed chairs and beanbags. Boys mostly, but girls too. Their hands limp in their laps, holding game controllers. These were the children of the world who, like Artie Kingfisher before them, loved *Otherworld* the video game. The nerds, the would-be elves and orcs and battle mages, the Dr Pepper heads, as Kay liked to call them.

Soon they would get a surprise.

Merlin tented his fingers and smiled. He turned his attention to a steel pedestal with a bowl mounted on top. It looked like a modern interpretation of a holy water stoup that one would see in the narthex of a church.

The stoup contained liquid sangrealite. Trailing from the backside of the pedestal was a tangle of bright wires, some of which led to the computer, but the bulk of which led to an archway made of stone. This archway was nestled about a dozen feet from the computer and the stoup between a row of twinkling mainframes. Twisting around the stone portal were coils of solid sangrealite. Everything was connected—the computer to the stoup, the stoup to the archway. It was an arrangement that Merlin had been experimenting with and was now ready to use in earnest.

Merlin pounded some more commands into the keyboard, and the images of kids continued to spill across the screen. But then they stopped, and a boy with dark hair and green eyes sitting in a folding chair appeared. He was about twelve and had on beige cargo shorts and a plain white T-shirt.

"Hello, child," Merlin cooed.

The wizard slid to the pedestal and held his hand over the bowl. He wiggled his fingers just above the liquid's surface.

"You will work this time. I can feel it."

Then, Merlin went completely still and each of his eyes rolled into his head sideways, parting away from the angular bridge of his nose toward the temples.

He dipped his fingertips into the rippling sangrealite. The wires jumped as power shot through them. The sangrealite twisting around the archway glowed bright, and the space between the rocks went completely black.

The face of the child on the computer screen widened

with an expression part terror, part elation.

Merlin's smile grew even more sinister. The very air filled with power—magical, magnetic, electrical.

And then the child on the screen disappeared.

IN WHICH A DANGEROUS CHAIR NEARLY KILLS SOMEONE

𝕿𝖍𝖊 𝖒𝖔𝖔𝖓𝖌𝖆𝖙𝖊 𝕬𝖗𝖙𝖎𝖊 𝖍𝖆𝖉 𝖔𝖕𝖊𝖓𝖊𝖉 from the key room led them to a very unexpected place: about ten feet above the round table. Artie had been the first to go through, and he was pretty surprised when he appeared in midair, fell on the table hard, and then rolled to the ground. Seconds later, Kay fell right on top of him.

"Ouch! What's up with that moongate?" Kay demanded.

"Dunno. Maybe it's because the gravity in that room was so messed up."

Shallot came next, and while she was also surprised, her fairy instincts kicked in, helping her to land gracefully.

"Sire, what is happening?" Bercilak called, clattering across the hall. "Why are your knights raining from the very ether?"

"Bunk moongate," Artie said. "Can you catch the others?"

"Certainly, sire." As soon as he had spoken, Lance materialized overhead. Bercilak reached out, caught the archer, and put him on the floor.

"That was weird," Lance said. "Thanks, Bercilak."

"No problem."

Lance looked at the moongate. "Heads up."

"But I don't have a head," Bercilak protested as Erik and then Bedevere fell one after the other on top of the Green Knight. Bercilak helped them to their feet and said, "Aha, *heads up* as in *look out*! Now I get it. Clever, Sir Lance, quite clever."

"Thanks. Heads up again."

Bercilak spun, but it was too late. Dred was right there. He landed hard on Bercilak's back and bounced with an "Ooof!" several feet toward the edge of the room.

Dred had fallen directly onto the inconspicuous black chair pushed to the wall of the Royal Chamber and was now slumped over, looking unconscious.

Bercilak turned again and brought his hands to his chest in a gesture of shock. "Oh no! Sire, that's—"

"Nobody touch him!" yelled Numinae, who had just entered the room with Thumb.

Artie frowned. "Why not? Wait—*that's* the chair you were going to tell me about, isn't it?"

"It's the Siege Perilous!" Thumb said quietly.

"What in the heck is the 'siege perilous'?" Kay asked.

Numinae and Thumb advanced cautiously toward the motionless Dred. "It was a seat reserved for the Pure Knight, lad," Thumb said. "Merlin made it. It was kept in Arthur's court as a reminder of what could befall any person who was not pure of heart."

"Well, what *could* befall any person who was not pure of heart?" Erik asked.

Bercilak said cheerily, as if he were announcing the rising sun, "Oh, he or she would perish—instantly!"

Artie walked briskly toward his brother, his heart pounding. "*What?* Dred is . . . dead?"

Numinae stopped him with an outstretched hand. "M'lord—"

Artie pushed past Numinae, who had to restrain him with both hands. "Please, sire!"

"*Dead?*" Artie cried, Numinae's crooked, treelike hands still holding Artie back. "What a dumb way to die! In a chair!" He paused, wiping a tear from his cheek. "It shouldn't be here. I want it removed immediately!"

"But no one can touch it, sire," Bedevere pointed out.

"I *can* touch it," a voice said.

They spun. Numinae gasped.

Dred sat awkwardly across the chair, a leg thrown over

an armrest. He wasn't dead at all. He had a big bump on his head and a tiny trickle of blood ran down the side of his cheek, but that was it.

"Dred!" Shallot shouted, sounding strangely relieved.

Thumb couldn't believe it. "How . . . ?"

Artie rushed to his brother, but Dred held up a hand and said, "Don't touch me! This chair is in effect. It didn't kill me, but so long as I'm on it, any contact with me would kill you."

Thumb nodded. "He's right. There is only one Pure Knight. That's the way it has always been; that's the way it will be forever. And even if it weren't true—would you be willing to take a gamble to find out?"

"Uh, no," Artie said. He stared at Dred with wonder. "Man, you're pretty lucky."

Dred stepped free from the Siege Perilous. "I'll say. That thing feels like . . . death itself." He shivered.

Just then Thumb jumped and did an excited little spin in the air. "Artie, do you know what this means?"

Numinae clapped his hands. "The Sword of David!"

"The Pure Blade," Bedevere cried. "He who can take the chair can draw the sword and live to tell of it."

"By the leas," Shallot chimed.

"Guys," Artie said. "Back it up. You know Otherworld history inside and out, but the rest of us don't, and Excalibur hasn't given me any information on this thing. So what's the Sword of David?"

Thumb's eyes widened. "The Sword of David is not a regular sword. It is not even meant for battle. It is subtler. It is safe to hold—so long as it stays sheathed."

"What happens if you unsheathe it?" Kay asked.

"Well," Numinae said. "Whoever draws the Sword of David is greatly weakened. This person cannot fight, or work magic, or flee. They are stuck—waiting for death."

"Hold on," Erik interjected. "David, like David and Goliath? The one David used to kill the giant?"

"That's it," Thumb confirmed. "And like David, only the Pure Knight can draw the sword safely."

"Which means *I* can draw it," Dred said, finally understanding.

Thumb snapped his fingers. "We have to get the Sword of David. Dred—you must seek it out!"

Erik sighed. "Great. Another harebrained quest for some ancient blade."

"Well, we *are* the New Knights of the Round Table, Erikssen," Kay pointed out. "But I still don't get how some weapon that only Dred can use is going to help us. He already has a sword."

"It *is* powerful," Thumb said. "For that reason alone, we should have it."

"Also, Merlin won't expect it," Numinae added. "Just as he did not expect you to blow Scarffern. It is obvious how the dragons can help us defeat him. If we're smart, we may be able to find a less obvious way for the Sword of David to help us, too."

Artie shrugged. "All right. . . . Hey, speaking of the dragons—are they here yet?"

Thumb shook his head. "Not as of yet, lad."

"But by sunup they will be," Numinae said. "I can sense Tiberius's location. It was a great thing you did, Artie, bringing him back. I am forever in your debt for that."

"Ah, no sweat, Noomy. We all love Tiberius." Artie looked to Kay. "We may have one other surprise, now that I think of it. Kay . . . you've *got* to read Cassie's letter. Like, now. It can't be coincidence that Cassie's key opened that padlock."

Kay explained to everyone what Artie was talking about. "Read it to us, read it to us!" several of the knights insisted, but Kay remained hesitant.

"I'm sorry, guys. . . . I need to do it alone. I promise to read it tonight. If there's anything important in it, I'll tell you."

"Good," Artie said reassuringly. "Now, I don't know about you guys, but I am totally pooped. I'm going up to my room. Tomorrow morning we'll talk more about this

Sword of David and get going into that King's Gate for the Grail. Merlin isn't gonna be sitting on his hands so we can't sit on ours. We *have* to find a way to head him off." Artie looked each of his knights in the eye.

Kay clicked her tongue. "Dang, Art. You sound like a king."

Artie winked. "That's because I am."

𝕿𝖍𝖆𝖙 𝖓𝖎𝖌𝖍𝖙 𝕶𝖆𝖞 𝖈𝖑𝖎𝖒𝖇𝖊𝖉 𝖎𝖓𝖙𝖔 a huge four-poster bed, a fire crackling in the hearth, and set the small box from her mother on top of the covers. For a while she did nothing but stare at it. Her mind crawled with questions.

Finally she reached down and opened the lid. She pried out the piece of paper and unfolded it. When she got to the last fold, she paused, closed her eyes, and took a deep breath. Then she opened it and held it in both hands.

And there was nothing there!

She turned it over hurriedly, and over again, but there was no denying it. The paper was blank.

Her nerves morphed into sudden anger. "Mom! What? Why did you leave me a *blank* note?" Kay was never one to complain about fairness, but this was different. This piece of paper wasn't just disappointing, it was insulting. It *wasn't* fair. She crumpled it and threw it away, but it hit one of the bedposts and bounced back onto the covers. "Ugh!" she blurted, kicking the ball with her feet. "Go *away!*" But just as it eclipsed the edge of the mattress, something caught Kay's eye.

She flopped over and grabbed the wad of paper. She pulled it open. There was a mark! "What the—?" And then, before her very eyes, blue-green strokes filled the middle of the sheet. When they were done, they had formed a single word.

Kay?

"Mom?"

The word disappeared, and new marks, in random order, took shape over the page. Within seconds it said, *Yes. It's me. Pamela gave you your gift?*

"Uh, yeah. . . . Where are you?"

Somewhere safe. Somewhere pleasant.

Kay almost said snarkily, "Isn't that nice for you," but she resisted and just said, "Good. But how are you doing this?"

It's magic, like so many things in the Otherworld.

"But where did you get magic paper when you left us? That was a long time ago, before all this stuff happened."

The words disappeared, and there was a pause before the answer came. *We have always had magic in us, sweetie.*

Remember how Artie came to us. . . .

Just then a horrible thought crossed Kay's mind. "Mom, I'm sorry to ask this, but can you prove that you're who you say you are?"

The words came almost instantaneously: *Kynder's middle name is Bell. Yours is Orleans. Your left eye is blue, the right green, as are mine. When you were born, you did not cry. Your favorite stuffed animal growing up was a white rat you called "Ratty."*

Kay raised her eyebrows and her heart quickened. It was all true. "What else?"

At the Great Sylvan Library, when I was swallowed by the forest, you and I locked eyes. We didn't say anything, but we understood each other's thoughts perfectly. I thought, I'm so sorry, and you thought, I forgive you, Mama.

"All right. But how do I know Merlin isn't controlling you?"

You'll have to take my word, dear. Like I said, I am safe and happy, and I will never see a witch or wizard again. Besides, if I were his prisoner, I would be dead. He wants Morgaine dead, after all—and I am a direct descendant of the Lordess of Fenland.

These last words lingered on the page before disappearing. Kay was flabbergasted. "Wait—what? You? That means . . . *I'm* related to Morgaine?"

Yes. As I said, we have always had magic in us.

"Whoa."

There is more, dear. There was a pause. And then, *Morgaine was the first Arthur's half sister.*

"So what? That was a long time—" But then she got it. "Holy dragon turds! That means that Artie is—"

Morgaine's biological half brother.

"But how?"

Igraine—Artie and Dred's genetic mother—was also Morgaine's mother so many years ago. Her father was a man named Gorlois, who, incidentally, was killed by Arthur's father, Uther.

Kay whistled. "Things were pretty mixed up back then, huh?"

Yes.

Kay paused as this new information washed over her. "So Artie and I . . . Kynder and me . . . the three of us were meant to be together, weren't we?"

Naturally.

"That's why Artie and I had our special connection!" Kay said, more to herself than her mom. "Because we really are related!"

Yes.

"It makes sense now. More sense, anyway."

I'm glad, dear.

Kay paused as she worked up the nerve to ask the most important question there was. "Mom . . . why did you leave?

If you're a long-lost child of the Otherworld, why couldn't you handle Artie?"

The page went blank and stayed that way for half a minute. Kay fretted that the connection had somehow been cut, but then the marks started to fill the page. *The apple fell far from the tree, dear. I'm not like you. I'm nervous and insecure. I rarely felt comfortable around other people, and when Artie appeared, I was pushed over the edge. Somehow, I crossed over and ended up in Fenland. . . .*

"How did you have that key? The one with the horse on it?"

It was a family heirloom, passed down from Morgaine to our forebears many centuries ago. It was a tradition, passing the key, so I was passing it to you. Tell me—did it open the door to the Grail?

"What? No. It opened a lock on some crazy chest."

Oh. We were always told it was the Grail key. "The key for the door. The door for the King. The King for the Grail.'" *That was the line.*

"I guess that's kinda true. We used it to get the Grail key, which is bigger and shaped like a crown."

Doors always lead to more doors. I am glad you are closer to the cup, since you seem to want it.

"We do, Mom. Merlin almost killed Kynder—who's frozen in rock for safekeeping—and we're going to use it to bring him back!"

Kay shook with anticipation. Just the thought of Kynder made her want to jump from bed and run into Artie's bedroom so they could get the Grail right away, but it didn't seem appropriate, not with this maternal message maker in her hands. Not since she was having a real conversation with her mom for the first time in forever.

"Mom . . ."

Instantaneously the page read, *Kay, I'm so sorry I left you. It has been the greatest regret of my life.*

Tears filled Kay's eyes.

Don't cry. Get the Grail. Save your father. Tell him I'm sorry too. I never meant to hurt him.

"What about . . . What about Artie?"

I never really knew him. But after you, I owe him the biggest apology. Please give him my heartfelt regards.

These words lingered on the page, and Kay read them over and over. Finally she asked, "Mom, will I see you again?"

The page went blank and remained that way for a while. *No.*

Kay's chest heaved silently. She drew a breath to speak but then thought better of it. She waited. A minute passed.

Are you still there?

"Yes."

I love you, sweetheart. I am so proud of you. Continue to make the world as you live it. I love you.

"I love you, too." She paused. "Mom, will I be able to use this piece of paper again to—"

But as she spoke, the sheet began to shake as if blown by a breeze. Then the edges caught fire. Kay jumped out of bed and moved toward the fireplace. As the page burned more, the words *I love you* grew bigger and bigger. Kay worked her fingers around the paper so they wouldn't burn. When she couldn't hold it any longer, she dropped it onto the logs.

After it was gone, she said, "Well, that had to be the strangest reunion ever."

Then she ran as fast as she could to her brother.

While Kay was opening the box, Artie lay his head on the pillow of his Tintagel bedroom and fell immediately to sleep. Within minutes his eyes darted back and forth as an intense dream overtook him.

He was inside the King's Gate, standing in front of the door with the crown-shaped keyhole. He inserted the key and opened the door. First nothing was there, but then a great flock of birds bolted out. They flew around him, beating their wings against his body. He held his ground. When the air was clear Artie stepped through the doorway, and a face took shape in the near distance.

The face was Erik's, his eyes completely white. Then the head turned all the way around, like an owl's, but instead of the back of his head there was just a repeat of Erik's white-eyed face, as if he had two. The image filled Artie with base fear.

The head made another half revolution. Erik's face was gone this time, replaced by one that was older, the nose long and pointed. It had white muttonchops, and the skin was dark with inked tattoos. The eyes were closed.

Merlin.

The eyes opened. One was completely red. But the other was as Merlin's eyes had once been—bright, alive, even cheerful. Merlin wore an oily cloak draped over his shoulders, and his leather hood dived down in a sharp V over his forehead.

Artie recoiled. Merlin laughed and brought his hands down quickly. In them was a sword. It looked exactly like Excalibur.

The blade sliced into Artie's neck, and everything went completely white.

The brilliance of this dream-death was as terrifying as anything Artie had experienced on either side in his young, ancient life. He tossed and turned but couldn't wake up. Eventually, the light dimmed and Merlin was gone.

Artie sat bolt upright in a cold sweat, his stare fixed on the far wall. It took him a few seconds to realize that Kay was in the room, saying, "Artie, hello? Are you there? You were having a dream!"

Artie spun to his sister. "Kay—I think I figured out a way to—"

"I just talked to Mom!"

"A way to— *What?*"

Kay explained what had happened with the note, and all that Cassie had said. When Artie learned that he was related to Morgaine, he cringed. "Gosh. I hope Dred doesn't figure that out. It would be pretty strange to learn the woman you thought was your mom actually was your half sister."

"Whoa. I didn't think of that."

Artie was much, much more delighted, however, to discover that he and Kay also shared some blood. In a sense Artie realized that he wasn't an orphan at all. He belonged with Kay and Kynder. If they could get their dad back, that lone fact would make all of these adventures worth the trouble.

But they still had a long way to go. "Kay," Artie said, thinking again of his haunting dream. "I think I have a plan to defeat Merlin."

"Really? What is it?"

"I'll tell you tomorrow. I want to think it through a little. I'll run it by Numinae in the morning. Will you join us for breakfast?"

"Heck yeah. I'll be there with bells on." She turned to leave and then paused. "Artie, Cassie said she was sorry for leaving us—and for leaving you."

Artie lay back down and pulled the covers to his chin. He was glad to hear it, not so much for his sake but definitely for Kay's. She didn't deserve losing her mom. No kid ever does. "I'm happy to hear it, Kay. And just so you know, I forgave her a long time ago."

She pushed the door open. "Me too, I guess. G'night, Art."

"G'night, Kay."

And then she left. Artie was so exhausted that even with this exciting news he fell back asleep quickly. Blessedly, he had no more dreams.

"𝔐𝔬𝔯𝔫𝔦𝔫𝔤, 𝔑𝔲𝔪𝔦𝔫𝔞𝔢." 𝔄𝔯𝔱𝔦𝔢 𝔞𝔫𝔡 𝔎𝔞𝔶 walked into the Royal Chamber, dressed and ready to go. Bran had laid out a breakfast of fresh fruit, hot coffee, cold Mountain Dew, and hard-boiled eggs at three places around the table.

"Sire. Miss."

Kay plopped into her chair, while Artie sat next to Numinae. Artie looked to the far end of the room at the shimmering portal that was the King's Gate. Soon enough, he'd be going through it again, this time with friends.

Kay pointed at the open book in front of Numinae. "Whatcha reading?"

"An obscure Leagonese text on what might guard the Grail. Most of it is in fairy verse, which is needlessly verbose.

It's funny—in person fairies are very direct; witness Shallot le Fey. But in writing, they dance around things in half measures and allusions."

"You don't have to worry about half measures anymore. Artie's cooked up some kind of a plan!"

Numinae turned to Artie curiously. "Beyond getting the Grail, you mean?"

"Yeah, but we're still doing that." Artie poured a cup of coffee and began to peel the shell off a brown egg. "In fact, I was hoping you'd come with Kay and me."

Numinae breathed in, making a sound like a breeze blowing through a pine forest. "I'd be honored, m'lord."

"I'm glad. I was going to ask Thumb, Bedevere, and Bercilak to join us too."

Numinae nodded his approval. "A good party for the mysteries surrounding the Grail. Bercilak is hungry for action."

Kay chuckled. "It'll be good to see wheat he can do, besides eat and drink like there's no tomorrow. Pretty funny how an 'empty knight'"—she made little air quotes with her fingers—"can be so darn hungry."

They laughed. "And what about the others, sire?" Numinae asked.

"That's where my plan comes in. It involves Dred and this Sword of David."

"Ah. I was thinking about that last night too, sire."

"Oh? How so?"

"Well . . . if we could somehow trick Merlin into drawing the Sword of David, it would weaken him without his knowing it. Not until he tries to make some magic, anyway."

"And once he's weakened, he might be vulnerable," Artie said, seeming to finish Numinae's thought. "That's what I was thinking, too."

"It would be risky, but if for some reason we could not best him in battle, it might be our only hope."

"Like a fail-safe," Kay said, snapping her fingers.

"That's right, sis. But tell me, Numinae—in what corner of the Otherworld does this sword live?"

"Ah, that's the thing, sire. None of them."

Artie took a sip of coffee. "What do you mean?"

"The sword of David is on *your* side. In some place called Turkey."

"Like the country?" Kay asked.

"Yes."

Artie shrugged. "At least it won't be guarded by a giant or witch there."

"Quite, m'lord."

"Do you know where in Turkey?" Kay asked.

"According to Master Thumb, someplace called Topkapi Palace, in the village of Istanbul."

Kay couldn't help but laugh. She'd done a unit on foreign cities in seventh grade that included Istanbul. "Oh, that's not a village, Numinae. Well over *ten million* people live there."

"By the trees! There is no place in the Otherworld like that."

"No, there isn't," Artie said. "Dred will have to go there, obviously. I was going to ask Lance, Shallot, and Qwon to join him."

Numinae nodded his approval. "And while they are there, we will seek the Grail."

Exactly. And here's how I think we can trick Merlin." Artie smirked at his two conspirators, and they huddled close over the table. "Listen carefully, and don't tell any—I mean *any*—of the others about this."

Kay's eyes went wide. "What is it, Art?"

"We have a traitor," Artie said.

"A what, sire?"

"How do you know?" Kay breathed, sounding shocked.

"I saw it in a dream."

"Seriously, Art?"

"Seriously. Trust me."

"Who is it?" Kay asked.

"I can't tell you. If I did, you might treat the traitor differently."

"Understood. Very prudent, sire."

Kay tilted her head at Numinae. "I'm assuming it's not him, right?"

"No. It's not."

"And it's not her either?" Numinae countered with a little smile.

"No, not Kay."

"All right, so it's *someone*," Kay said. "I'll try not to let the suspense kill me. But what's this plan?"

"The traitor is going to help us." Artie's voice dropped to a bare whisper. The fire crackled in the hearth. There was no other sound. "Here's how."

After formulating their plan and going over it again and again, Artie, Kay, and Numinae called for the others to meet them in Tintagel's courtyard.

It was a bright, cloudless day. The Otherworld sky was bluer than it was purple, and high above the castle walls two dragons turned in the air, occasionally diving playfully at each others' tails or wings. Tiberius—majestic and motionless—roosted on top of the gable end of the main building, completely asleep.

The knights congregated around Kynder's stone in the middle of the yard. Next to it was Morgaine's stone. Thumb paced in a tight circle. Lance checked his quiver of arrows. Bedevere ran a cloth over the edge of his claymore. Shallot squatted, drawing pictures in the dirt with the tip of The Anguish. Erik was next to her, whispering something that made the fairy smile. Bercilak stood off to the side, whooshing his great battle-ax through the air. And Dred stood thoughtfully against the rock that held Morgaine, a hand resting on it.

With his sword and mussed hair and long legs, Dred looked pretty impressive. As Artie crossed the yard, he realized that he, too, must have appeared impressive from time to time, and this made him feel that much more kingly.

"Call Tiberius, please, Numinae," Artie said as they walked out of the dragon's shadow.

Without responding, Numinae pointed his face toward the sky and cooed. The green dragon's rainbow eyes shot open, and his wings unfurled. He leaped off the roof and snaked to the ground, landing silently.

When they were all together Artie clapped his hands. "First things first—Lance, would you cross over and get Qwon and Pammy?"

"Now?"

"If you don't mind."

Lance stashed his bow next to Kynder. "Not at all. Any special instructions?"

Artie nodded. "Have them load their laptop with

whatever they can find on a place in Istanbul called Topkapi Palace. Come back quick. We'll wait for you."

Lance gave Artie a funny look at the mention of Istanbul but took off at a jog and passed through the open crossover to the Kingfishers' backyard.

Artie turned to Tiberius. "How many dragons so far?"

"Hmmmph. Three. The others'll be here by nightfall. We'll number seven."

Kay's face brightened. "That's good! That's great!"

"It *is* good," Artie said. "When they arrive, have them gather on the castle walls, Tiberius. Tell them to be ready for battle at the drop of a hat."

"Hmmph. Dragons're always ready."

"Excellent." Artie spun to Erik. "I have a solo mission for you, Erik. It's important, but I don't think it will be very dangerous."

"What is it?"

"Go to Sweden, find Sami, and bring him back. If he's out hunting, wait for him. We're going to need his strength when we confront Merlin, which will be sooner rather than later."

Erik shoved Gram into its sheath. "On it, Art."

"Good." Artie used Excalibur to open a moongate to Sweden. "We won't close this until you're back. See you soon."

Erik smiled at everyone, slapped a few hands, and disappeared.

A few minutes later Lance reappeared with Qwon and Pammy. Qwon gave Artie and Kay each a kiss on the cheek. Then she strutted over to Shallot and Dred and gave each of them a big hug.

Artie went about introducing Pammy to everyone she hadn't met. It was hard for her to accept Numinae and the dragons, and she squeezed Artie's hand *really* hard when Tiberius first spoke, but all in all she took it pretty well.

When they were finished, Artie knelt in the middle of the group. "Here's the plan: Dred, Qwon, Lance, and Shallot—you're going to Turkey, to a place called Topkapi Palace in Istanbul. Once you're there you'll have to find and retrieve the—"

"Sword of David," Dred interrupted.

Artie nodded. "Bingo."

Shallot whined.

"I know you don't like our side," Artie said, "but I need you there, Shallot. Think of it as, like, an honor. You're the only fairy to go to our side in thousands of years! Not counting Tom, of course."

"Thanks, lad."

"Don't mention it."

Lance added, "Your scentlock may be all we need to deal with any guards, Shallot. And you're a heck of a fighter. I'd love to have you there."

Shallot grunted. "All right. I'll go. But your side is strange to me. Too strange."

"Man," Kay said, "talk about the pot calling the kettle black. You have pink hair, Shallot. It grows that way!"

The group shared a much-needed giggle.

"All right," Artie continued. "Obviously, be careful with the sword once you find it. Remember, only Dred is allowed to touch it, okay?"

They agreed.

"Now, while you're doing that, me, Kay, Bedevere, Bercilak, Tom, and Numinae will go for the Grail." Artie paused.

"And after we're all back here, we visit Merlin."

Qwon snapped her fingers. "Good. He's up to no good, Artie."

"Why? has something happened?"

Qwon stepped to the middle of the circle as Pammy said, "The day you left, there was a news report that a girl in Peoria nearly disappeared while playing her Xbox."

"What do you mean, 'nearly'?" Artie asked.

"Well, she did disappear, but then she came back. She didn't know where she went, but she went *some*where."

"Get out!" Kay said. "That sounds like when we flickered back and forth at Mont-Saint-Michel."

Qwon jumped in. "Minutes after that delightful news item, we learned of a boy in Paris, France, who was playing a game on his computer when his screen flashed and then his keyboard melted, almost burning off his finger."

Artie gulped. "What game were these kids playing?"

"*Otherworld.*"

Artie's head fell forward. Pammy put a hand on his shoulder. "It gets worse."

"How?"

"Last night," Qwon said, "a boy in Fresno, California, *did* disappear from his bedroom. For good."

"Where did he go?" Dred asked.

"No one knows," Qwon answered.

"Merlin knows," Thumb said darkly. "As sure as he used that game to contact you, Artie, he is using it to get to these children."

There was a pause and then Qwon said, "Guys, since then *hundreds* of kids have gone missing while playing *Otherworld*. Hundreds."

Artie was disgusted. Why would Merlin do this?

"Do you two have *any* good news?" Kay asked.

Pammy tilted her head to the side. "Actually, we do."

Qwon opened the laptop. She clicked through some screens, and eventually a map of western Britain popped up. "Here's a picture from a weather satellite taken a couple months ago." It looked perfectly normal—it had been a clear day and they could see the patchwork farmland of the countryside. "Here's one from yesterday." It had also been a clear day, but the land below was blotted and blurred.

"I don't understand. Merlin's taking out the countryside?" Artie asked.

Qwon shook her head.

"He's not taking it out—it's still there. He's erasing it," Pammy explained. "Not literally, but from the minds of people."

"Are you saying that as far as anyone is concerned, western Britain never existed?"

"That's exactly what we're saying, Artie," Qwon answered. "There are *no* news reports from this part of the UK dating back three weeks. Not one. We cold-called over five hundred numbers in the UK. In London, officials had never even heard of Wales. When we started calling places *in* Wales, people were clueless. None could say where they lived or worked, and a lot could barely remember their last names. The closer we got to here"— Qwon zoomed in on a jagged strip of coast called St. David's Head—"the more incoherent people became. They could barely speak. When we asked if there was anyone nearby that we *could* talk to, the only words any of them mumbled were—"

"Myrddin Emrys," Artie interrupted. It was one of the names Excalibur had shared with him somewhere along the line. "Aka Merlin."

Pammy pointed at Artie. "Yes!"

"That's it, lads!" Thumb confirmed in a low voice. "I can't believe I'd forgotten. . . . In the old days, Merlin would sometimes retreat to Wales. On the northern side of that headland there are several deep, fingerlike cuts into the cliffside. The sea gathers there. At the end of the third one, counting from the west, there is a small opening at low tide. In there was a cave. *His* cave."

"The Bunker," Artie said.

"Aye, lad."

Artie rubbed his thighs and stood quickly. "All right. That's where we're going to throw down. We'll try to surprise him. But God, I hope he isn't hurting those children. . . ."

"Hmmmph," Tiberius said, as if he knew the answer— but no one had the heart to ask if he did.

"Tiberius—when the time comes, will you and the dragons cross over to Wales for me?"

"Yes, lord kingling."

Artie breathed a sigh of relief. "We'll have that going for us at least."

"And the Seven Swords!" Qwon pointed out.

"I will arrange for several packs of dire wolves from Sylvan," Numinae said.

"I spoke with the black dragon, Snoll, and she can muster a flock of Fenlandian dragonflies," Dred added.

Bedevere beamed. "And there's my sabertooth!"

Kay whooped as Artie said, "That's a pretty decent army, guys. Thanks. We've got a shot at beating Merlin fair and square. But we can't underestimate him. And for that, we'll have the Sword of David."

As the group cheered, another dragon showed up and lit on the wall—a silver one they had never seen before. Tiberius eyed him. "'Tis Darg, from Surmik."

The sun shone bright as it reflected off the newest dragon's scales. Artie held up Excalibur and saluted him. "Ho, Darg!" he shouted. The silver dragon lowered its head and roared, the ground shaking beneath Tintagel.

Artie grinned hard. He was the Dragon King. "Friends, arms in."

A song of steel rang out as everyone produced their weapon of choice. Cleomede and The Anguish; Kusanagi and the Peace Sword; the Welsh *wakizashi* and Bercilak's battle-ax; Lance's bow (Orgulus stayed in its sheath); Bedevere's claymore and Numinae's gnarled, moss-covered hand. Tiberius came closer and raised his head over the group.

"'New Knights of the Round Table' on three! One! Two! Three!"

"NEW KNIGHTS OF THE ROUND TABLE!"

They hoisted their weapons, and a wind, cool and fierce, rose from the circle. It was dotted with golden sparkles like little stars. These went higher and higher and dissipated over Avalon.

Artie looked each of his knights in the eye. "A storm is coming, my friends. A big one. Be prepared for anything."

𝔚hile the knights waited for it to be the middle of the night in Turkey, they made final preparations, copying maps and notes from Pammy's computer about Topkapi Palace. The Sword of David mission looked like it might be relatively easy, because the item in question was a museum piece—just a relic from another age.

When it was time, Artie opened a gate for Team Sword. Dred, Qwon, Shallot, and Lance wished everyone else good luck, and stepped through, Dred in the lead.

They emerged from the moongate shoulder to shoulder in the recess of a large hollowed-out tree. The tree stood in a courtyard that was in much better shape than Tintagel's. The night air was warm, and a few stars struggled in the sky against the relentless glow of Istanbul.

Dred poked his head out and peered around.

"Anyone there?" Qwon whispered.

"Not a soul." He stepped onto the packed dirt and walked halfway around the tree. A crisscross of white stone paths led to various buildings. It was unlike any palace Dred had ever seen. The buildings were low and long, with countless arches. Many had domed roofs, and a few minarets pointed at the sky like spears. There were tons of pillars, and ornate screens carved from stone or wood covered many of the windows.

"All clear," Dred said.

After the others emerged from the tree, Qwon blurted, "Shallot—your hair! It's glowing!"

"What?" Shallot pulled her long ponytail around her neck and stared at it. Sure enough, her pink hair glowed brightly. "Ack. Another consequence of your world. I'm telling you, fairies don't belong here."

She twirled and went invisible, as if in protest.

"You're still glowing!" Dred whispered.

It was true. Shallot was all the way invisible except for her hair.

"It looks like a jellyfish or something," Qwon said, and Shallot hissed her disapproval.

"What about your scentlock?" Lance asked. "Does it work?"

Shallot tried. Rose and orange and anise and lavender

and lemon filled the air, and her three companions went helplessly stiff. She released her invisibility and, perhaps foolishly, tossed her ponytail in pride. She'd retained her fairy essence—all was not lost.

But as her hair traced through the darkness, a voice called out in a language she'd never heard before. She wheeled and released her scentlock. Her friends came back immediately. The voice yelled again.

Weapons drawn and flickering in the night, all four hustled to a nearby bush. The voice continued to bleat in their direction, accusatory and urgent. It was far off. But another voice, closer and on their side of the courtyard, answered.

"Anyone speak Turkish?" Lance asked.

"Nope," Qwon answered.

"I can speak to the bird named turkey, but I don't recognize any of those sounds," Shallot said.

"Why *is* this land called Turkey, anyway?" Dred wondered.

"Got me. I always thought it was a funny name for a country, too." Lance pulled a piece of paper from a pocket on his thigh, hastily unfolded it, and traced his finger over the map. "We need to go here." He pointed at a mishmash of jammed-together buildings on the western side of the palace. "According to all the web pages, it's in a room called the Privy Chamber. Qwon, you got our position?"

Qwon fiddled with her mom's smartphone, pulling up Google Maps to get a location. Within seconds a large circle pulsated over greater Istanbul and then got smaller. She held it out. "Sure do, Lance."

Lance peeked over the bush. "There should be a fountain in that direction. Just past it is the main section of the palace."

Lance trotted past a palm tree into a row of crape myrtles. The fountain—with a stone-and-concrete facade inlaid with gold and lapis—was on his left. Across the path was another bush, which had been cut into the shape of a cone. Qwon bumped into him as he scanned the low rooflines surrounding the courtyard for guards.

Lance pointed past the fountain. Wedged between two older colonnaded buildings was a white building with a wooden double door under a plain triangular pediment. "There," Lance said.

Just then two beams of light streaked the courtyard. More nonsense in Turkish as the guards called back and forth.

"Think they have guns?" Qwon asked nervously.

"Most likely," Lance answered.

Dred turned to Shallot. "Distract them, fairy. Go invisible and streak that pink hair of yours all around."

"But they'll see me, Fenlandian."

"That's the idea! While they're watching you, we'll head into that building."

Qwon snapped her fingers. "He's right. They won't shoot. They'll think you're a ghost—or something from another world."

"Which technically you are," Lance pointed out.

Shallot clicked her tongue. "Oh, fine."

Lance nocked an arrow. "Don't worry. If they *do* decide to shoot, I'll wing 'em."

"Stay clear. I'm throwing scent too." Shallot stepped onto the white paving stones and spun like a top. Then she took off, bolting between the trees. She *did* look like a ghost. The flashlight beams honed in and tried to follow her without much success. She flashed to the far side and slalomed between some pillars. The guards continued to shout in suddenly awestruck voices.

"C'mon!" Lance trampled over a bed of flowers onto the path, Dred and Qwon hustling behind him. They made the double doors in seconds, but they were locked.

"I got this." Qwon slid Kusanagi's thin and beyond-razor-sharp blade between the doors and jerked it up. The bolt and latch were cut effortlessly. She brought her sword out and pulled open the right-hand door. "After you, gentlemen."

Lance slipped into the darkness, Dred following.

Qwon turned to the courtyard and whistled like a bird. The fairy stopped dead. She was twenty feet away to Qwon's left. "Wait," Qwon said quietly. She knew from her captivity with Shallot at Castel Deorc Wæters that Shallot le Fey had incredible hearing.

Qwon held out Kusanagi with both hands, pointing its gray tip at the treetops. "*Kaze!*" she hissed.

Immediately, the trees bent over like they were actors taking bows. A whirl of sound shot from Qwon's blade as well, and debris was thrown into the air. Qwon had better control over Kusanagi's power this time, and as she moved the blade over the yard, the breeze moved with it.

The flashlights swung from Shallot's rose-colored hair to the treetops. The men called out again, now more desperate, wondering what was going on.

Within seconds Shallot slipped into the doorway and disappeared, taking her scent with her. "*Shizume'ru*," Qwon said. The breeze died. The trees sprang back up. Qwon stepped through the door and pulled it shut.

Lance flicked on a small flashlight mounted to his bow. An arrow nocked, he swept the room. It was empty. He eased out the string and pulled the paper map from his pocket. "There."

Qwon stepped toward the door to the north. "I'll lead."

"I'll cover you," Lance said. "Shallot, you take the rear. You hear anyone, freeze 'em."

"With pleasure."

They moved out. The first door was padlocked, but Kusanagi made quick work of that. They passed through a plain room with white marble walls and high windows. On their right side they saw the guards' lights dancing through the trees.

They came to another set of double doors. These were tall and regal-looking. An expanding pattern of stars was carved into each, and each was fitted with elaborate brass rings. Qwon carefully tried to open them, but they were also locked. She got ready to slide Kusanagi into the breach when Shallot said, "Wait. There are voices on the other side."

"I'll be careful," Qwon whispered. She pushed Kusanagi between the doors only an inch and carefully slid it up, searching for resistance. When she hit the bolt, she flicked the blade, pulling the sword free. She reached out and grasped one of the rings. Lance pulled his bow-string. Shallot held out The Anguish, and Dred readied the Peace Sword.

Qwon inched the door ajar and peeked in.

The dimly lit room contained several glass display cases. The walls, covered with ornate blue-and-white tiles, stretched high into the second story of the building. The ceiling was arched and covered with more tiles and painted all over with geometric patterns in gold and green and red. Flowing Arabic script wrapped around the room at the ten-foot mark. It was beautiful—something right out of a Middle Eastern dream. At the far end of the room was a low stage, on either side of which were two more glass cases. Inside these cases were swords.

But in the middle of the room were four guards, each toting submachine guns and wearing head-to-toe *Call of Duty* body armor. Troublingly, they stood watch over what the knights knew to be a crossover gate that must have sprung open when Artie first drifted through the King's Gate. Worse still, they were wearing gas masks, so Shallot's scentlock would have no effect on them.

Qwon pulled the door shut. "We got a problem," she whispered, and explained the situation.

"We could rush them and take them by surprise," Shallot said.

Lance shook his head. "Not with trained soldiers like that. Even if we succeeded, at least one of us would probably get shot. We can't take that risk."

"How about one of those fireballers?" Dred asked.

Qwon shrugged. "But what if it destroys the sword? That would really suck."

"I have a flashbang arrow. That would stun them, but I'm not sure how much time it would buy us."

Shallot put a hand on Qwon's forearm. "Wait—maybe we should use the crossover."

Lance raised his eyebrows. "Go on."

"It's a stretch, but what if I sneaked through to the

Otherworld and brought something back with me?" Shallot asked. "Something that would cause a commotion and enable the rest of you to come in and either knock them out or just take the sword?"

"Okay," Lance whispered. "So you go in there and come back with what—a bunch of fairies?"

"That would be ideal, but it could be anything. A flock of birds, a bear, anything to get their attention and hold it long enough for you guys to surprise them."

"How'll you get past them without them seeing your hair, though?" Qwon asked.

"I'll make a hood."

Lance slapped his forehead. "Duh." He pulled a hand-kerchief from one of his cargo pockets and Shallot wrapped her hair into a bun. Qwon helped tuck it under the kerchief, making sure no strands leaked out.

"Ready," Qwon said.

Shallot blinked her huge eyes, smiled with her jagged teeth, and went invisible. "I'll be back in five minutes. Anything past that, you can assume something happened. You'll have to come up with another plan in that case."

"Understood," Lance said.

Then they watched as a small pebble floated into the air in Shallot's invisible grip. She pushed the door ajar and the pebble sailed into the room, clinking against one of the sword cases. All of the guards looked in the direction of the noise. In a flash the door opened enough for her to pass through it and then closed just as quickly.

There was no commotion. She had made it. Now, all they could do was wait.

At that same moment, Artie stood in the Royal Chamber looking up at the King's Gate, turning the dark, crown-shaped key in his fingers.

Behind him, the knights of Team Grail were tethered together, mountaineer-style, with a single rope. Artie was first, then Kay, Bedevere, Thumb, Bercilak, and, finally, Numinae. "Who knows what we'll find in there," Artie had warned as he looped the climbing rope around each of them. "If it's like last time, we'll just drift along until we get to the end. We might not be able to hear each other, either. . . ."

When they were ready, Artie slipped the key into his shirt. He pointed Excalibur at the portal, and a howling breeze swirled around the room. A strand of Excalibur's darkness shot from the blade and connected with the abyssal spot. This was black and empty, but then it flashed white, blinding Artie and his knights. They were lifted from the ground, the rope straightening as the knots tightened into unworkable clumps, and were pulled magically into the King's Gate.

For an indeterminate amount of time nothing happened. They could see their own bodies and a foot of rope in either direction, but past that it faded into nothing. Artie asked Excalibur for light, but even that couldn't pierce the dark. As before, there was no sound—all they could hear was the thumping of their own hearts. Bercilak, who didn't even *have* a heart (or eyes, or a mouth), heard nothing at all.

Since there was nothing to see, Artie closed his eyes. He willed himself to be calm. With all that had happened, this wasn't so hard anymore. The boy he had been only six months before—a skinny kid who couldn't even stand up for himself, who'd been scared of something as insignificant and cowardly as a bully, who preferred the basement game room to the outdoors, who never really tried in school, who relied on his headstrong sister to stick up for him, who loved his dad without fail—that boy was gone. Parts of him remained, of course—he still loved his dad, and he still admired Kay—but they were like stones in a foundation, not the building itself. He had grown. He wasn't a man, not yet, but he knew without question that there weren't many kids his age who could do what he could do. There weren't many kids who were fated to find the Holy Grail, or hang out with fairies, or call dragons, or battle an all-powerful wizard.

His mind turned to Merlin. No more games, Artie thought, remembering what Merlin had etched on the little tag that hung around the sabertooth/rhino's neck. And then Artie realized that Merlin was being literal. What it should have said was, *No more video games.* It had been a warning, since somehow Merlin was kidnapping children using *Otherworld.* How many had he taken? What would they be used for? Only time would tell.

Artie steeled himself against a budding nausea. He swallowed, trying to convince himself that this wasn't all his fault. If Merlin has hurt even one of those kids, I will kill him, Artie vowed.

Just as he was making this grim promise, Artie bumped into something. The other knights came into view as they too slammed into what turned out to be a long wall, as black as the void surrounding it.

They still couldn't hear one another, but they could see. Each was fine. "Find the door," Artie mouthed.

The knights moved their hands up and down the black

wall, looking like mimes in outer space. After several minutes they still had no leads. As they searched, Artie had a small thought: What if they didn't find it? It then occurred to him that he had absolutely no idea how to get *out* of the King's Gate—the last time, he was there one minute, and the next he was falling through the air over the Lake. His heart began to race. Was this some kind of elaborate trap? Did Merlin have anything to do with this? Was the Grail a whatchamacallit—a red herring—meant to lead Artie astray?

With a questioning look, he tugged the rope that led to Kay. She shook her head. "Keep searching," Artie mouthed again. It didn't feel like they'd been looking for long, but nevertheless Artie started to lose hope.

After a while longer, a noise grew in Artie's ears. At first he thought it was his heart getting more anxious, but then he realized that it was too fast. He glanced over his shoulder and saw nothing. The others seemed not to hear it. He tried to ignore it and continued searching. But then the sound became deafening. It was not the pounding of a heart but of hooves.

He wheeled in place. Rushing toward him was the ghost of King Arthur, galloping on his warhorse, and carrying a long lance at his side. Steam billowed from the horse's flaring nostrils; saliva streamed from its mouth and dripped from the tackle. Arthur's visor was up. His face was twisted and mean. He glanced at the people and creatures Artie had brought with him with a look of stern disapproval. The message was clear: They should not be here. The King's Gate is for the king.

"Too bad!" Artie said defiantly. "I'm the king, too, you know!"

Arthur snapped his head and dropped his visor into place, ready to joust. The faceplate was gleaming and terrifying and shaped like the pointed beak of a carrion eater. In a second the lance's point hit Artie in the side, looping through the lifeline that tethered Artie to his friends. Artie reacted quickly, swiping Excalibur at the rope and cutting it, and the horse galloped away. As it left, sound returned to the knights.

"Who are you talking to, lad?" Thumb inquired.

"And why did you just cut the rope?" Kay asked.

"You guys didn't just see the ghost of King Arthur rush by on a huge warhorse?"

"I think we'd notice that, sire!" Bercilak said.

"Well, I saw him. He disappeared into the darkness. I hope he comes back. He can show us where the door is. He did before."

"Um, Artie . . . seeing ghosts that other people can't see—that might be a little, you know, cra—"

Artie held up a finger and shushed Kay. "He's coming back."

The horse then reappeared and came to a screeching halt in front of Artie. "There—can you guys see that?"

"Uh, no." Kay said. "Any of you see what Art's talking about?"

The others shook their heads.

"Whatever. Let me talk to him."

"Ah! This will be entertaining," Bercilak said.

Artie turned to the old king. Arthur had raised the face-plate of his helmet. He still looked peeved.

Artie stepped forward. "I'm sorry if I broke some kind of code, but I had to bring them. They're my knights—no—they're my friends. You remember what *friends* are, right?"

The expression on Arthur's face softened. "Yes," came the response, though Artie knew that he was the only one who would ever hear it. "I remember that some of my friends turned out to be my worst enemies. And some of my enemies, my best allies."

"Yeah. I'm learning that too."

"Are you sure, young king?"

"I think so."

Arthur nodded toward the wall, and there, where it hadn't been before, was the outline of the door, the crown-shaped keyhole clearly visible. "Take your friends and go through, Artie Kingfisher."

"Thanks, Arthur Pendragon."

"Get the cup. Use it wisely. And don't end up like . . . like part of me did."

"I'll try not to. No offense, but I really don't want to end up guarding a door in some weird bottomless void for a thousand years."

"Nor did I, but fate can be funny. Now listen carefully."

"What?"

"The answer is *me*," Arthur said cryptically. "Godspeed." And then, in a blink, he and his horse were gone.

Artie committed it to memory, even though he was totally unsure of what it meant. He turned to his friends, who stared at him in confusion.

"What did he say to you, lad?" Thumb asked.

"He said get the cup. Which is exactly what we're about to do." He went straight to the door and fit the black key into the crown-shaped hole. He tried turning left and right with no luck. "Oh, come on." Artie sighed. He pushed it in another quarter inch. A small click came from within, and he was about to try turning it again when the key was sucked from his hand. "What the—?"

"Look, lads!" Thumb said. The entire door moved

silently inward a few inches and stopped. Then it began to glow, getting so bright that they had to shield their eyes. With the light came a frigid gust of air that stung their nostrils and throats. After a few seconds the light subsided. Before them was an open doorway. On the other side was a stone cave.

Artie pulled out Excalibur and asked for light. Numinae converted his right hand into a maul and charged his left with a green and twinkling spell. Artie put a foot across the threshold. "Here we go." They stepped into the opening single file, Bercilak bringing up the rear.

As soon as they were all safely in, the cave shook so violently that they had to brace themselves against the walls. When it stopped they found that the door had shut and sealed the exit off completely. As if to emphasize that they were stuck there, the key pushed out of the smooth rock and clunked onto the ground, leaving no trace of a keyhole.

Bercilak picked up the key and touched the stone with his metal fingertips. "Sire . . . how exactly are we to escape this place?"

"Let's find the Grail first," Artie said, holding Excalibur to light the way. "We can cross that bridge when we get to it." He spun and walked briskly away.

"What bridge is he talking about?" Bercilak whispered,

but no one felt like explaining the expression to him.

The cavern sloped up at an easy incline. It was only a few feet wide, but well over fifteen feet high, and the upper reaches were shrouded in shadow. Little drips and squeaks came from here and there. Bercilak's armor made an unholy racket, and Bedevere said, "I hope we don't have to do any sneaking on this mission. It's like you're toting a dozen pots and pans, Bercy."

Artie turned one corner, then another and another. As he made his way through the cave he got more and more excited and began to pick up speed. He moved so quickly that he put several paces between himself and the others. Finally he turned one last corner and stopped short, and after a few seconds the rest of the knights barreled into him.

Artie crept into an enormous, cathedral-like cavern. About thirty feet away was the edge of a vast underground lake, the water inky and as still as death. A few torches flickered along the walls.

Bedevere pointed over Artie's shoulder. "Look there!"

Sitting at the water's edge was a large man in tattered rags. They hadn't noticed him because he was incredibly still and also because his skin was so ashen and drab that he blended in with the water and rock. His broad shoulders were curled up and his neck bent over, as if he was holding something precious in his hands. His hair was white and scraggly. At closer inspection they could see that his arms were crisscrossed with scars and lesions. He sat with his legs out in front of him, the heels of his feet nearly touching the water. A stream of purple blood led from his leg into the lake. His rib cage rose and fell slowly with deep breaths.

"Sir?" Artie asked carefully.

No answer came.

"Sir, can you hear me?"

Still nothing.

"Maybe he's a deaf-mute," Kay whispered, her voice echoing.

Artie was within a few feet of the man now. He could see that the man's profile was statuesque—a large, crooked nose jutted from under an overhanging brow. He held something in his hands admiringly. His inner thigh had an oozing gash that went from his knee all the way up to his groin, which was covered with a rank and filthy loincloth. "Sir?" Artie said more loudly this time, his own voice bouncing around the cave for many seconds.

The man turned to Artie. His eyes were as white as snow, just like Bran's. His lips were thin and chapped and he didn't appear to have any teeth. He looked like a ghoul.

Artie's heart raced. "My name is Arthur Kingfisher, sir," he offered, trying to get a better look at whatever was in this man's hands.

"*Kingfisher?*" the man demanded.

"That's right."

"*I* am the Fisher King, Kingfisher!" He bellowed, and the wound on his leg gushed blood, swirling in the water.

Artie choked back his disgust and said, "I'm a king too, my friend. I have something that can help you."

"King?" He sniffed the air like a dog. "Ha-ha. He says, 'King.'"

"I can heal your wound."

The man spun and regarded whatever was hidden in his massive hands.

"What're you holding, Fisher King?"

"It is something. Something I take care of. Something that was supposed to take care of me, but that has only ever just sustained me. . . ."

"May I—" Artie's voice cracked high then low, reminding him, at a most annoying time, that he was still kind of a child. He coughed, feeling stupid, and repeated, "May I see it?"

"Yes. As a matter of fact—you can have it." The injured caretaker raised his gigantic hands and opened them. Artie reached out. The Fisher King held a simple metal cup. It was not shiny or adorned in any way. It lacked either a handle or a pedestal. It didn't look like the magical, legendary chalice Artie had imagined.

"Is it the—"

"It is. I have been trying to rid myself of it for an age. Here."

Artie took it gingerly and pulled the Holy Grail to his chest. There was no moment of revelation with it like there had been when Artie first got Excalibur. The grail was just a plain little cup.

He stepped away from the Fisher King and noticed that the wound on his leg began to spray blood. The man placed his hands behind him and leaned back, and he sighed with relief.

Kay stepped forward. "Nice work, Artie. That was a cinch!"

Artie didn't answer. Something felt off. He looked from the Grail to the Fisher King and back. Just then, the old guardian began to laugh.

"Uh-oh," Numinae said.

"What is it?" Kay asked.

The Fisher King answered, twisting his neck at a gruesome angle. "The quest is changed, good sir knight."

"What does that mean?" Artie demanded frantically.

"Ah! Such freedom! Freedom for the body to die, for the spirit to soar!" the Fisher King said. "Give that cursed vessel to the Pure Knight as soon as you can, young king. Only he can keep it properly." And then the man's arms broke, as if his bones were made of dry twigs. He flopped back, his head whiplashing against the ground.

A smile crossed his face.

"Mordred? You mean Mordred?" Artie asked desperately.

"In my day he was called Galahad," the man whispered. His face aged, his stomach sank—and then his leg stopped bleeding. "I am done. Blessed death, I am finally done."

Thumb bolted toward the expiring man. "How has the quest changed?" he asked pointedly.

"Getting the Grail—easy. Leaving with it—not so easy. Godspeed." And then the ancient man's skin went from white to gray to charcoal in a flash. His cheeks hollowed, his eyes disappeared, and his hair fell from his head.

The Fisher King was dead.

His body was dragged hastily into the water by unseen hands, and when it disappeared the lake began to bubble and boil, and all the torches puffed out.

Artie handed the Grail to Kay, who slipped it into the infinite backpack. They had to get out of there. He unsheathed Excalibur and said, "*Lunae lumen!*"

Nothing.

"*LUNAE LUMEN!*"

More nothing.

"Dang it," Kay said.

The lake hissed and the room became hot and humid.

"Light!" Artie ordered. Excalibur lit with purpose. The knights stared at what they were faced with.

"Super dang it," Kay said.

What they saw before them was not a welcome sight at all.

Lance, Qwon, and Dred stood outside the double doors at Topkapi Palace, waiting for Shallot to come back with her distraction. Two minutes passed. Three. Four. And finally, five.

"What do we do?" Qwon asked.

Lance tapped his watch. "Wait some more."

Six minutes. Seven.

"Fairies," Dred said scornfully. "Probably bailed."

Qwon shook her head. "Not Shallot."

"Yes, Shallot," Dred said.

Lance said, "All right, change of plans. I still don't think we can risk a fireballer, so I'll put in a flashbang. We're not going to kill any of these guys—they're just soldiers doing a job."

"I don't want to kill anything, ever," Qwon insisted.

"Good. As soon as the grenade is off, you whip up a nasty storm, Qwon. One that will really put them on their butts."

"And Shallot?" Dred asked.

Lance shrugged. "Hopefully she'll show up and lend a hand. We can't wait around all night. If she doesn't show, we'll rendezvous with her back in the Otherworld. You guys ready?"

Dred scowled. "Ready."

Qwon held out Kusanagi. "Ready as I'll ever be."

Lance pulled the flashbang arrow from his quiver and placed it on the string. He pulled it to his cheek, slid the door open with a foot, and let the arrow go.

A bright flare erupted, followed by four rapid rifle shots. Qwon shouted, *"Arashi!"* The doors flew open as dark clouds and lashing rain and crackling lightning streamed off the blade. Lance and Dred wasted no time rushing in, but as soon as they passed Kusanagi they were sucked into the storm. Qwon had her hands full—this one was strong, really strong.

"Resu," Qwon implored, and the tempest calmed enough that she could steady herself. Lance and Dred bounced to their feet. One of the guards had been lifted up in the initial gust of the storm, and had crashed into a rafter, wrapping around it like a rag doll. He was out cold.

Two of the others had been thrown to the back of the room and were climbing from behind the glass cases, their gas masks blown clean off. One still had his rifle, and the other was unholstering a pistol from his thigh.

The guard with the rifle took aim at Lance's head in the same moment that Lance let an arrow fly. It sailed across the room and, in the shot of a lifetime, went straight into the rifle's barrel, pushing the guard backward. Lance nocked another arrow and spun as the guard with the pistol made a bead on him. Lance wasn't going to be able to shoot quickly enough.

Qwon concentrated on the guard with the handgun. A bolt of lightning shot from the tip of the blade, crackling through the air, and hit the guard square in the chest. He was flung to the ground, completely knocked out, the pistol twirling away and out of reach.

The one with the ruined rifle was vaulting toward Lance, an anodized knife in his fist. Lance dropped his bow, unsheathed Orgulus, and ran at the guard. The rapier's tip glanced off the knife and the two men came face-to-face. Lance took a hit to the gut, ducked a swipe of the knife, and then jumped back, wielding Orgulus like a musketeer. He twirled his wrist and the blade made a series of whip-fast curlicues that hit the guard across the cheek and knuckles. The knife clattered to the floor as Lance brought the rapier upright, drawing the cage to his face. Just as he was about to knock the guard out with a punch, another of Kusanagi's lightning bolts sizzled past and, with pinpoint accuracy, struck the guard in the side. He shuddered and fell to the wall in an unconscious heap.

As this happened, Dred looked frantically for the fourth guard. At first he didn't see him, but then Dred caught glimpse of a watery image on the other side of the cross-over—the guard hadn't crossed, of course, he couldn't—but just being on the other side of the portal helped to hide the guard from Dred.

Dred dropped to a knee. Three quick shots came from the guard behind the crossover and ricocheted off the Peace Sword, rattling Dred's wrists painfully. He rolled across the ground and then came up, throwing the Peace Sword directly at the guard's rifle. It spun end over end through the air, and the hilt came down hard on the muzzle, knocking the weapon to the floor.

"Qwon!" Dred called, hoping she could shoot this guy with one of her lightning bolts, but no answer came. And that was when Dred realized that the storm was gone. He chanced a look over his shoulder. Qwon was fighting with two *more* men over twice her size!

Dred ran for his sword—but the guard who he'd thrown it at was holding it—and running toward him!

Unarmed, Dred took off for the crossover gate and

disappeared. He suddenly found himself standing in the middle of an endless field of spring wheat. "Shallot!" he called, just in case the fairy was nearby, but no answer came. Forgetting about her, he put his face right up to the surface of the crossover and saw the guard standing there, baffled as he tried to figure out where Dred had just gone. Dred dropped to a knee and thrust his hands through the gate, grabbing the guard by the ankles. Dred pulled hard, and the guard slammed onto his back. Dred vaulted to the Turkish side of the gate, snatched the Peace Sword from the startled guard, and hit him on the forehead with the pommel. He moaned and passed out.

Without hesitating, Dred rushed to Qwon, but she was so deft with Kusanagi that by the time he got there she had defeated her two attackers, leaving one unconscious and the other on his knees begging for his life.

"Nicely done, Q!" Dred cried, panting with excitement. Qwon stepped back, bowed respectfully, pointed the sword at the frightened man's face, and barked one more word. A fist-size hailstone materialized and flew from the metal, striking the man hard in the head. He too slumped over and passed out.

Qwon spun to Dred, beaming. "I did it! I did it! I won my first fight with this thing!" Then, without thinking, she jumped forward and landed in Dred's arms.

Dred blushed.

"Hey, guys," Lance said, sauntering up.

Qwon let go of Dred and peeled away from him awkwardly, her round cheeks turning rosy. "Oh, hey. Good, uh, good fighting, Lance."

"Yeah, really good!" Dred said a little too enthusiastically.

"You too—both of you. That was smart using the crossover, Dred. And the lightning, Qwon—that was really something. Although I had that guy, you know."

Qwon shuffled her feet like a schoolgirl. "Oh, I know. Just thought I'd give you a hand."

"Well, I appreciate it. Now—"

Lance was interrupted as Shallot bounded through the crossover, The Anguish flashing in front of her. "Ah-har!" she announced, sounding more like a pirate than a fairy. Her scentlock was so strong that Lance, who was closest, swooned and fell over.

"Where ya been, Tinker Bell?" Qwon managed to ask in a nasally voice, a finger jammed up each nostril.

Shallot looked around desperately. She dropped her scentlock and asked, "What happened?"

"You said five minutes, fairy," Dred said, sitting on the ground. "We waited seven."

"But it's been five minutes."

"And I came over there for a second," Dred said. "I didn't see you at all."

"I was there. I was looking for a creature to distract the guards, but I couldn't find one. It was just a huge field of wheat."

"Whatever; it's over now. We went ahead without you."

Shallot looked around and saw the beaten men and the damage done by the storm. "Looks like it was a good fight. Sorry, I really didn't mean to miss it. I swore it was five minutes."

"Don't worry about it," Lance said, waving his hand. "Everything worked out. Let's get what we came for and bounce. You'll get to fight soon enough when we go up against Merlin."

They walked to the sword cases at the far end of the room. The one on the right was still intact and held two blades. Both were unsheathed, so neither could be the Sword of David, since the act of unsheathing it was suicidal for anyone but Dred. The case on the left had been shattered by the storm. There were three swords there, all unsheathed as well—but there was also a blank spot where a fourth sword had clearly rested.

Dred's eyes widened. "Guys, the Sword of David is—"

A guard screamed, coming out of nowhere. His face was bruised and his hands were wrapped around the scabbard and hilt of a long sword. He ran straight for Dred, drawing the cursed weapon, and swung the blade through the air. Dred parried with the Peace Sword, but it wasn't necessary, because as soon as the guard had finished his misguided attack, he fell over, his skin green and withered, his cheekbones and knuckles protruding like he'd been dead for weeks. He thumped to the ground, and the fearsome Sword of David clanked harmlessly on the tile floor.

"Omigod!" Qwon exclaimed. "That poor, poor man . . ."

"Yes," Lance said solemnly, walking slowly to the deceased guard. "That was *not* a soldier's death."

Shallot stared reverently—and a little fearfully—at the sword. "Well, we found it, that's for sure."

Lance scratched his head before giving Dred a worried look. "Guess it's time to pick it up and get out of here, right, kid?"

"Suppose so." He knelt next to the Sword of David and held his hand over the hilt nervously. "Here goes nothing."

"Wait!" Qwon yelped, running toward Dred. She dropped next to him, grabbed his face with both hands, and pulled him close. It was a short kiss—but it was still a kiss. "Just in case," Qwon said with a grin.

"Thanks." Dred was *really* blushing now.

But the kiss had given him a little oomph. With renewed resolve, he wrapped his fingers around the hilt and picked up the blade. Nothing happened. It didn't even feel special.

"No sweat!" He walked around the case and sheathed the weapon. Just to be double sure, he pulled it out and resheathed it. "Yep, totally fine." Lance and Shallot shared a sigh of relief as Dred placed a hand on Qwon's shoulder and whispered, "But maybe I should almost die more often."

Qwon nudged him with her hip. "C'mon, guys. Let's go back to Tintagel!"

The four knights trotted back through the palace. They could hear sirens wailing in the distance, but as they made their way back to the moongate, they met no resistance. They stepped into the hollow of the ancient tree, and just like that, their mission was done. All they had to do now was wait for Artie and the others to return too—with the Holy Grail.

𝕬𝖗𝖙𝖎𝖊 𝖆𝖓𝖉 𝖍𝖎𝖘 𝖐𝖓𝖎𝖌𝖍𝖙𝖘 𝖌𝖆𝖟𝖊𝖉 over the expanse where the lake had been, their mouths agape. In the water's place was a valley of mud. And rising out of the mud like trees were dozens of long and writhing tentacles, blindly searching for prey.

Kay gasped sharply, and Artie reached over and squeezed her hand.

All across the muddy field, in between the tentacles, lay dozens of men in different kinds of clothing or armor spanning many different eras: English plate armor; a Spanish cuirass; a few flouncy French-looking shirts; and one guy in a tan button-down shirt, leather jacket, and a wide-brimmed hat. All of their heads hung forward, obscuring their faces. And each was completely legless and armless.

Then at the same time, they moaned.

Bercilak pointed across the lake bed and said, "Hark! Your brothers in amputation, Sir Bedevere!"

"*Those* are not my brothers, Sir Bercilak."

"Lad!" Thumb pointed the Welsh *wakizashi* at the far end of the cave. There, a crude stairway rose out of the drained depths of the lake. The knights followed it with their eyes and saw a figure standing at the top. Its face was obscured, and it stood in front of a pair of heavy-looking iron doors.

Above the doors were written the words *Way Out*.

"Guess we know what we need to do next, huh?" Kay asked.

"Looks like it," Artie answered.

"Right. How hard could it be to cross a muddy lake full of limbless zombies?" Bercilak said. He swung his ax and walked to the edge of the muck. A tentacle shot out in his direction and he swiftly cut it down. "No sweating!" he announced.

"No *sweat*," Kay corrected.

"Right you are, Sir Kay."

Just then the figure at the end of the cavern started to laugh. It held out a hand, and as it lifted the hand higher and higher, the amputees rose from the mud.

"So they do have legs!" Bercilak called. But as soon as he said it, he choked on his words. "Oh my!" he said faintly.

The legs weren't legs at all. They were tentacles, long and sickly gray, with puckering suction cups. Then the figures' bleeding shoulder stumps grew tentacles too, and all at once, in a din of creaking bone, their heads swung up. Their faces were blank and puffy, as if they'd drowned hundreds of years ago. Snails and clams and worms filled their eye sockets and mouths.

"Gross!" Kay exclaimed, readying Cleomede.

And then the far-off figure called, "You cannot pass! These former Grail seekers will see to that!"

"Numinae, give him a shot," Artie ordered quietly.

"With pleasure." Numinae punched the air, and a green bolt of energy leaped forward, arcing across the chamber. But just as it reached the guardian, it hit an invisible wall and spread out flat like a pancake. Numinae recoiled, and the spell fizzled.

"Looks as though we'll have to fight our way across, lad," Thumb said.

"Fine with me. Phantoma!" Bedevere ordered, and his powerful ghost arm sprang to life. Before anyone could stop him, he pulled out his claymore and marched to the front of the line.

As Bedevere fired up his arm, Artie eyed the ground sternly. There was the indentation where the Fisher King had sat, and his trail of blood that had drained into the lake. It disappeared where the mud began. . . .

The mud!

"Bedevere," Artie said urgently. "Wait!"

Just as Artie said the word, the foot of Bedevere's parabolic leg touched the muck. The undead men nearest to Bedevere pounced—which is to say, their arm tentacles stretched and groped, their suckers making little kissing noises. In an instant, Bedevere's fake leg was pulled into the mud to the knee. If he hadn't reached out with his phantom hand to unfasten his stump, the rest of him would have been sucked in as well, and he would have turned into a Grail-seeking zombie like the rest of those sorry souls.

"By the trees!" Bercilak ran forward and grabbed Bedevere by his shoulders and pulled him out of harm's way. The tentacles and the zombies grew calm. They resumed waiting.

"Ack!" Bedevere punched the ground with his real hand. "Phantoma," he said weakly, turning his fake arm off for the time being.

Kay knelt next to him, pulling the infinite backpack off her shoulder. "Don't worry. I have your backup somewhere in here."

Bercilak pointed at the guardian, who laughed. "Sire, not to belabor the point, but pray how *are* we going to cross this infernal suck pit?"

"I don't know, Bercy," Artie said. "I wish I still had

Rhongomyniad. I could just chuck it over there and make a rope bridge. . . ."

"Like back in Sweden," Kay mused, helping Bedevere strap on the spare leg.

Numinae cleared his throat.

"Lads, lads," Thumb said. "Don't forget who we have with us."

"Oh yeah!" Kay yelped. "Noomy, you can just fly us over there on some kind of magic green carpet, right?"

"Well, no, Sir Kay. I don't know any flying spells. But that doesn't mean I'm useless."

Artie snapped his fingers. "Your vine thing! Like when you took Cassie! Can't you shoot a bunch over there and we'll climb across?"

Numinae grinned. "I can do better than that, sire." He closed his wild eyes and held out his arms and began to hum, low and sonorous.

Numinae then changed before their eyes, shedding every part of him that looked human. His legs joined and his hips thickened as his lower half turned into a stout trunk. His arms shot out for the stone walls, and his fingers turned to many-branched roots that grabbed the rock, working their way into it, and from the waist up, he grew. With a loud cracking sound his body stretched out, reaching across the cave in an arc. Little branches sprouted here and there and leaves uncurled and bark hardened. He was a tree, growing in a sunless cave. Over the mud he went, the Grail zombies not even bothering to look, because why would they? Zombies want brains, not leaves.

Farther and farther he went, growing thinner as he reached the promontory at the top of the stairway. The figure at the other end grew hushed and dropped to the ground, his legs crossed. After a couple of minutes, Numinae's tree form hit its target, and in an explosion of green the part of him that had been his head lodged itself onto the stone.

The bridge was complete.

"Bet you didn't see that coming, dude!" Kay yelled, her voice echoing across the hall.

Artie put a hand on her shoulder, "We're not out of this yet, Sis."

"No, lad. But we're getting closer," Thumb said, sheathing his *wakizashi* and climbing onto Numinae.

Artie clambered on next, then Kay, Bedevere, and finally Bercilak. As they walked across, the poor creatures below them writhed and reached with their tentacles, trying in vain to capture the knights. Kay pointed at the one with the wide-brimmed hat. "Check it out. Indiana Jones wants to know where we're going with the Grail!"

Artie looked. He wanted to laugh but couldn't. How does she stay so upbeat? he wondered of his sister. There was no way he could have gotten through everything without her. "Yeah, he sure does," he said quietly.

"You all right, Art?"

"I will be when we're out of here." He watched his feet. Crossing the Numinae bridge was like moving over a forest path strewn with roots and divots. If they weren't careful, they could turn an ankle—or worse, fall into the lethal muck below.

After a few moments Bercilak chimed, "I always enjoyed walking alongside you, Lord Numinae . . . but never did I think that I would walk *on* you!"

They were very near the end when Artie said, "Tom, I think you're smaller."

"Me too," Kay seconded. "It's like we're half in the Otherworld and half in our world."

"Yes, lass. We are nearing some point between the worlds. I can feel it."

Artie eyed the man who was waiting for them and realized, as they drew within fifty feet, that his face had not been obscured. Instead, he had no face—or rather, no eyes or nose. Only a mouth, and for ears only little holes, like on a lizard.

Once they'd all crossed, Numinae set about bringing himself over. They watched in awe as the end closest to them became thick while the other end became thin. It looked very painful, and when this process was done, two strong branches shot out close to the knights, grabbing the rock on their side. Then Numinae's body released the ground where the Fisher King had been, and telescoped up and over the zombie mud pit. Finally he was with the others. The leaves and branches withdrew into his body, and the bark of the trunk softened and became mossy, like his skin usually was. His head and neck re-formed, followed by his arms and chest. Last, his legs separated and he planted his feet wide. He cracked his neck and opened his eyes and looked at Artie.

"Nicely done, Numinae."

But before he could answer, the guardian of the mud pit, not more than a dozen feet away, began a slow clap. "Nicely done, indeed." He waved his hand at the pitiful monsters below. "None of those adventurers thought to bring a creature as freakish as you."

Kay stepped forward, "You're one to talk, face-off!"

"Am I? I can see, you know. Not like you do, but I can see everything in here. So you brought some kind of alteration mage. Congratulations. That doesn't mean you're leaving with the Grail."

"Yeah, it does," Kay said defiantly. She felt for the invisible wall that had stopped Numinae's spell and found it in seconds. Then she pulled out Cleomede and held its tip against the barrier. "This cuts through anything, chump."

"Sir Kay, wait—," Numinae said, but there was no stopping Kay Kingfisher.

She pushed. Cleomede's tip slipped to the side, and she

fell awkwardly forward into the wall with all her weight, smashing her cheek against it.

The guardian laughed. "Nothing can breach this wall, m'lady."

"He's right," Numinae said. "That spell was the same I'd used on Morgaine's dragon bubbles. If it can't break this thing, nothing—"

The guardian stood. "Did you just say *Morgaine*?"

Artie stepped forward. "Yep."

The guardian pointed at the knights. "So you did not come here through the secret tunnel—the one in the church in Glastonbury."

"Glastonbury, England?" Thumb asked dubiously.

"Yes—that's the one," the guardian said.

"No, we did not," Artie said forcefully.

"Then how did you get here?"

"The King's Gate. Heard of that?" Kay blurted.

The guardian took a couple of steps back. "The King's Gate . . . I . . . I can't believe it."

"Believe it, good sir faceless man!" Bercilak said.

"But that would mean that one of you—"

"Is King Arthur. Bingo. Now step aside," Kay said.

Artie drew Excalibur for emphasis and said, "I am the king."

"But . . . how?"

"Never mind that. I am the king and I demand that you

let us pass."

The guardian was silent for a few minutes as he processed all this. Then he crossed his arms and said, "I am sorry, but . . . none shall pass."

"Bollocks!" Thumb yelped. "*We're* passing. This is the king of both worlds you're talking to."

"None shall pass," the guardian repeated.

Artie stepped back and swung for the fences at the wall with Excalibur for good measure. It put off a few sparks but accomplished nothing.

And that was when the sword told him something: *Answer.* Artie stepped away from the wall, his face twisted in thought. Answer? Answer? What did that mean?

Hadn't the ghost of King Arthur I said something about an answer? That meant . . .

"You're supposed to ask us a question!" Artie blurted.

"None shall pass."

"That's right, lad! Perceval hinted the same thing back in the olden days!"

The guardian stammered, "I . . . I . . ."

"Ask us the question," Artie insisted.

"It's just that, well—no one's come for the Grail for eighty-two years, and besides, no one has made it as far as you have since this Perceval that the little fellow just mentioned. . . ."

Artie bristled. "Are you trying to say that you've *forgotten* the question?"

The creature hung his head. "Y-yes."

"*What?*" Kay yelled. "You have got to be kidding."

"Perceval and the Grail knights—they were here so long ago!" he cried defensively.

Artie turned a small circle, thinking.

"Did Sir Perceval ever tell it to you, Master Thumb?" Bercilak asked.

"No, of course not. The Grail was one of the biggest secrets anywhere, at any time."

"Guardian," Numinae announced in an officious voice, "you are derelict. If you cannot administer your duties, lower this barrier and let us leave. Since you are not fit, we *shall* pass!"

Artie waved his hand. "It's all right," he said loudly. Everyone was quiet, including the flummoxed guardian. "Because I know the answer."

"Lad, how would you know the answer to an unasked question?"

"A friend told it to me," Artie said. "Listen, guardian: If I give you this answer, then you will let us go?"

The guardian stroked his chin. "I suppose I have to. But you just get one try! I do remember that. Get it right, and you may leave with the Grail. Get it wrong, and you will be stuck here forever!" He pointed to the undead knights in the mud pit below.

"Understood," Artie said confidently.

"You sure about this, Art?" Kay asked.

"Don't worry. I got this."

"Okay, lad," Thumb said. "Let him have it."

Artie took a deep breath and said, "The answer is 'me.'"

The faceless guardian didn't speak at first. But then he laced his fingers together proudly and said, "Wrong."

Artie stamped his foot and pointed to the exact spot where the Fisher King had sat. "No! That man was . . . King Arthur Pendragon. Or it was his body, at least. His ghost told me. And I am King Arthur remade, so the answer is 'me.' If you want to be technical about it, the answer is 'King Arthur,' plain and simple. But that is who I am. That is me!"

In spite of his facial handicap, the man appeared shocked. "That's . . . that's correct. And now I remember: the question was, 'Who had the Fisher King once been?'"

Kay pumped her fist silently. The guardian stepped to the side and said quietly, "You may pass."

"Well done, lad!"

"Huzzah!" Bercilak buzzed.

Artie beamed, super proud of himself. But then he had a terrible thought. "Wait; all of us can go, right?"

"Yes, Grail King," the guardian said.

"Whew!" Artie walked to the giant doors and put a hand on them. They opened easily, revealing a stone spiral staircase. Before leaving, he looked at the guardian and said, "Thank you. Thank you for keeping it safe."

But the man didn't say anything. He couldn't. His mouth had sealed shut. The zombies below wailed and cried as they were sucked into the muck, their bodies falling apart, as if some spell had released them from their misery. And then, right before Artie's eyes, the guardian turned to dust and fell into a pile on the floor.

"Whoa!" Kay said. "Looks like you did everyone here a solid, Art."

Artie tilted his head. "I guess so." He grasped Kay by the arm. "Now let's go revive our father."

"Heck yeah!"

Artie bounded up the stairs, Kay on his heels. The rest followed in a tight formation, Numinae hoisting Thumb onto his broad shoulders. As Artie ran he tried a *lunae lumen*, but it still didn't work. They ran for the equivalent of six flights of stairs before Artie stopped to catch his breath. "Man, I hope it's not much higher," Kay said.

"We're getting there," Thumb announced, even smaller. "If my size is any indication, we're closer to somewhere on your side."

They continued on. It was *way* more than six more flights. Twenty at least. By the time they reached the end, they were soaked with sweat. Even Bercilak, who had no obvious reason to get tired, announced, "That's going to smart in the morning!"

The end of the line was a wooden trapdoor. Artie reached out and pushed. It was locked. No problem—he sliced it to pieces with Excalibur. Wood and nails rained down on them, but they didn't care, for the light of a bright sunny day streamed into the stairwell. Artie clambered out.

The door opened atop a stone tower built on a tall, round hill, with a picturesque countryside sprawling out in all directions. Big clouds marched lazily across the sky like white elephants. To the west and north a far-off storm was brewing. Looking around, they found that the building was roofless and hollow, and that they were in fact standing on what was essentially the wall of a square tower. Driving home that they were not in the Otherworld, a few tourists with cameras and cell phones milled around at ground level taking pictures.

"Where are we, sire?" Bedevere asked.

"Looks like England," Artie said.

"This is Glastonbury Tor," Thumb said assuredly.

"Ah. Smashing," Bercilak said.

Numinae took cover near one of the crenellations. "We shouldn't stay. Can't have any of those poor people seeing me." He pointed at the tourists.

Artie shook his head. "No. Or you, Bercilak."

257

But Bercilak didn't hear him. He was too busy craning his torso over the edge, his massive metal hands planted on the stone. "It's grand, sire! Just grand. Much nicer than I thought it would be."

"Lad, we should be going," Thumb said, staring at the dark part of the sky.

"I know, I know." Artie prepared to open a moongate back to Avalon.

"No, I mean it. We should be going!" Thumb insisted. Numinae risked standing, and in that same moment the sky went completely dark, as if someone had switched off the sun.

"Merlin!" Kay yelped, pointing high above.

Artie spun frantically in every direction. "Where?"

And then a terrible form fell from the clouds—a giant birdlike thing shrouded in mist—and simply plucked Bercilak from the edge, pulling him into the sky, screaming like a child and clanking like the empty suit of armor that he was.

Kay reached after the Green Knight, but Bedevere restrained her. Lightning cracked overhead.

"Lads, now is not the time to save our friend. We must leave here, gather our army, and stick to the plan!" Thumb insisted.

It bothered Artie to abandon Bercilak so quickly, but Artie knew that Thumb was right. "*Lunae lumen!*" he said quietly, and the pommel stone glowed. A moongate crackled open and then closed around the group, carrying them away from the ancient hill called Glastonbury Tor and back to the secret isle of Avalon.

"**The Grail! The Grail! Congratulations** to them, I suppose. But it won't stop me. No, it won't stop me at all!"

Merlin paced in the computer room near the array of sangrealite stones and still-humming mainframes.

"It *can't* stop me," he said to himself. "And now that the fool Green Knight, the one called Bercilak, is on his way to me, Lord Numinae will know exactly where to find me. Ah, I am good. And I am ready."

He clapped his hands greedily and stopped pacing. The floor between the stones was pockmarked and worn as black as pitch. The wires leading from them were frayed and the sangrealite in the stoup was gone, used up.

Merlin looked over this array proudly. "I am *very* ready."

It had worked. He'd mustered the foot soldiers of his army. They were aboveground, waiting in a giant field tent overlooking the sea. They had been outfitted with simple armor and all manner of weapons. Battle was in their future. A strange battle that Merlin knew he would win.

He reached over and threw a big electrical switch. Lights twinkled off and fans ceased to spin and drives stood still. The computers shut down, having served their purpose. All the years spent learning code and programming had paid off. The game called *Otherworld* had been an unequivocal success. It had brought him Artie Kingfisher, and now it had done this.

He left the computer room and made his way to the chamber with the huge cage. "*Agorwch*," he said when he reached it, and the cage door swung wide. Lights simultaneously beamed on from all corners of the enclosure. The creature had never seen so much light. It jostled and hissed as its black eyes adjusted. The hooves of its hind legs banged the cage's floor. It reared, scratching the air with forepaws each the size of a compact car. Its neck writhed, and its head knocked into the cage's uppermost bars.

"Easy, pet, easy." Merlin pointed his cane at the earthen roof of the chamber. It cracked open, revealing a gray sky. Rain fell into the room.

The creature roared and then settled.

"Come out. You are free now. Free to serve me."

Its head emerged from the cage. From the tip of its nose to the base of its neck it was a black snake, scaly and smooth. Pale, cambered fangs as long as scimitars dived from its upper mandible, dripping with a translucent liquid like mother-of-pearl. Its head was the size of a dinner table. The snake tongue darted in and out as it sniffed the air.

Merlin rubbed his fingers together. "It's all right, dear. Come out and play."

From the shoulders to its sternum the creature was a giant, dark-spotted leopard. Its fur was nearly black, its darker spots like ebony eyelets. The head lowered to Merlin's level and the tongue sniffed some more.

A gurgle came from its stomach.

"Hungry, eh? Let's go inspect our forces. There is sure to be a morsel or two for you."

The creature exited the cage completely and switched its short white tail back and forth. From the sternum to the rump it had the high, powerful body of an enormous white stag. Merlin held out an open hand, and the snake head lowered over his fingertips. He scratched its chin. Its eyelids drooped with pleasure.

Merlin peeked around his creation. From nose to tail it was sixty feet long. A thin line of sangrealite marked where the snake met the leopard, and where the leopard met the stag, as if the animal were stitched together with the mercurial element.

"My Questing Beast. The dragons will have met their match with you and your Questlings."

On cue, a chorus of wails and bleats erupted from a room in another section of Merlin's caves where the Questlings were kept. All together there were one hundred creatures just like the Questing Beast in every way but size.

The worlds had not seen a creature such as this since the days of Arthur the First. But this beast was different from that medieval monster. In addition to its increased size, Merlin had outfitted it with a set of massive wings identical to those found on a magnificent Argentine bird. This Questing Beast could fly. Best of all, at the back of the creature's mouth, there was a small tube that curled into its throat, through its sinuses, and into its ear canal. Plugged into its ears were little receptors that were sensitive not just to sound but also to Merlin's spellcasting. At his choosing, Merlin could channel any magic through the creature's head and out of its mouth. It was like having a dragon with unlimited breath attacks. Fire, ice, poison, acid, slime, mud, bees, snowflakes, odors—the attack was only limited by Merlin's imagination and his ability, the latter of which had no limits, not now, not since he'd reached full strength.

Fifty of the little Questlings had similar contraptions built into their heads.

All together they would be unstoppable. "Bring your dragons, King," Merlin cooed. "I have them beat." Then Merlin thrust his owl-headed cane to the ceiling. "Up, pet!"

The Questing Beast gathered its haunches and peeled its wings from its body. As it took off, Merlin grabbed a hind leg. Up it went. Spry as a cat, Merlin climbed onto the Beast's rear end. He worked his way over its back and dug his fingers into the leopard fur at its midsection. "There!" he pronounced, indicating an opening in a crisscross of leather and rope strung across the chamber. The Questing Beast flew for it and threaded its long neck through the opening. The straps and ties met its skin and drew tight. At the apex of this arrangement was a simple leather saddle with a high horn, shiny and smooth as if it had been ridden for years. Merlin waved his cane left then right, and the straps wrapped around the neck and behind the front legs and buckled themselves. Merlin jumped into the saddle and effortlessly slipped his feet into the stirrups. Blunt metal spurs extended from his heels like claws. He kicked the creature so hard he drew blood. "Go!" Merlin shouted, pointing the cane toward the heavens. The creature bellowed and beat its wings and pulled into the sky, rain pelting Beast and rider.

Merlin deposited his cane in a sheath at his ankle so that it stood upright and at the ready. He grabbed the saddle horn with both hands and guided the creature toward the field tent that fluttered in the sea-borne wind.

They reached it in seconds, and the Beast pulled up and settled on the ground.

The tent—the same gray color as sky and sea—was shaped like a circus big top and was three hundred feet across. Its flaps were closed. Merlin knew it was full, but no sound came from within.

He pulled the cane from its holster and swiped it through the air. The flaps flew open. It was very dark inside. Little glints and round silhouettes could be seen here and there, but nothing was clear.

"Food," he called. A shuffling from within as two human figures came into view. They were each about four feet tall and skinny but covered in chain armor from head to ankle. On the feet of the smaller one—a girl—were pink-and-purple sneakers; while the other—a boy—wore scuffed Vans. A thin sword hung from the girl's waist, and a mace nearly as long as the boy's leg hung from his belt. They walked side by side, together holding something.

"Like Artie and Kay, a brother and a sister. Beast, I give you Henry and Maggie Marks."

The Marks children stepped into the light. Maggie was eight or nine, and Henry was a couple of years older. They had fair skin and light hair and big, empty eyes.

They did not speak. They held out their hands, which contained a rope. The rope led into the darkness of the tent.

"Food," Merlin repeated.

The Questing Beast lowered its head, but the children, who appeared not to be aware of the hellish thing leaning over them, didn't so much as budge. The snake head unhinged its jaw. Its fangs dripped. The tongue darted from its mouth and slipped over the crown of Henry's head. It got closer and closer to the children. Its foul breath puffed visibly on the cool air.

"Now, now, pet," Merlin said. "You know they're not for you."

Henry and Maggie raised the rope higher. With lightning quickness the snake head stabbed down and came back up, the strand in its mouth.

The children still stood there, completely unfazed.

The Beast sucked the rope into its mouth like spaghetti. It ran limply over Maggie's shoulder before drawing tight. When it did, a squeal came from inside the tent. The Beast kept sucking. The thing at the other end came into view. It was a pig, fat and round, stolen from a nearby farm. The animal strained to get away from the monster pulling it closer, but it was useless.

The poor creature wedged between Henry and Maggie and pushed them apart. It cried loudly now, aware of what was happening, and young Henry seemed to take a flicker of notice. His eyes widened when the pig finally reached the lips of the snake head. The Questing Beast bit down, impaling its prey with its long fangs. The pig stopped moving. The Questing Beast tilted its head back and in three gulps swallowed its meal whole.

At this, Henry let out a small yelp, but Merlin chanted a low incantation and the boy's arms fell limply back to his sides. Maggie, still oblivious, didn't make a peep. The color faded from Henry's face and his eyes once more took on the blank stare that he'd worn when the Marks siblings exited the tent.

Henry and Maggie turned in unison and scuffed back inside.

With a loud series of cracks, the meal slid through the snake's neck and passed into the cat portion of the Questing Beast, directly beneath Merlin's saddle. The wizard grinned.

"Surprises, Artie, surprises." He looked to the southeast. In the distance was the form of a great bird, made of clouds. In its talons Merlin could see the green dot that was Sir Bercilak. "And like I said—no more games."

𝕿eam 𝕲rail tumbled into 𝕿intagel's yard in a heap, Numinae heavily and uncomfortably landing on top.

"Bercilak! Why Bercilak?" Kay whined as she and the others pulled out of the pile.

"Better him than the king," Bedevere observed.

"Well obviously, but—omigod! The backpack!" Kay spun in a circle. "Artie, the backpack!"

"This backpack?" Artie said with a grin. He sat on the ground, the bag between his legs, his arm in it all the way to the shoulder. "There you are!" He pulled out the Grail and let it fall in his lap.

Kay dropped to her knees. "Man—we did it, didn't

we?" Artie nodded, a big smile on his face. "But we need to save Berc—"

"He'll be fine," Artie said, cutting Kay off. "Merlin chose him on purpose."

"Yes," Numinae said. "The wizard is sly."

"What are you talking about?" Bedevere asked.

"Bercilak is a knight of Sylvan, Sir Kay," Numinae explained. "And since I am the lord of Sylvan, he and I are connected. Wherever Bercilak goes, I will be able to find him—even on your side."

"Merlin *wants* us to find him, doesn't he?" Kay asked unenthusiastically.

"Aye, lass."

"The others!" Bedevere said, pointing at the main building of Tintagel.

"Artie! Kay! You're back," Qwon called, running full tilt, Dred right behind her.

Artie waved as Kay slung the backpack over her shoulders. The two groups rushed toward each other, and as they did, Artie noticed the dragons. Six were perched along the walls, looking down on the knights like uncaring statues. There was Tiberius; another green dragon from Sylvan; the silver one, Darg; a black one, Snoll, plus a blue one and a white one.

The sight of the dragons pumped Artie up, but it also

made him a little more scared. Things were coming to a head. They had the Grail, the dragons were here, and the others had made it back from Turkey—presumably with the Sword of David.

Which, of course, they had. Everyone was safe, and most of them were there—although Shallot had gone to Leagon with the golden dragon (making seven total) to gather the fairy platoon. To make up for her absence, Erik had returned with Sami, and when Artie saw the giant Swede, he gave him a huge hug.

"I was wondering when you'd call," Sami said. "This outfit needs a big man like me."

Artie laughed. "We've been fine without you, actually. But Merlin—we'll definitely need you when we go up against him and his minions."

"Can't wait."

Kay tiptoed over. "Sorry to interrupt, but I was wondering . . . Artie, should we—"

"Dad."

"Yeah. Dad."

The Kingfishers turned toward the pair of black stones in the middle of the yard.

"Should we do it now?" Artie asked, his gut churning with sudden nerves.

"I think we should."

"You *absolutely* should," Sami said, eyeing the plain cup

that Artie casually held. "No reason not to."

Numinae appeared next to Sami and placed a hand on Artie's shoulder. "I agree. The Grail is here. It should be used."

Artie turned to the group. "Everyone, please." The hubbub of storytelling and catching up subsided. "We're going to revive Kynder—now. There'd be no better way to celebrate getting the Grail and the Sword of David."

A hush fell over the group. Even the dragons became more solemn.

"Dred, you're the Pure Knight, and you need to be the one to do it," Artie said, holding out the Grail. "Are you up to it?"

Dred swallowed hard, conveying some trepidation. Artie understood—if for some reason it didn't work, Dred might blame himself, which would be a terrible thing. Still, Dred said resolutely, "Of course I am, Artie."

"Then let's do this."

Artie and Kay led everyone to the stones. As they walked, Artie gave Kay a warm smile. But she did not smile back. "Artie, I'm so . . . scared."

"Me too." He squeezed her hand. "It'll be fine." And for maybe the first time in his life, Artie Kingfisher felt like he had helped his sister Kay, who was always so strong, to be stronger.

It felt awesome.

Tiberius came down from his perch and landed on the far side, while Numinae, Thumb, and Dred joined Artie and Kay next to the rocks. The others kept some distance, arranging themselves in a semicircle. Qwon held on to one of Pammy's hands with both of hers, as if she would fall over otherwise. She had begun to cry.

Artie handed the Grail to Dred, who looked most nervous of all.

Numinae knelt. "Do not fret. This is going to work. It has to."

"You got that right," Kay said, immediately trying to guard her emotions.

Artie squeezed her hand again. "It's okay. Everyone here is family."

It was true. They'd been through so much together. *Too* much. Kay stood frozen for a few seconds and then did the most improbable thing ever: Kay Kingfisher started to bawl.

Everyone was shocked. Artie wrapped her in a hug. Fighting through his own tears, he whispered over and over, "It's going to work."

Finally Kay stopped and they pulled apart. "We're ready," Artie said. "Are you?"

Dred held out the Grail. "Yes."

Artie looked at his dragon. "Do your thing, Tiberius."

"Hmmph. As you wish, lord kingling." Tiberius stooped over Kynder and began to lick the rock away. After several minutes Kynder's body revealed itself in bits and pieces. Numinae stepped forward, cradling Kynder's listless head. Tiberius kept working. A few minutes more, and Kynder Kingfisher was there, on the ground, just as he had been in Fenland: his leg broken, his skin ashen, his breath nonexistent.

Numinae ran a huge hand over Kynder's head. "Now, Sir Mordred. Artie, bring Excalibur's scabbard."

The twins stepped forward and the other dragons began to hum eerily. Artie pulled Excalibur from its scabbard. The steel hissed. He handed the leather sheath to Numinae as Dred held the Grail directly over Kynder. Numinae put the scabbard on Kynder's leg and then reached down, repositioning the broken limb, pushing the bone back into place with a gnarly snap.

One minute passed. Two. Two and a half.

Kay fidgeted. "What's hap—"

"Sh!" Thumb hissed, grabbing Kay's hand.

The dragons' humming grew louder, and a flock of small dark birds burst into the sky beyond the castle wall.

Three minutes. Three and half. Four.

Dred looked inside the Grail. It was still empty. Dred shook his head slowly.

Artie stared at Kynder's unseeing eyes. It wasn't working. Frustrated and scared, Artie said, "It's me, Dad—it's Arthur."

The dragons went suddenly silent.

"There!" Numinae whispered.

Dred leaned over the Grail. A few drops of red liquid—blood? wine? cranberry juice?—seeped from the bottom of the cup. Then, very quickly, it filled.

"Give it to him, Dred!" Numinae implored.

Dred and Artie knelt at the same time, like mirror images. Artie parted Kynder's lips, and Dred tipped the Grail. The liquid poured in, filling Kynder's mouth. Artie stroked his dad's hair. Kay fell next to him and grabbed Kynder's hand.

And then his body seized. It shook so violently that Artie, Kay, and Dred had to hold it down. Numinae slipped one of his long wooden fingers between Kynder's teeth so that he wouldn't bite his tongue off. Kynder foamed at the mouth; his eyes shot open; his voice returned in a harsh rattle.

"Come back to us, Dad. Come back!" Kay begged through tears.

"It's me, Dad. Your son."

Then Kynder's body froze and went completely limp. Artie and Kay ran their hands desperately over his face and body. There was no breath, no life. Dred stood, full of fear and shame, the Grail slowly slipping from his fingers. "I . . . I . . . ," he stammered.

The Grail fell to the ground. When it hit, a great sound

rang over Tintagel, like a huge church bell had been struck.

Kynder's mouth opened wide as he inhaled fully. His pupils contracted and his hands gripped those of his two children. His chest began to rise and fall, and his skin filled with living color.

"Dad!" Artie and Kay yelled. Numinae pressed the scabbard hard onto Kynder's leg wound. Blood flowed from it for a few seconds before the skin and muscles magically closed and reformed around the exposed bone.

Kynder's kids fell forward, and the three of them locked in a tight embrace. Dred jumped up and down and pumped his fist. Pammy and Qwon ran forward, followed by all the others. When Pammy got there, she dropped to her knees, pushed Numinae out of the way, and grabbed Kynder's head. She stroked his hair and planted a huge kiss on his forehead.

Lance, Bedevere, Erik, and Sami stood abreast, their arms thrown over the next man's shoulder. They laughed and cried all at once, without a dry eye among them. Sami got so caught up that he squeezed Erik's shoulder a little too hard, and Erik had to remind him not to crush his arm.

Kynder's eyes darted over the group before landing back on his children. "How long . . . Who . . . What . . . Where's Merlin?"

Artie said, "Merlin's not here, Dad. You're safe."

Kynder nudged his kids off his chest. He was equal

parts happy and confused and desperate. "Arthur—I have to tell you something. I realized it right before I . . . I . . . Did I die?"

"Almost, my friend," Numinae said. "But Tiberius preserved you. It nearly killed him, too."

Kynder's gaze swept the yard. "Thank you, Tiberius."

"Hmmmph. My pleasure to've done it. Thanks be to the kingling for calling me back."

Then Kynder sat bolt upright, as if stricken by something. "Arthur—you have to confront Merlin."

"I know, Dad. We're going to. Tomorrow. We had to bring you back first."

"He's half devil, Son."

"We know."

"And Excalibur—"

"We know, Dad," Artie said. "Excalibur wants to kill him. And I have to be the one to do it."

Kynder shook his head. "No, Artie. Not exactly. The sword doesn't want to kill him. It wants to *free* him."

The knights stared at Kynder with wild eyes.

"You have to cut the devil out of him, Artie. You must save Merlin—from himself!"

Artie frowned and let his fingers rest on Excalibur. The sangrealitic metal of the blade buzzed at his fingertips, as if to verify Kynder's words.

"Of course!" Thumb yelped. "Why couldn't I see that?"

"He enchanted all of us," Kynder said.

There was a moment of silence, and then Numinae took Kynder and, with Artie, helped him to his feet. The other knights welcomed Kynder back, giving him hugs and handshakes and a few more kisses. Finally, Kynder looked to Artie and said, "Arthur, not to ruin the mood, but I'm starving."

Artie laughed out loud. "I am too, Dad. Come on, everyone, let's eat."

IN WHICH ARTIE DONS HIS TRICKSTER CAP

𝕭ran had gone all out and made quite possibly the best platter of mac and cheese in the history of mac and cheeses. It was smooth and buttery on the inside, flaky on top, and crunchy at the edges where the cheese and pasta pushed against the roasting pan. For dessert each got a custom-made ice-cream sundae. Most were typical flavors—chocolate, vanilla, butterscotch, strawberry— but Numinae's was green and brown and sprinkled with dirt and leaves. "Whatever floats your boat," Kay said as the forest lord dug in.

As they ate, they told each other the gritty details of retrieving the Sword of David and the Grail. Since Team Sword had gotten to Tintagel first, and since they were super anxious waiting for Team Grail to arrive, they had busied themselves.

Along with Shallot going to Leagon on the newest golden dragon, Dred had taken the black dragon, Snoll, to Castel Deorc Wæters to gather some war bears and dragon-flies. He did all right on the insects—he got a contingent of 143—but he could find only a dozen able bears. Tiberius had done a similar thing in Sylvan, rounding up two packs of dire wolves and three saber-toothed cats, including Bedevere's. All of these groups were ready, and they would take moongates opened by Artie directly to Tintagel, where everyone would muster before heading off to Wales.

Naturally, they were thrilled that things were going so well.

After dessert came tea, coffee, and an endless supply of Mountain Dew. While the knights drank, Dred went to the far side of the room and showed off the Sword of David, forbidding anyone else to even come near him. "It works," Lance confirmed. "It works *really* fast." They toasted the poor guard who'd had the misfortune of pulling it from the scabbard, and Artie promised that he would not have died in vain. Kay wondered if it would work as quickly on Merlin, and Numinae answered, "Doubtful, because his magic is so strong. But it will compromise him. All we have to do is convince him that it's Excalibur."

"But how?" Sami asked. "If he's as powerful as you say he is, won't he know what we're up to?"

Artie's palms went clammy as he said, "You're right, Sami. He might figure it out. We just have to hope he doesn't. As to how—this is how." Artie was nervous because he knew that Merlin had done something to Erik, something that, Artie guessed, enabled Merlin to see or hear whatever Erik did. And now it was crucial that Merlin heard what Artie was about to say. Everything hinged on it—it was essential.

"Merlin will expect me to have Excalibur, the sword he wants more than anything. We have to fight and really try to beat him, but if we can't, then eventually we should surrender."

"*What?*" a few of the knights asked together.

"Arthur," Kynder said, leaning forward. "I don't think that's a good idea."

Artie held up his hands. "I know it doesn't sound smart, Dad. I saw what he did to you on that beach, but hear me out. If we surrender, then Merlin will want to speak to me. He's too much of a jerk to just kill me. He'll want to say something all evil-wizardy, rub defeat in my face and all that. Trust me. I know how bullies operate."

"Artie," Lance said, "I think your dad's probably right."

Artie took a sip of black coffee. "Let me finish, Lance. So as a last resort we surrender, and Merlin and I, we'll be close to each other. Merlin will take my sword, thinking it's Excalibur, and try to cut my head off with it." A chorus of startled breaths went around the table. "Wait—think about it: there are a million ways for him to kill me, but what better way than to do it with my own sword? It's—what do you call it—poetic justice, right?"

"Or irony, lad," Thumb said glumly.

"Right, or that. But here's the thing: it won't be Excalibur! It'll be the Sword of David, disguised to look just like Excalibur. I'll have it strapped to my back in battle just for show, but I won't use it." Artie's hands were shaking now, and he slid them under the table to hide his nervousness. Erik, and Merlin, who was using him, had to understand this point perfectly. If not, the whole plan would fail.

Kay, who was one of three who knew about the traitor, even though she was still ignorant as to *who* was the traitor, leaned forward. "Artie, that's crazy. If you don't fight with Excalibur, then that means no scabbard—and no scabbard means no healing power! You're going to go into a full-on boss battle without that? Would you ever do something so stupid in *Otherworld* the video game?"

Artie shook his head. "Of course I wouldn't. But this isn't a video game, Kay." Artie realized in that moment that truer words had never been spoken. "None of *you* have a scabbard like Excalibur's. It's not fair to you guys if I can get healed on the spot. You're putting your necks on the line too."

"Yes, lad. But you're the king!" Thumb protested.

Kay threw up her hands. "Artie, this is stupid."

Artie planted his hands on the table. "It isn't. Once Merlin draws my sword—the one he thinks is Excalibur but is actually the Sword of David—he'll be weak. He'll strike out for me, and then, at the last minute, I'll hit him with Carnwennan, which I'll hide in my sleeve. This won't kill him, of course. Only Excalibur can do that. So at that moment, Numinae will bring me my sword, which he will hold safe for the entire battle, and together Excalibur and I will free Merlin. Just like you said, Dad."

There was a silence. "It sounds like a good plan," Erik said. It was the first thing Artie could recall him saying all evening.

"Thanks, Erik," Artie said, his heart racing. "Dred, Numinae—will you work on disguising the sword tonight?"

"Gladly, Brother," Dred said, uneasy about the whole idea.

"Yes, sire. We will do an incomparable job of it."

"I still don't like it," Kay said, playing along a little to help sell this idea to the traitor. "I mean, maybe I'm being the protective big sister and all, but it sounds crazy risky. Outside of the fact that he's been stealing kids, and mashing sabertooths with rhinos, we have no idea what Merlin is planning."

Artie stood. "Maybe not, but it's all been moving to this moment. All of it, from the very beginning, even before Dred and I were born." Which was true. Artie understood now that while he was a king, and a boy, he was also a cog in the machine of fate. They all were. Even Merlin. "We'll find out what Merlin has planned soon enough—just as *he* will find out what *we* have planned for him. He told us: no more games, and he's right. We're not playing anymore." Artie paused. "Now, if you don't mind my giving an order: except for Dred and Numinae, I need all of you to go get some sleep. Tomorrow morning, at seven sharp, we gather the troops—and then, we go to war."

𝕶𝖞𝖓𝖉𝖊𝖗 𝖈𝖆𝖒𝖊 𝖙𝖔 𝕬𝖗𝖙𝖎𝖊'𝖘 𝖗𝖔𝖔𝖒 that night, intending to talk him out of the surrender plan. But Artie told Kynder everything—even that the unfortunate and unwitting traitor was Erik—and Kynder left feeling that maybe Artie was right. If Merlin had somehow used Erik to spy on their strategy session, then Artie had a chance. "Besides," Artie added as Kynder left the room, "I think we can beat him. Remember, we have the dragons on our side. That's not nothing, you know?"

"Yes, but even dragons can be killed," Kynder said, and then left.

The next morning was bright and crisp. Artie went outside extra early, greeted the dragons, and wasted no time: he opened a gate to Leagon, and one to Fenland, and one to Sylvan, and King Artie's army poured into the court-yard at Tintagel. Here came the bears; the dragonflies; the wolves; the saber-toothed tigers; and Shallot, with Chime, the golden dragon, at the head of a line of thirty fairies. As the forces arrived, the dragons took off and turned a multicolored wheel in the sky. The other knights arrived, and Artie assigned tasks to everyone: Kay briefed the fair-ies; Sami took charge of the war bears; Dred managed the dragonflies; Thumb, mounted on a new dog-size bunny from Sylvan, rallied the wolves; Bedevere attended to the sabertooths; and Lance and Erik handed out the last pieces of armor to whoever needed them.

While this happened, Artie consulted with Numinae, Pammy, and Kynder, pinpointing Bercilak's—and there-fore Merlin's—location in Wales. Then Artie opened three huge moongates onto a Welsh bluff a mile south of the place called St. David's Head, taking care to hide them in a depression. Artie dispatched Sami, three bears, and the blue dragon, called Azur, to keep watch. If Merlin showed any sign of an ambush, they would report back and everyone would spill through to fight.

So far, though, the coast had stayed clear.

During the night, Numinae and Dred had labored tirelessly to disguise the Sword of David, which had not been a walk in the park. Since it was going to stay sheathed until the last minute, they worked hard on the hilt. Dred stripped the Sword of David down to the tang and built the hilt back up to look just like Excalibur's, and were lucky enough to get a glass bauble from Bran that looked exactly like Excalibur's pommel stone. They then went to work on the scabbard, which wasn't too hard to deal with: both were worn and unadorned and made of ancient leather; the Sword of David's just needed a few tweaks here and there to make it convincing. When they were finished, the sheathed swords were dead ringers.

Artie was talking quietly with a group of knights when Numinae approached, holding out the blades he would carry.

"Here you are, sire. Avoid all temptation to draw it in battle."

Artie took the Sword of David and slung it over his shoulder. "Don't worry. I don't want to die from stupidity."

Kay and Erik laughed. "No way," Erik said. "You wouldn't want the kids at school to learn that's how you went down."

Kay punched Erik. "Ha! School. That's a good one, Erikssen."

"What? We *are* going back there, right?"

Artie clapped his friend on the shoulder. "Yes. We are. We're fighting for a lot of things today, but that's a big one. In my book, anyway."

"Sweet," Erik said. He turned to the lord of Sylvan

and, nodding at the sword in Numinae's hands said, "Keep Excalibur safe, Numinae."

"I will, Sir Berserker." And then Numinae repeated the painful-looking trick of pushing the sword—sheath and all—into his leg, leaving the hilt and pommel exposed just above his hip. "Just in case," Numinae said with a wink.

Artie scanned the yard. "Guys!" he announced, his voice sounding deeper than he ever remembered. The army came to attention. "Dragons!" He yelled into the sky, and all of them stopped cruising and pulled into low-altitude hovers. He thought of all the comics he'd read, all the heavy-handed stories in RPG video games, even a bunch of his favorite books. He was about to give a speech, and it had to be a good one.

"Thanks for coming to Avalon! It's an honor to have you here. We've been through a lot to get to this point. Some of us have been enemies"—he eyed the wolves and drag-onflies and war bears—"others have always been friends. Now we will be united in war! Now we have to fight Merlin Ambrosius!"

A general roar of fury at the wizard's name.

"We will stick to the plan. Expect anything! Numinae and the dragons will attempt to combat Merlin's magic, but don't count on it. He is treacherous! If at any time it looks to me like we cannot win, then we must give up so that I can get close to Merlin." He held up Scarffern.

"If I think we have to do this, I'll blow the whistle three times, and Numinae will send up a green flare—this is the signal of our surrender." The crowd grumbled. "But don't think of that now! Think of victory! As long as I live, and as long as I hold this"—he tapped the hilt of the Sword of David that peeked over his shoulder—"we *will* win! Remember, we're fighting not only to send Merlin packing, but for the fate of both sides of earth. For mine, which needs the clean energy that sangrealite can provide; and for the Otherworld, so that the sangrealite that Merlin has hoarded can be given back to you and your homelands— so that magic will not die! Now! Be ready! It is a good day for victory!" Since he couldn't draw the sword from his back, he yanked the cutlass, Flixith, from its sheath and shook it overhead.

The knights yelled out, and the soldiers rattled their weapons, and the creatures lowed and growled, and the dragons flapped their wings in support. Kynder and Pammy clung to each other, staring with a mix of pride and worry at Artie and Kay and Qwon. Both of the parents were staying in Tintagel, and it was clear from the looks on their faces that they wished that their kids were, too.

Artie stood high on his toes. "I *said*—IT IS A GOOD DAY FOR VICTORY!"

And the crowd went wild. Artie beamed; his heart filled; his eyes welled. Kay stepped next to him, Cleomede shining in the morning light. "You've come a long way, Art."

"I know." Together they looked at Kynder.

"I love you," their father said loudly, tears in his eyes. "Now go get that wizard. Make his evil side pay for what he did to me—for what he did to us all."

𝕎𝕒𝕝𝕖𝕤 𝕨𝕒𝕤 𝕔𝕠𝕝𝕕 𝕒𝕟𝕕 𝕝𝕒𝕤𝕙𝕖𝕕 with freezing rain. A stiff wind blew in from the sea, taking their breaths away if they faced it. The clouds were low and dark and spun in a vortex whose center was off to the northwest. Artie's army gathered in a stretch of open field between a footpath and a low ridge of bald, pockmarked rocks. To the south were emerald sections of farmland; to the east the craggy outlook called Carn Llidi. A mile to the west, past a shallow valley and over a thin stream, was the stony peninsula of St. David's Head. The land between was open and overgrown with purple scrub brush and green-and-brown grass. Lichen-covered rocks of all sizes—from pebbles to rough slabs as big as school buses—were littered everywhere.

It was harsh but also beautiful. Too bad it was going to be marred by battle in about thirty minutes.

Artie took Kay, Numinae, Thumb, Dred, and Lance to an outcropping to survey the field. Tiberius followed, sauntering along on all fours, careful to keep his head and body as low to the ground as possible.

"Specs," Artie said, lying on his stomach in the grass.

"You talking to me, Your Royalness?" Kay asked.

"Uh, yeah—the binoculars, please."

Kay rummaged in the backpack. She passed out three pairs of binoculars and kept a fourth pair for herself.

They scanned the countryside. Over Merlin's field tent were about a hundred dark, winged creatures turning in the air.

"You guys see Merlin?" Kay asked.

Lance shook his head. "Could be in that tent."

Artie clicked his tongue. "I doubt it. My bet is that whatever nasty army we're about to go up against is in there. Probably a bunch of hybrid animals that have been snacking on the kids he stole."

It was a gruesome image that no one wanted to entertain. "Speaking of nasties—what are those things in the sky?" Kay asked.

"I can't be sure," Numinae said a little ominously. "But they appear to be—"

"Hmmmph. Questlings. The wizard has made Quest-lings."

Kay looked back at Tiberius, whose eyes were darting all around, looking for signs. "I kinda don't want to ask, but what's a Questling?"

"The Questing Beast was a mythical creature from the old days, Sir Kay," Thumb said. "Head of a snake, mid-section of a leopard, hind section of a stag."

"That doesn't sound so bad," Kay said.

"None of those animals have wings, though, Tom," Lance observed.

"No, lad. Merlin must have added them. And it *was* bad, Kay. It was a magical thing that was nearly impossible to take down—or so the rumor went. Not many ever fought the Questing Beast, though many searched for it."

"Hence the name," Artie observed, lowering his binocu-lars.

Before Thumb could respond, Numinae exclaimed, "There!" and pointed across the plain.

The others followed Numinae's finger, bringing their binoculars back to their faces. It took a few seconds to find what he was pointing at, but then they saw it. Bercilak. He had been divided into two sections, which hung on two tall wooden posts twenty feet apart. The arms of his top half and the legs of his bottom half kicked and whirled in pain or protest.

several moments in the clouds before reappearing a few hundred yards away. He hovered over the plain and let out a spine-tingling roar that sounded like a car crash. Black smoke sprayed from his mouth and resolved into little pebbles that pelted the huge tent. The Questlings were tossed into a frenzy and flapped wildly before drawing into a line over the tent.

The swirling clouds crackled with lightning, which was followed immediately by claps of thunder. "He's in the clouds, Brother," Dred shouted.

"No more games!" Artie screamed. "Do you hear me, Merlin? I am the Dragon King! No. More. Games!"

A hearty laugh boomed from the sky above.

The other green dragon, Aquilia; the silver one, Darg; and the white, Smila, shot into the air to join Tiberius. The dragonflies buzzed out of the depression where Artie's army had gathered, their wings making a noise like a thousand pieces of paper being torn at once. And then Artie's impressive and motley army moved out. They were over two hundred strong, not counting the seven dragons, which counted as a hundred soldiers or more each. Chime and Snoll marched with the ground forces, keeping the formation tight. Behind the dragonflies, Artie walked at the head of his battalion, a general and a king.

This was it. This was the beginning of the end.

𝕿𝖍𝖊 𝖘𝖔𝖚𝖓𝖉𝖘 𝖔𝖋 𝖙𝖍𝖊 𝖆𝖉𝖛𝖆𝖓𝖈𝖊 were intoxicating. The snorts and huffs of bears. The howls and whines of dire wolves. The roars of tigers. The march of feet. The swish of clothing. The jangle of armor. The staticky hiss of rain across the field.

Artie smiled, and Kay did too. "This would be really awesome if it wasn't so freaking scary!" Kay blurted.

"It's awesome *because* it's scary, Kay!" Artie said.

As Artie's forces covered the first hundred yards, Tiberius and Aquilia took turns spraying the ground with their breaths, creating short walls for cover here and there. Smila and Darg made circles around each other, waiting for something to happen.

And for a little while, nothing did.

But then, as the ground forces crossed a small stream, half of the Questlings burst forward, and as many dragonflies launched up to meet them.

The dragonflies used their powerful mouths to snap off the wings of several Questlings, sending them hurtling to the ground, but the advantage did not hold. Merlin's strange creatures used the hooves of their hind legs to kick holes in the dragonflies' exoskeletons, and the claws on their forepaws to tear into the papery wings, and their long snake necks to wrap up the bugs' abdomens and crush them like fruit. For a time the fight seemed even, but then three of the Questlings did something unexpected. They broke above the melee and began to breathe a white mist over it. The Questlings were immune to whatever this was, but the dragonflies definitely were not. Their very bodies began to disintegrate, falling to the ground in slimy chunks.

Smila and Darg flew in. They were also immune to this mist and they succeeded in taking out several of Merlin's beasts, either eating them whole or downing them with their breath attacks—a stream of ice and frost from Smila, and one of jagged stones the size of baseballs from Darg—but the majority of the Questlings broke back to their ranks, which still hovered over the tent.

Artie's army was much closer to Bercilak's two halves now, and Artie yelled, "Numinae, get Greenie off those posts!"

Tiberius took off, and as he drew close, Numinae rose in the saddle and shot two jolts of green at Bercilak. His lower half hit the ground running, making its way to the upper half, which lay on its back, its fingers twiddling wildly. When the legs reached the torso, they fell over, and Bercilak's hands grabbed his hips and pulled his body, such as it was, back together. The knights couldn't see any of this, but they could see a green flash of light in the brush, and then a few seconds later Bercilak was up and running toward them, waving his arms like a madman.

"Is he trying to call us off?" Dred asked.

Artie frowned. "I don't know."

Before they could reach Bercilak, though, the Questlings screeched all at once, and the tent flaps flew open. Artie and the knights could see nothing but blackness inside. But then a dozen very large sabertooth/rhinos, like the one they'd fought in the Kingfisher house, bolted out of the tent and ran full tilt down the slope. Three of them had riders, but the animals were so fast, and their stride so violent, that these riders flopped along more like dolls than soldiers.

"Sami, Erik—go and meet them!"

Sami, who rode the largest bear, kicked his animal. It bolted forward at full speed, followed by six more bears. Erik jumped into a frenzy and grabbed the scruff of a large wolf as it took off, leading a pack of five lupines. Together, the wolves and bears broke through the wall of dragonflies, and made headlong for the onrushing sabertooth/rhinos.

"Double time!" Artie commanded, and the whole of his army stepped faster.

"Show yourself, Merlin!" Artie cried to the heavens, but there was still no sign of the wizard.

And then a light flashed on the far side of the plain, up high on St. David's Head, forcing the knights and creatures to close their eyes momentarily. When they reopened them, the tent was gone, and finally, they saw what they were about to tangle with.

It was an army easily four times larger than theirs, organized into tight squares of foot soldiers. In between the lines of pikemen and swordsmen were columns of more sabertooth/rhinos.

"There're a lot of them, lad!" Thumb said.

"Sure are," Lance added. "But at least they don't look that big."

It was true. It was hard to tell at this distance, but the human part of Merlin's army didn't appear to be all that horrifying. The animals and the Questlings certainly were, but the soldiers just . . . weren't.

It was at this moment that Bercilak came within earshot, yelling, "Sire, sire, sire!"

"Oh no," Qwon said, as she peered into the mass of people they were about to engage.

"They're children, sire! The wizard has enslaved an army of children!"

Artie's heart sank as he raised the binoculars to his face. Bercilak was right. Artie scanned as many faces as he could, and all of them belonged to zombified boys and girls his age or even younger.

"We're about to face a bunch of *Otherworld* gamers!" he yelped in disbelief.

"You're joking. That's an army of Dr Pepper heads?" Kay asked.

"Yes," Artie said. "Bercy, head to the moongates, near that blue dragon. Help her guard our flank, and find a weapon."

"Yes, sire. Thank you for coming for me, sire. The wizard is—"

"Don't mention it. Now go!"

Bercilak took off for the moongates. Artie turned his attention back to the battlefield and saw Sami and Erik fighting the sabertooth/rhinos. Sami jumped from his bear and skidded into the ground, punching two of Merlin's creatures square in the nose and sending them soaring, their faces crushed. Erik launched from his wolf and flew into an immediate rage, and pieces of tiger and rhino went flying too. The bears and the wolves attacked ravenously.

Their teeth flashed and their hides shook as they went about taking down their much larger but slower adversaries. The second skirmish of the day would belong to Artie and his knights.

In the breakaway group of sabertooth/rhinos, Artie could just make out the three riders who he now knew to be children. Their movements were clumsy but harsh as they swung great swords and spears in all directions. Sami disarmed two, and another got caught in Erik's rage before cartwheeling out of the melee.

"Don't hurt them!" Artie yelled.

"*What?*" Shallot asked. "How are we supposed to fight?"

"Numinae! Relay the message!" Artie shouted. "These guys cannot be hurt! Anyone who kills or seriously hurts one of these kids will have to answer to me personally! We are responsible for them, do you understand?"

"Yes, sire," Numinae hollered, and then he and Tiberius moved out to spread the order.

Just then, Merlin's army let out a war cry and broke into a dead sprint.

"Smash it!" Shallot said in protest.

"The animals, the Questlings, and Merlin are fair game," Artie shouted. "Immobilize the children, but, I repeat, do not hurt them! They're just innocent kids!"

"Fairies, come," Shallot barked, running to Chime and vaulting into the saddle strapped to her neck. "Take the wolves and meet these poor souls. Full-up scentlocks! Nothing moves! All animals die! Go!"

Before Chime could make a break for it, Kay jumped behind Shallot and wrapped an arm around the fairy's ultra-slim waist. Shallot gave Kay a hard look, but Kay didn't care.

"Don't worry, sister. I'm going to stuff my nose good. Scentlock away. Now let's fight!"

Shallot cooed at Chime, and the golden dragon, which was by far the most beautiful of all the dragons, spread its slender wings and glided into the air.

Qwon and Dred fell in close to Artie and jogged up the incline. Sami and Erik had regrouped with the bears and wolves and ran across the field to meet the others. When Tiberius and Numinae were done informing everyone not to hurt the children, they broke toward the front line, Aquilia joining them. As soon as they got in range, the two green dragons sprayed the kids with their black smoke-rock breath, freezing them in basalt midadvance. These children would be fine. The rock breath didn't even hurt, and being frozen had the added benefit of protecting the kids from whatever craziness might happen once Merlin showed up. Smila and Darg, their attacks more purely offensive, refused to engage the children at all, and darted forward to meet the Questlings.

The black dragon snorted and reared fifty feet to Artie's

left, plainly eager to join the fight. "Stay with us, Snoll. We're going to need your strength!"

And then the two armies crashed together.

The sounds of marching and lashing rain and wind were gone, replaced with steel on steel and tooth on tooth and claw on claw. Qwon raised Kusanagi and slapped away sword after sword, knocking several children onto their backs with the blunt end of her katana. When she reached a little clearing in the action, she planted her feet and asked Kusanagi for wind, fierce and howling. The blade blew out and away, and she sprayed the kids and beasts with a gale, disabling scores in one fell swoop.

Dred planted his back against Qwon's, wielding the Peace Sword to disarm children and slice the legs off as many sabertooth/rhinos as he could.

Lance, riding high on a bear, shot arrow after arrow into the eyes of Merlin's creatures. Many died; many others were struck blind and sent into furies that set them on their fellow creatures. These were dangerous, as they posed a threat to the children, so Lance finished them off immediately. When he was greeted with lulls in the action, he placed flashbang arrows in the crowd, knocking some of the smaller kids unconscious and diverting animals toward Qwon's gale or a hovering dragon, which would pick the creatures up and tear them to pieces.

Near Lance, Bedevere and his own saber-toothed tiger

fought alongside a pair of Sylvanian she-wolves. Bedevere hadn't wasted any time activating his phantom arm. He used it freely to punch children this way and that, knocking them out cold on contact. With his real hand he expertly wielded his devastating claymore, slaying any animal that got too close to him. The she-wolves likewise concentrated on the creatures, slicing off noses and biting into necks.

The children, in spite of their zombie state, were decent fighters. It was not easy for the knights to exercise restraint in fending them off, but they tried their best. As for those who suffered an errant blow, or found themselves underfoot of a blind hybrid creature, Tiberius would freeze them in basalt, preserving their lives until the battle was over and they could get help.

After several minutes of frenzied fighting, Lance reached the bottom of this quiver. All he had left was an infinite arrow—which literally had Merlin's name on it, since Lance had whittled it into the shaft during the muster—and three fireballers. He looked over the battlefield. The fairies had driven a wedge into Merlin's ranks, leaving whole platoons frozen in strong scentlocks. Chime sprayed any Questling that got too close to her with her glitter breath, and the unlucky monstrosities disintegrated into showers of fairy dust that blew away on the wind. But the Questlings fought back. Around half seemed to possess breath attacks of their own, and these came in many different varieties. There were fire and ice and smoke, as anyone would expect, but also oil and spikes and thorns and shrapnel. Darg and Smila were trying to deal with these, but there were so many Questlings that it was difficult.

At one point, as these two dragons broke into the clouds to regroup, a flock of Questlings giving chase, Lance saw an opportunity. He pulled his bow back and called, "Snoll, light it up!" The black dragon swung its massive feathered head as Lance aimed his fireballer, and let it fly. When the arrow exploded among a group of breath-enabled Questlings, Snoll shot a huge ball of black oil at them. The sky detonated in oranges and yellows and blues. All of the Questlings in this area burned to a crisp, and fell wailing and dying. Several more also caught fire and began to whirl around in a panic, but the rush of air only fed the fire and made their burning worse. Snoll used these as targets for more oil balls, and when they hit, each Questling burst like a winged bomb overhead.

"Lance—there!" Artie yelled. Up the hill a few fairies were engaged with the two largest sabertooth/rhinos, each animal easily as big as a double-size elephant. Lance strung his penultimate fireballer and pulled the bow extra hard. The arrow raced over the field and went into the soft side of one of the creatures, stopping somewhere in its guts. A few seconds passed and then the thing just blew up, sending blood and skin and bone all over the place, and catching the other sabertooth/rhino off guard. This attack provided just enough time for the fairies nearby to gather themselves and finish it off.

After ten minutes of fighting this way—an eternity in close-range, hand-to-hand combat—Artie was able to take a break. He was covered in blood and sweat and grime. His body ached. The graphene shirt had taken more than twenty hits. His nose had been broken along with at least two ribs. "Thumb!" he called. The little man bounced here and there, checking on the well-being of felled children. "Have we won this round?"

Thumb stopped. "Aye, lad. We have."

There were still about a hundred children farther up the field, but the dragons and fairies had broken their ranks. Qwon's storm also was doing a lot of work, cutting a wide swath up the middle. Artie realized that Kusanagi was the most powerful of all the Seven Swords, Excalibur incuded. Not only was it simply an awesome sword, but this storm thing was the bomb.

As Artie thought this, Qwon let the storm go. It rose from the ground into the clouds and disappeared. As soon as it was off, she joined Dred to check on the hapless kids, helping those who needed assistance. Merlin's earthbound creatures, almost to the last, were either dead or maimed.

Wails of dying things echoed over the landscape as the drag-ons picked off whatever was left. Darg, the silver dragon, had suffered a cut on his wing, and he lumbered over the scrub and rocks spraying his breath where it was needed. Chime, too, had a bad gash along the length of her tail, and as she flew overhead, blood trailed from it like fuel leaking from a plane.

But all in all they were okay. So far, they *were* winning. Except . . .

"Where is Merlin, Tom?" Artie asked.

"I don't know, lad."

Artie had to find him. He ran toward the black dragon, a finger pointed to the sky. "Snoll! We're going up." The black dragon growled in anticipation. "Numinae, Tiberius—join us in the clouds!"

"Yes, sire!" Numinae leaned forward, and Tiberius bolted headfirst toward the vortex that swirled in the mid-dle distance.

Artie slid his fingers into the quills around Snoll's neck and pulled himself on. The dragon picked its head off the ground, and Artie held tight. He dug in his heels. Snoll let out his wings and launched upward.

The temperature dropped as soon as they gained some altitude. As they rose higher, Artie searched for Kay, who, with Shallot, rode Chime. When they saw each other, their eyes locked. Even at a distance of four hundred yards or more, they suddenly could feel each other and make out each other's faces as if they were only a few feet apart. Something about the rush of battle had restored their connection. There was no explaining it—it was simply magic.

Kay looked triumphant but confused. Artie knew that Kay thought Shallot was the traitor—that was why Kay had decided to stay close to the fairy. Artie wanted to tell her that she was wrong, but couldn't. Besides, there was still a chance that they could beat Merlin without resorting to Artie's risky surrender plan.

As Artie and Snoll passed out of view and into the gray cloud cover, he held up his hand, indicating that Kay, Shallot, and Chime should stay near the others. He hoped that they would.

Then, for a few seconds, grayness surrounded them before a large blot grew on their left, pressing through the mist. It was Numinae on Tiberius. The forest lord had a swirl of green energy in both hands, and his legs had melded with Tiberius's neck. They were as one. "Into the vortex, sire?"

"You know it!"

The dragons clicked at each other and bolted forward. Rain streaked their bodies and faces. The dark clouds spun in front of them, and then lit up as a crack of thunder rang out.

And then, the vortex stopped spinning, and the rain shut off, and the wind ceased to blow. Tiberius and Snoll came to a dead halt. A thousand feet away, the sky lightened.

There you are, Artie thought, his nerves tingling. Come and get me.

Artie expected the clouds to part, and to have Merlin appear before them riding some kind of conjured fiend.

Instead, a jolt of electricity surged between Snoll and Tiberius. The air smelled of ozone and singed flesh and hair as both dragons banked defensively. Numinae let his spell fly. Blindly it slammed into the clouds, and the sky lit up in greens and yellows. Snoll peeled through a barrel roll and when he'd righted himself, the air was clear. Clouds stretched as far as the eye could see below them, but above them visibility was unlimited.

And what they saw was not a welcome sight.

Artie yelled, "Is that a—?"

"Hmmph. A *real* Questing Beast, lord kingling."

The creature was like the Questlings but huge, and its

310

size made it about a hundred times more grotesque than the little ones. Its black-eyed gaze bore down on them, and its leopard claws pawed the air as its massive wings flapped up and down and up and down.

"Merlin!" Artie shouted.

"Child." His eyes were like fire, and even though his skin was covered in the sangrealitic ink, images crawled across it like writhing insect larvae.

Artie pulled Snoll's neck feathers, and the dragon darted forward, Tiberius immediately following. They snaked through the air, slaloming past each other. The Questing Beast just waited.

Smug wizard, Artie thought.

When he got in range, Snoll breathed a steady stream of oil at Merlin and his monster. But before it could do any damage, the Questing Beast unhinged its jaws and let out a jet of freezing-cold water; when the two liquids met, the oil broke into pellets and fell to the clouds below.

Water? Artie thought. Why would we be scared of water? Snoll strafed the Beast, trying to gouge its side with sharp hind claws, but the Beast slid away and kicked at Snoll with its stag hooves. Rib bones cracked under Snoll's left wing, and the black dragon cried out.

Numinae and Tiberius attacked the other flank. Tiberius blew puffs of black smoke all around, which hung in the air like flak explosions in a World War II movie.

Numinae threw a flurry of rapid-fire spells at Merlin, hoping to overpower him. At first Merlin fended them off, knocking them out of the sky with orange counterattacks. Then a few broke through and hit Merlin, but he just laughed as though Numinae's onslaught was nothing. He absorbed the hits like a sponge soaking up water. As the Questing Beast dodged Snoll on the other side, Tiberius blew a giant cloud of smoke, aiming to encase the right wing of the Beast in stone and send it and Merlin falling to the ground. But the Beast was unfazed. It finally beat one of its wings, and the smoke wafted harmlessly away. Tiberius did manage to whip the hindquarters of the Beast with the barb on his tail, but the result was not much more than a flesh wound.

The dragons regrouped side by side. Artie yelled, "All it does is breathe water! Hit it again!"

Snoll and Tiberius each let out massive breath attacks. Numinae shot a burst of energy into this mix, and Snoll's oil lit up in green flames. These twisted together like a braid, shooting at Merlin and the Beast at lightning speed.

But when it reached them, Merlin held up his cane, and the attack hit an invisible barrier. It curved around the Beast's head and fell away.

"We can't touch him, sire!"

Artie stared across the sky. "Come on! Is that all you've got?"

Merlin moved his mouth, but Artie couldn't hear the words. The Beast reared. Artie prepared to get drenched.

But this time was different. A cloud of locusts sprayed from the Beast's jaws and were on the dragons in a flash. The insects clicked and clawed all over Artie and Numinae, and got caught in the dragons' eyes and nostrils.

Numinae spoke an incantation. Instantly, the swarm flew away. He wasn't the forest lord for nothing.

First water, then bugs? Artie thought. What's next?

"Next" was not fun. Fire and ice and electricity and several huge rocks hurtled toward them. Snoll and Tiberius parted, trying to dodge the attack—but it bent and turned toward Tiberius! Numinae raised his hands and magic shot from them, and Tiberius blew smoke into the air. They were able to either combat or evade the fire and ice and electrical power, but several of the rocks got through. Both Tiberius and Numinae were battered hard and struck unconscious. Tiberius rolled over in the sky and fell. Within seconds they passed into the cloud cover below and disappeared.

Artie knew it was time to surrender. He yanked Scarffern from his pocket and blew it hard three times, signaling that it was over.

"What is that for, child?" Merlin's voice boomed all around, as if it were part of the weather. "Calling *more* dragons, are you?"

"No, Merlin. You have—" But just as he was about to say that Merlin had won, Smila and Azur burst through the clouds behind the Beast. And then, on the other side, came Chime—still carrying Shallot and Kay—and Aquilia!

"Ack!" Merlin sputtered, caught off guard. He spurred the Questing Beast, and it spun in midair. Smila let out a stream of ice and snow. The Questing Beast didn't flinch. It countered with a blast of orange fire so hot that Artie, over a hundred yards away, felt it on his face and chest. The ice melted and steamed, and the Beast let out another blast, an order of magnitude hotter than the last. It caught the white dragon and instantly burned it to a crisp.

Chime came in close to the Questing Beast, spraying the golden glitter that would disintegrate anything it touched. But Merlin waved his cane, and a gale blew out, scattering the glitter in every direction. "Kay!" Artie yelled as the Beast whipped its snake head and caught the golden dragon in its massive mouth and very simply bit it in two. Shallot and Kay were unharmed, but scared. Artie watched in horror as they clung to Chime's lifeless head as it too fell through the clouds and out of sight.

Azur and Aquilia shot into the breach. The blue dragon had possibly the strangest attack of all. It spit light, blinding and blue. Aquilia was next to her, her eyes closed, hoping to use the light as cover. But Merlin held up the cane again, and the Questing Beast opened its mouth and expelled a huge cloud of darkness that swallowed the blue dragon's light like a black hole eating a star.

"Kill!" Merlin hollered. The Questing Beast attacked the airborne dragons with lightning quickness, using more columns of sun-hot fire. Azur succumbed first, catching fire along her right side. Her wing simply evaporated in the flame, and the rest of her sizzled and turned to ash. Aquilia was next. She tried to fight the Questing Beast's fire with her smoke breath, but what was the point of that? There was no point. The wizard's power was too great—*far* too great. Aquilia lit up, from nose to tail, and fell, crackling, to the ground.

"Get us out of here!" Artie said to Snoll, suddenly very afraid. The plan would never work if Merlin just incinerated him.

Snoll dived. Artie dug his fingers into the thick feathers and squinted against the wind and rain. They were on the ground in seconds. Snoll landed near Lance, Dred, Qwon, and the other knights, who were all frightened and disturbed to have seen the dispatched dragons raining from the sky. As Artie jumped down and ran to them, he saw Tiberius and Numinae in the distance lying in an unconscious heap. Kay and Shallot were in a little gully to the east, also knocked out. Artie was about to tell the black dragon to stand down, but Snoll spun and took back off, driven mad with fury over the fate of his kindred. At the same moment, Merlin and his Beast dropped through the clouds. Snoll gave Merlin a jet of scalding oil, and the Beast counterattacked with more fire. Snoll's oil stream lit up and retraced its way into his head and body, and like Scarm before him, the black dragon exploded.

The knights watched, crestfallen and horrified, as feathers and chunks of flesh churned to the ground.

The dragons were dead. Artie was the Dragon King, and it didn't make a lick of difference. Merlin was something different, something more.

Artie was about to yell his surrender, when Qwon screamed, "Look!"

Uphill, dust and leaves flew in a ball of commotion. "What is *that*, lad?" Thumb asked, his voice shaking with excitement and fear.

"It's Erik," Artie said. "He's fighting with something." Do it, Erik, he thought. *Betray me.*

Artie looked to Merlin, who had stopped to watch the fight below with as much curiosity as Artie and his friends.

"Kid, I've got an infinite arrow," Lance whispered, nodding in the direction of the distracted wizard.

"Do it."

Lance calmly nocked it. He took a knee behind an

awestruck Bedevere and eyed the wizard's head. Lance relaxed his fingers and breathed. And then he let go.

The arrow shot forward, air twirling over the fletching and picking up speed. The shot was true. But at the last split second Merlin spotted it, and the wizard morphed into a puff of smoke before re-forming. He smiled down on the archer and held up his cane. The knights saw nothing—no bolt of electricity or waft of air or string of fire—but Lance's bow exploded in his hand, the pieces flying everywhere. The force of the impact sent both Lance and Bedevere to the ground, knocked out cold.

Qwon and Dred raced to check on them as the Questing Beast landed.

"How are they?" Artie asked.

"Lance is fine," Dred said.

Qwon held Bedevere's hand. "Bedevere too."

They returned their attention to Erik, who was still fighting some unknown foe. But then there was a flash of recognition in the melee, and Dred gasped. "Erik's fighting *Sami*?"

"Sami was defending Numinae," Artie whispered. "Erik wants the sword Numinae's carrying. Erik has betrayed us."

Qwon blurted, "Betrayed us. But why wou—"

Artie sliced a hand through the air. "Shh."

Then, unbelievably, Erik bested Sami with a direct hit

to the side of the Swede's head. As Sami fell over and rolled away, Erik hustled to Numinae and labored to pull the sword—sheath and all—from his hip. Then Erik walked briskly across the field. When he got to within a dozen feet of Merlin, he stopped.

"You've won," Artie finally yelled, moving toward a tumbledown Neolithic stone structure thirty feet away.

"I know, fool king," Merlin said smugly, eyeing the same spot. "Slave, give it to me." Erik held the sword out, and Merlin took it.

"No one say a word," Artie ordered in the barest whisper.

Thumb obeyed, but Qwon blurted, "Artie!" as Dred clapped a hand over her mouth.

"Go, Brother," Dred said, understanding something that Qwon didn't.

Artie winked at Dred, who held Qwon tightly.

"Thanks," Artie said.

He dropped Flixith and raised his hands. As he neared Merlin, Artie thought, Poor Erik. He doesn't even know what's happening to him.

Artie stopped when he was only a few feet from the crazed wizard. "You've won," he repeated. "You've gotten everything you wanted."

"No, not everything. Not yet."

Artie fought back tears. "Please, spare my friends."

"We shall see."

Artie put his hands together. "Please."

But the wizard just smiled and said nothing.

𝕸𝖊𝖗𝖑𝖎𝖓 𝖍𝖊𝖑𝖉 𝖚𝖕 𝖙𝖍𝖊 𝖘𝖜𝖔𝖗𝖉 that Erik had handed him. "That is all, thrall. You are dismissed." Erik collapsed to the ground, unconscious. Artie felt relieved. Whatever part Erik had played in this final act was done.

The wizard and the king now stood opposite each other, not ten feet separating them. Next to them were the two Neolithic stones, one upright and the other at an angle, forming a triangle of empty space big enough for a man to walk through.

"Do you know what these rocks are called?" the wizard asked.

"No idea."

"Arthur's Quoit, which is a fancy way of saying Arthur's Tomb. Some of the fools of this side believe that King

Arthur is buried here. Of course, we know better, don't we—*sire*." He said the last word with such heavy-tongued disdain that it nearly made Artie laugh.

"Sure we do. The real Arthur is long gone."

Merlin snickered. "That's right. Still, it's fitting that you will die here. If you wish, I can bury you under these rocks. I wouldn't mind it, really. It will be nice to have a reminder of my triumph so close to home."

"If it makes you feel good, Merlin. Go for it."

Merlin smiled. "You gloat, young Arthur."

"It's just whatchamacallit—gallows humor. I've got no reason to gloat. Not by a long shot."

Merlin turned the sword in his hand. "Because I have this."

"Yeah," Artie said heavily, letting his chin fall to his chest. "Because you have that."

"Erik was under my control this whole time."

"*Wha—?*"

Merlin held up a hand and cut Artie off. "Through his eyes I saw that you would be carrying David's silly sword into battle. I know you thought I would pull it from its scabbard, right off your back, and try to strike you down."

Artie fidgeted; his pulse raced. "I . . . I really wish that hadn't happened."

"I'm sure you do. Anyway, now I have Excalibur. Why you gave it to that mad tree man is beyond me."

Artie gulped. "He's not mad. You are."

"Ah. Perhaps." Merlin licked his lips and inspected the sword in his hands. Artie's heart quickened even more.

"You *should* be afraid, boy."

"W-why?"

"Because I am going to kill you with your own blade. It was brave of you to go into battle without Excalibur and its healing scabbard—but it was also stupid."

Artie didn't speak for a few seconds. "I had to try. Carrying the Sword of David was a calculated risk."

Merlin chuckled. "'Calculated risk'? My, my, listen to you. You've come a long way, Artie Kingfisher."

"Not really," Artie said uneasily, his voice cracking. "You want something from me, just like you always have. Only now, it's my life."

Merlin cocked his head to the side. "Right you are." He took the sheath in one hand and wrapped the dark fingers of his other hand around the hilt. "But tell me— how foolish did you think I would be? Don't you know I've been watching you since you gated here? You haven't so much as touched that sword on your back. It is poison. Evil. The Sword of David is even more insidious than me. It was idiotic of you to put so much faith in that blade. No matter how well disguised it is to look like Excalibur."

Artie eyed the ground. "Another calculated risk, Merlin. I figured you're so powerful now, it was my only chance."

"That is true, young Arthur. And I will say that I did not foresee the purity of your brother, Mordred, or his willingness to defy Morgaine. The very fact that you retrieved David's Sword, and concocted this far-fetched plan, is impressive."

"Maybe—"

"But now your planning—and your luck—have run their course."

Merlin tilted his head, and Artie's legs gave out from under him. He fell onto his hands and knees. He looked up at Merlin, suddenly afraid to die. "Merlin, please, don't. . . ."

A long and sinister smile broke across Merlin's face. "Meet your end with your face up, king. Let me see your eyes as your head rolls across the ground!"

And with that Merlin unsheathed the sword and threw the scabbard into the purple brush of St. David's Head.

At that moment, Kay Kingfisher clawed her way out of the gully she and Shallot, who was still knocked out, had fallen into. Kay wiped her eyes as she searched the battlefield. The vibe she was getting from Artie—who, she was so happy to discover, she had been reconnected to—was off the charts. It was so confusing that she didn't know what was going on. It didn't take long for her to see what was happening, though. Merlin stood over him with a sword.

He was going to chop Artie's head off! It was just like Artie had predicted!

"No!" Kay shrieked. Merlin hoisted the blade and sliced through the air. Qwon, Dred, and Thumb reached out and screamed.

Artie closed his eyes as time slowed. He tried to dodge the blade, but Merlin was fast, even in the slow-motion world. The edge caught Artie and sliced deep, striking his jugular and the strong muscles in his neck. Blood jumped from the wound, and he fell over sideways in agonizing pain, but he still had his head. Artie curled on the ground and gazed at Merlin. The wizard was shocked that Artie had been able to move at all, and so quickly to boot. Artie rolled out of the way as Merlin brought the blade back into the air, readying for the death stroke. Artie rolled twice, three times, four. And when he finally sprang to his knees, he had his hands on the hilt of the sword strapped to his back. Merlin bore in on him, brandishing the weapon that Erik had delivered.

Artie pulled out his sword—the sword that everyone believed to be the Sword of David—and held it over his head, Conan-style. The metal of the blade was shiny and bright, and the blood channels glowed with anticipation. Merlin's expression went from shock to fear as he saw that Artie's neck . . . Artie's neck was healed!

Merlin stumbled to his knees. He looked at the sword in his hand. The metal of the blade was dull, and there were no blood channels. It didn't look anything like Excalibur!

"You tricked me!" Merlin cried, his face awash in disbelief. "This is not Excalibur at all! How did you—?"

"I knew Erik was under your sway, Merlin. I knew he would betray us all along. I revealed a fake plan in front of him, knowing you would think that Numinae had Excalibur. But I switched the swords—and you fell for it! Maybe I'm smarter than you think."

Merlin's power had drained from him like water from an unplugged sink. Artie walked to the wizard. For everyone watching—Kay, Qwon, Dred, Thumb, even Numinae and Tiberius, who were both coming back around—it happened in a blur. Artie put a hand on Merlin's shoulder and the tip of Excalibur over the wizard's heart. He looked into Merlin's eyes and said, "You're free!"

Artie pushed the sword bodily through the old man, and it emerged black and stained on the other side. Then Artie pulled it out, and with it came a clump of black and rotting flesh: *Merlin's demon heart*. Excalibur lit up and burned this foul pith to a white ember. It exploded with a pop and disappeared.

In that instant the skies cleared and the Questing Beast cried out and fell into three pieces, its parts no longer bound by Merlin's magic.

For Merlin had no more magic.

Artie released the wizard's shoulder, and Merlin fell over sideways. Kay hollered with joy and pride and disbelief, jumping up and down. Qwon and Dred and Thumb fell to their knees and hugged and cried and laughed. Numinae and Tiberius were smiling, smiling, smiling.

Artie used Excalibur to knock the Sword of David away where it wouldn't hurt anyone else. Then he knelt next to the wizard and said, "I'm sorry, Merlin. I had to do it. Excalibur had to do it, too. Nyneve was right. Kind of. But you know who was more right? Kynder."

The ancient man looked up at Artie. His eyes were no longer red. They were white, and brilliant blue, and his pupils were as dark as deep pools. "Sorry?" he managed to say. "*You're* sorry?" Merlin smiled—not an evil smile, but a real one. "You have saved me. I am the one who is sorry. With my dying breath, I thank you. I thank you and hope that you can forgive me."

Artie wanted to say so many things but didn't. He stroked Merlin's bald head, still dark with the marks left by the liquid sangrealite.

"Artie," Merlin whispered, "I was not all bad. Even to you. I hope you can see that."

"I know, Merlin."

They paused, staring intently at each other. The king and his ancient wizard. Then Merlin said, "Oh, by the trees!

Those children! What did I do to those children?"

Artie smiled. "We didn't kill any. They'll be all right."

Merlin coughed, and black blood ran from his mouth. "Artie, listen carefully. Follow Thumb into my caves. Find the sangrealite. I have gathered so much. Take it. Take it. Make the worlds whole." And then Merlin reached out and touched Artie's hand, and in that one touch Artie learned all the secrets to melting the magical element. "Use that, Artie Kingfisher. My last magic. Use that, my king."

Merlin withered before Artie's eyes. Artie took Excalibur's scabbard from his back and laid it across the wizard, but he knew it was futile. The old man was finally free. The old man was finally, and blessedly, dead.

Artie reached out and shut Merlin's eyelids. "Thank you. Thank you for everything."

Kay Kingfisher watched all this, frozen and in awe, a smile so big and toothy that her face already hurt. "*That* is Artie Kingfisher," she said out loud. "My awesome little brother."

She looked down the hill to Qwon, Dred, and Thumb. She held up a fist and shook it. They returned the gesture. In the distance, where he had been sent to guard the moongate, Bercilak jumped and clanked with unrestrained pleasure. She turned to the gully and saw Shallot making her way out. Kay didn't say anything. The fairy would learn about what had happened soon enough. They had done it. *Artie* had done it.

As Kay turned back to her brother, a small voice came from her left. "Excuse me, miss?"

Kay couldn't remember ever being called *miss* before. She turned to the voice. Two kids a little younger than her, both with light hair and large eyes, walked toward her. The smaller one, a girl, had a bruise on her head. The larger one, a boy, limped badly and had a big abrasion on his right forearm. Both were clearly kids who Merlin had taken and forced to fight for him. "Hey, guys," Kay said gently.

"Where are we?" the boy asked with an American accent.

"What're your names?"

The girl looked around, as if the answer were in the air. Then she said, "Maggie Marks, miss."

"And I'm Henry, her brother," the boy said.

"Well, Henry and Maggie, my name's Kay Kingfisher, and we're on earth—in the United Kingdom, not *that* far from America. Don't be scared. Everything's going to be fine. Come and look. That kid over there is my brother, Artie Kingfisher."

Henry and Maggie put their heads together and stared along the length of Kay's outstretched arm. "Artie?" Henry asked.

"That's right. And my name's Kay. Don't worry, guys. Everything's under control. Everything is going to be fine." Kay paused, and then she said, "Yep, from now on, everything is going to be just fine."

𝕿𝖍𝖗𝖊𝖊 𝖜𝖊𝖊𝖐𝖘 𝖑𝖆𝖙𝖊𝖗, 𝖑𝖎𝖋𝖊 𝖋𝖔𝖗 the Kingfishers was back to normal.

Or normalish, at least.

Sure, there were a lot of odds and ends to tie up. Like how to dispose of a bunch of dragon carcasses; and how to explain to the people of Wales and England that they'd been under the spell of a wizard; and how to convince Bercilak that, no, there was no such thing as Mount Pepsi. And Tiberius had to unfreeze all the kids he'd put in stone, and Artie had to help them get back home. And finally, Artie, Kay, Dred, and Thumb had to go into Merlin's caves and find the ball of sangrealite.

Within a week, Artie and Kay and all the knights became instant international celebrities. They had their pictures in every single blog, magazine, newspaper, and website the world over. The people and creatures of the Otherworld sang their praises—literally, since countless songs were made up about them. Artie had a heck of a time explaining everything, and he knew that never again would a day pass without him having to talk about King Arthur, or the Otherworld, or sword fighting. Artie got to meet the president, which was cool, and he presented her with a volume of liquid sangrealite that would be sufficient to help all the nations of earth rejigger their power-generating systems. The rest of the sangrealite went back to the Otherworld, where Dred would make sure it got redistributed so that magic could once again grow and flourish. Dred would also guard a precious reserve that Artie or any of his knights could tap, for whatever reason. As far as saving the environment on Artie's side, there was tons of work to be done, of course, but the president promised to rally the leaders of the world to the task. It made Artie, Kay, and Kynder feel pretty darn good.

Perhaps surprisingly, the world accepted the Kingfishers' story—though it was hard to argue with a kid who had the Seven Swords at his back, and Thumb and Shallot and Numinae and Tiberius at his side. It was also hard to argue with the power of sangrealite—a power that Artie did not hoard. Before giving the president the goods, Artie, Kay, Kynder, and Thumb made a two-minute YouTube video demonstrating how the metal worked, and then shared it with the world. Within one week it had over 100,000,000 views. It was the most popular video ever posted to the internet (at least until the one of Bercilak and Tiberius chugging their "lifetime supply" of Mountain Dew in one sitting went viral).

This all worked because, just like when the invisible tower materialized in downtown Cincinnati and tumbled to the ground, people exhibited the uncanny and baffling ability to believe just about anything. People *wanted* to believe—they wanted to believe more than anything.

Slowly, sadly, the group said their good-byes. Artie, Kay, and Kynder buried Merlin in the Kingfishers' backyard, where Kynder planted a magical bed of ever-blooming wildflowers over it. Bedevere came to live with the Kingfishers, but Dred decided to return to Avalon as Artie's regent. Artie forgave Erik for being a traitor—because without him, after all, the plan would not have worked—and Erik went home to a gaggle of very happy Erikssens who had missed him dearly. Sami got a flat in Stockholm (but kept his camp up north). Numinae and Bercilak went to Veltdam to live and work at the Great Sylvan Library, and Tiberius split his time between his cave in the Sylvan woods and Castle Tintagel. Lance and Thumb renovated and reopened the Invisible Tower gaming store, where they sold video games and board games and books and toys to hundreds of kids a day (*Otherworld*, however, was recalled and discontinued). Shallot went back to Leagon, where she eventually became lordess. And Morgaine was given a quiet but respectful burial in Fenland, attended by all of Artie's knights.

Artie offered Excalibur to Nyneve for safekeeping, but she refused, since Artie was still very much alive. The Sword of David was FedExed back to Topkapi Palace, to the Turkish government's great relief. But no one was quite sure what to do with the Grail. For the time being it was in Avalon, buried in a chamber deep under Tintagel. And there it would stay—at least until someone had a better idea of what to do with it.

And after everything was said and done, Pammy and Kynder actually moved in together. Then, only weeks later . . . they got married! They chose the Kingfisher house to live in, keeping the Onakea house for Otherworld guests whenever they happened to cross over.

That meant Artie had a new sister—Qwon. Which was weird, because he still kind of liked her, even though by then it was obvious that Qwon (who, like all of them, visited Avalon regularly), was moony-eyed for Dred. The family kept a runt dire wolf for a pet, and Kynder constructed a backyard coop that housed a dozen passenger pigeons, all named Martha.

Eventually, Artie, Kay, Qwon, and Erik returned to school, where, as Pammy had predicted, they would be forced to repeat their year. Bedevere, who also had to go to school, tested and placed in the ninth grade. All in all, though, they didn't care. School was actually fun—and a lot easier than fighting huge battles for the fate of the world. It also didn't hurt that all of a sudden they were, and always would be, the most popular kids in, well, the world.

On a disturbingly warm January first—a Sunday that year—two days before they would go back to Shadyside

Middle School, Artie found himself in the basement game room. Since getting back from the Otherworld, he hadn't played a single video game—and neither, to the shock of all, had Kay. Artie hadn't even played *Ninja Caretaker* or *Monster Ate My Minivan* or *Angry Unicorns* on Kynder's iPad. The thrill, quite simply, was gone.

Artie looked around the room. Excalibur, Cleomede, Kusanagi, and Merlin's owl-headed cane were mounted in a glass case on one wall, and opposite it, in another glass case, were Flixith, Carnwennan, Bedevere's ginormous claymore, the infinite backpack, and a bag of moongate coins. Sitting on the coffee table in the middle of the room was the Otherworld cell phone that they used almost daily to call Dred, Bercilak, Numinae, or Shallot. Sitting at the far end, under the TV, was the Xbox, collecting dust. Artie stood there and stared at it, and as he stared he played with the two trinkets he kept on a single platinum-and-sangrealite chain around his neck at all times: the black key that opened the door inside the King's Gate, and the small golden disk that read, "No more games."

Artie turned these words over in his head.

After ten or more minutes of contemplation, he tucked the chain into his shirt and went to the case on his left. He opened it and took down Excalibur, pulling it from its scabbard, which he leaned against the wall. Taking the sword in both hands, he walked to the TV, looked down at the black plastic Xbox, and calmly and smoothly impaled it with the sword. Electricity shot up and down the blade and dissipated. Artie pulled the sword free, resheathed it, and put it back in the case. As he was closing the glass, Kay yelled from upstairs, "Hey, Art—whatcha doing?"

"Nothing," Artie yelled back.

"Well, get up here! It's so warm out, Kynder's making lemonade—in January! He's going to barbecue, too!"

"Cool. I'll be right up," Artie yelled back. Kay's footfalls pounded overhead and out the patio door into the backyard.

Artie looked at the vanquished Xbox, but all he could think about was his friend and enemy, the dead wizard, Merlin Ambrosius.

Artie smiled. "No more games," he said quietly.

Then he spun and dashed out of the room, and up the stairs, and outside, into the sun that had brought the New Year, to play with Kay and everyone else.

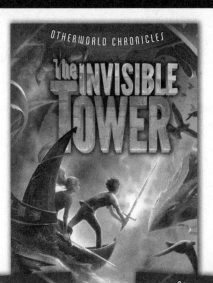